Glenda,

Thanks for reading.

Let me know what you think.

M

TATE DRAWDY
by Michael Ludden

ISBN: 978-1-978210-73-8

Cover artwork and design by Larry Moore
www.larrymoorestudios.com

TATE DRAWDY

MICHAEL LUDDEN

ALSO BY MICHAEL LUDDEN

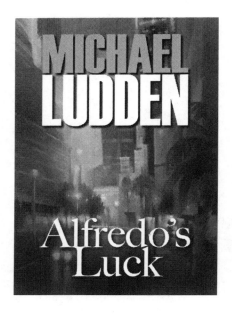

ALFREDO'S LUCK

Miami detective Tate Drawdy's girlfriend won't marry him. His boss can't stand him. And the hottest Cuban in the city has just been murdered on his watch.

Drawdy's about to discover the victim was the wrong man. A case of mistaken identity? He's going to find out, but it means surviving a terrifying encounter with an escaped con. And, ain't this a thrill? He's beginning to suspect the guy he's trying to protect is running some sort of expat conspiracy.

Drawdy's a rich kid who dropped out of med school to become a cop. He's impetuous. He's a blues fanatic—bring your earplugs. And his obsession with this case is about to get him killed.

A well written tale of honor, loyalty, impossible dreams and ultimate betrayal. Riveting, fast-paced story with characters you'll love and characters you'll hate. Buckle up and enjoy the ride...

Fast paced with plenty of twists and turns. Loved it!...

A page-turner that keeps the mind working with twists and turns and enough drama and complex characters to challenge the best of the crime genre...

The suspense grabs you with layers of possibilities. The perps, the victims and the cops are proliferating like weeds. You won't solve it, most likely, but keep your eye on Tate as he puts investigative instinct to work while risking his all...

I found Alfredo's Luck captivating from the very first page. As each chapter finished I was compelled to begin the next; until before I knew it — it was over. And I was like, "Whew, what a ride! Let's go again...

Fantastic twists and turns kept me turning the pages. The author clearly knows his territory and subject. The descriptions were vivid, the characters well-developed and varied, the plot engaging. Put it at the top of your summer reading list!...

Michael Ludden's recent contribution to the crime/detective genre is an undiluted pleasure. The pacing is fast, the language spare and the action taut...

Check out our website at
www.michaelludden.com

And see Michael Ludden's blog "Tales from the Morgue" at
https://michaelludden.net

CONTENTS

CHARACTERS

P.D.
Charlene Pinckney—juvenile officer
Tate Drawdy—detective
Tyree Lamonica
Jimmy Patterson
Ansley Newsome—head jailer
Russell—jailer

Savannah
Precious Gardner
Stan James—the prosecutor
Laura—Tyree's girlfriend
Vincent Palladino—the priest
Eugene Jorgenson
Emily, Dina—Eugene's wife and daughter
Barksdale Newman—Tate's girlfriend
Ken Fowler—Char's boyfriend
Sister Cacia

The hitchhikers
John Robert Griffin
Richard Allen Wigle
Jeanne Mabrey
Lisa Hillerman

Pittsburgh
Earl and Bernadette Griffin—the parents
Rose—owns a deli
Brian—rehabbing an apartment
George "Goo" Orbison—retired cop
Wynton Bonds—retired cop
Bobby Mayo—retired cop
Dino "Mooch" DiMucci—retired cop
Vasiliya Popov—bar owner

Part One

1

THE SUN was just beginning to edge over the treetops. Still cold in the shade of the tall pines by the side of the road. She could hear the car slowing as it came up behind her. She got in back beside the girl. There were four of them. A tall guy driving, long hair. A young woman in the passenger seat up front. She had creamy skin and high cheekbones, auburn hair, beautiful round eyes. A model, perhaps.

In the back against the window, the other guy. Short, nasty looking, edgy voice, complexion like the surface of the moon. His girlfriend, childlike, and so voluptuous it was almost lewd.

Precious Gardner wasn't sure why four young white people would pick up a rangy black woman shucking an arm full of bags from the Piggly Wiggly. But then they had lots of questions. How far was the beach? What was the weather like this time of year? Any good places to eat? Any good places to party?

She figured they had to be from someplace up north.

Precious had eyes as dark as night and they crinkled almost shut when she looked at you. Lips, chapped from smoking her daddy's Swishers. Stubborn hair, pulled back with a purple scarf one of the ladies had given her. A knobby gap between her front teeth. Bushy eyebrows and ears that clung tight to the side of her head. Skin, tough from the sun. A faint scar under one eye, like a freshly fallen tear.

Tomato sandwiches, with Wonder Bread and Miracle Whip. They'd made her grow tall. Strong hands and big feet. Men's feet.

Good for walking. Shoes from the church store and dresses the ladies gave her.

Once a week she made the trek into town on foot, getting up at dawn while it was still cool. Always the first inside the door, hoping to get back before it became stifling, heading home with three or four bags in each hand, enough for her and her mom and Donetta, next door. Donetta didn't get out much, with her back.

Unless somebody she knew came by, the Piggly was half a morning's walk and she was glad of a lift and then they were heading out of town. They had a lot of liquor.

It was a sweet day already, a few wispy clouds moving slowly across a pale blue sky brushed in with orange and pink, blind mosquitoes in clusters, hovering over the road and at the edge of the trees, gathered there by instinct. The sun, climbing higher now, warming the air. Spanish moss plucking up like waves late at night in a silk breeze. The gassy smell of the cord grass and pluff mud, oysters and crab, as the marsh came awake.

The guy up front, smiling at her in the rear-view mirror. He kept looking at her. Smiling. Being polite. It made her uncomfortable. He was speaking slowly, holding the wheel with both hands. Too polite. Her stomach began to churn. She wished she hadn't told them how far she was going.

And so she went along. Talking. Making nice.

At least it was good to sit. Precious spent much of her days on her feet, or her knees. The ladies didn't hire her to dust or load the dishwasher. It wasn't the easy stuff they wanted. She made her money doing the things the white ladies didn't care for. Getting underneath things. Getting wet or picking things up and moving them. The heavy cleaning.

Still pretty, despite the work. Six days a week, when she could get it. And there was a fair amount of bowing and scraping. Uppity black folk tended to move on. Savannah liked them docile, with an eye toward how things had been.

She was trying that now, keeping her head low, keeping her voice soft.

She thanked them for the smokes and for the dope. But she wasn't interested in making any money, not like that. She wasn't pulling her pants down for two young white boys and then the tall guy started yelling at her, calling her names, telling her to shut up.

He'd gotten angry fast.

And now he was turning around in his seat and reaching for her. He was really strong. She pulled back, trying to get his hand loose from her shirt. They were off the road now, bouncing on the shoulder.

And then the small one yanked her outside the car. She was crying and pleading, "please don't hurt me." Over and over again.

He punched her and then he stabbed her in the stomach. He stabbed her a couple of times with his little knife. She was down now, down on the ground, crawling, begging them to leave her alone. Then the big guy picked her up under one arm and started dragging her into the woods. She threw up on his arm.

He paused a moment, lifted her up, as if her were going to help her, whispered in her ear.

"You gonna want some fries with that?"

His little friend giggled and yipped like a kid on a carousel. And then he kicked her. On her knees now. One of the girls found an old garden hose somebody had tossed in the woods. They wrapped it around her neck. Each girl took an end. They ran in opposite directions. Precious choked and gasped and sobbed. They stabbed her a few more times and then they left.

She could feel the sun's warmth lingering on her face still. But when she looked, it wasn't there. And then it grew dark and cold.

They kept her groceries.

2

CHAR PINCKNEY was a juvenile officer, had her own cruiser, her own beat. She'd been out on the island, heading back toward town, when she saw the four of them. Hitchhikers, hair all long and stringy. They didn't exactly look like kids. She stopped anyhow and they started away fast. Char opened the door.

Later on, she'd replay it in her mind, half wishing she had just let them go.

"Just hold on there a minute," she said. "You folks just sit tight."

Their answers weren't too good. Char called in.

"I need two cars with cages. I don't want the boys riding with the girls."

The dispatcher sent somebody right away.

Old blue jeans and boots. Couple of backpacks. Woodstock, except one of the girls had a little flowery purse. They weren't saying much, but she had a good idea the girls were underage. Gorgeous young girls.

The boyfriends were another story. Their ID's looked phony. Char told the booking officer to ship their prints.

Then she called that new detective, Tate Drawdy, the one with the jaw. The bluest eyes. And that lean, hard frame. Char thought Tate was something special. It was her duty to help him get acclimated.

"You making any headway on the Gardner woman, the one they found out in the woods?"

"Zilch."

"I'm thinking we oughta look at these kids."

"Couple runaways and their boyfriends? You serious?"

"Yeah, I'm afraid I am. These kids are way more grown up than they need to be."

"Want me to have a look?"

"Wouldn't hurt. Tell you what. See the girls first, then the guys. Then tell me."

Tate worked Saturdays on a long shift. Young, already looking pretty smart. Pretty good. The jail wasn't far. He took the stairs two at a time and headed down the hallway. Lanky, a few inches over six feet, the lean muscle of a relentless runner.

A stride like he'd had a good life.

You might notice his hair, bushy, brown; his eyes, or, more likely, the nose, Roman, prominent bridge, just slightly hooked. It gave him something of the look of a hunter. More likely, it would be the expression that would seize notice. The high forehead, those piercing blues and a modest widow's peak combined to create a sense of clarity, a calmness. But that was an illusion.

The CO buzzed him in.

"Looking for the new girls in juvey."

The lead jailer and a couple of officers were standing in a huddle, whispering. They grinned and pointed.

Standing in the middle of the group, a head taller than the rest, Tyree Lamonica.

Tate knew him enough to say hello. A guy you wouldn't mind having your back. He could pick up the car while you changed a tire. Feet so big you wondered how he could get in and out.

Not a lot of patience with smaller folk, the look of a man who's climbed the hill and he's tired of waiting for the others to catch up.

"You heard, huh?"

"Heard what?"

"Right."

Then they laughed and slapped each other's backs and then one of the guys stuck his tongue out and put his hands behind his head and started pumping his pelvis.

"Tell you what," said Tyree. "Before you go in there, let's have a little side bet."

Tate walked over, popped his chin in the air, waiting to hear.

"I'm gonna trust you," the deputy said. "You don't get real interested in 10 seconds, you don't have to pay me."

Tate just shook his head. He walked to the cellblock door and waited. The guard buzzed him in.

Twenty minutes later, he found Char at her desk. Her office, not much bigger than a closet, but she'd made it her own. A nice watercolor, some flowers, a paperweight some kid had made out of clay.

He asked her if she wanted to get a coffee downstairs. She set down the papers she'd been reading, folded her hands.

"I'm guessing you ignored the bet," she said.

He just looked at her.

"Yeah. You're not the type."

They headed down. Tate took short strides so she could keep up. Char, a small purse over her shoulder, swinging her arms. She had on a trace of lipstick, pink.

"What is that you drive," she asked. "BMW?"

"Yeah."

"What's it cost?"

"I dunno. A lot."

"How fast does it go?"

"I dunno. A hundred and fifty maybe."

"You got a problem with these questions?"

"A little. What difference does it make?"

"Wake up. You coulda sold the car."

"Yeah... I suppose."

"So you got into trouble?"

"No."

"Bullshit. Rich kids from Atlanta don't come down here to be cops. What are you… slumming?"

"No. I like cops. I like police work. Why are you here?"

"I needed a job, asshole. So what did you think of the girls?"

THE SUN forced its way in. Tate got up early, threw on some shorts and his New Balance, headed for the park.

Wide sidewalks, spattered by eruptions from tree roots, crowded by azaleas pushing through wrought iron fences. Spanish moss hanging everywhere in spectacular clumps, like bits of torn awning billowing in the breeze. Facing Forsyth Park, some of the prettiest houses in the city, tall and statuesque, with flower boxes under arched windows. Resolute porches with broad steps, dressed in Adirondacks, Doric columns, brass lamps and beveled sidelights. In the windows, fancy curtains and little lamps.

Hedges and streetlights. And brick. Somebody had made a bunch of brick in this town.

He looped the park three times and headed home. He was renting an old house just a few blocks away, close to a corner where the tour buses passed in the mornings.

This city lived on its history, its blending of the past and present. People from all over, pouring in to feel the charm, to pass time in a place carefully set down on the water's edge; the river, the creeks, the marshlands stretching for miles in every direction. The sea.

It could be scorching in summer, muggy enough that shirts and shorts would stick to your skin like salty glue. But when it rained, the city took on a softness and a quiet and the still of centuries seemed to seep from the ground.

Tate's house, vintage gingerbread out front. Inside, tall mirrors surrounded by gilt and marble, fancy carpeting, pillows that matched, portraits with tiny lights overhead, elaborate wallpaper, crown moldings, fireplaces everywhere you looked, chandeliers that would take a week to clean.

Tate had rented the place furnished. Lots of mahogany and cherry, stuff you'd need help to move. He'd emailed a realtor, told her his price range. She called five minutes later.

He was getting grits and sausage at Clary's when Char called.

Out of style for a generation, Clary's had hanging fluorescent lights, tile, ceiling fans, bricks everyplace covered with dusty photographs, an honest to goodness soda fountain and a decent breakfast. It had turned out to be the ideal place to get situated. He found out who the big shots were, who was in trouble with the bank, who was sleeping out. A good place to get situated.

Char had an idea. She wanted Tate to back her up with the chief. Tate thought that was asking a lot.

"Hope you'll change your mind," she said. "And you'd better hurry up."

"What for?"

"We're due in his office in 10 minutes."

The boss had his feet up, shaking his head.

"This is just bizarre as hell."

"We can keep the guys," Char said. "No sweat. But I don't want those girls loose yet either."

"Not gonna happen. You need to ship 'em home. You find the parents?"

"The older one's been out on her own for a couple years, says she's been making money on the street," said Char. "The younger one lives with an aunt who's not real sure she wants her back. Not after all this. You believe it? She's 15 years old. She may not look it, but she's 15 years old."

"We're gonna just send 'em home."

"Don't be in too big a hurry just yet, please. I'm gonna charge 'em up. I just don't wanna charge em with anything too big right now. I want to see if they'll talk."

The words were confident, but the tone was pleading. The chief rubbed his bald head, scratched at his neck, crossed his arms, fussed his mustache.

"Not feeling it, Char."

He'd already spent one career in the Army. Making decisions was not an issue. He turned to Tate.

"Thoughts?"

"Ten minutes with those scumbags was enough to give me a migraine. Real sweet guys. Now that I've met 'em, I'm thinking about getting a Doberman."

The big guy, John Robert Griffin. Athletic, heavily muscled, thick sandy hair that fell over a tall forehead. He had a long nose, heavy jaw, that woodsy, blue-collar thing some women go for. Kept a smile on his face, like he knew what you were thinking, what you might do. The kind of smile that would give you some concern.

The little guy was something else. A purplish birthmark splashed across one cheek and half his nose. Wiry, matted hair, lots of acne scarring, the face just slightly lopsided when he spoke. Jellyfish lips under a sparse moustache. Kind of guy who'd be hunched over by his 40s from lack of exercise and a life of cringing away.

They were down from Pennsylvania. Wanted to see the old houses, the riverfront. Lying through their fucking teeth.

And the girls, strange. The older one was flat jaw-dropping gorgeous. Auburn hair, cut short, round green eyes and a chin that finished in small rounded edges below a soft mouth pressed lightly closed. Demure acting.

A good actress.

The younger one, some kind of genetic anomaly. Wide-eyed, with high cheekbones and a child-like smile. An hourglass body like one of those illustrations from a sci-fi fantasy magazine. Long-legged and broad-shouldered with jet-black hair that hung loose from her head, just slightly tousled. Sun-drenched, like she'd just come out of the water.

Just didn't seem right, them hooking up with these guys.

When they found out who the guys were, it wasn't going to make any sense at all.

Tate wanted to be good at this. He spent a lot of time reading the files, studying the crime scenes, re-interviewing the witnesses and the suspects. An older guy on the force, Jimmy Patterson, had been drumming it into him: Details. See the details.

They were sitting on Jimmy's front porch, drinking a beer. Jimmy had shed the work clothes for some corduroy pants and a sweater that used to belong to somebody. Jimmy's family had been around awhile. Jimmy was old Savannah.

His house, something nobody on the police force could afford. Wouldn't cost three million bucks, but not much less. Jimmy'd grown up in that house, the single child of older parents.

Both had passed away when he was a rookie on the force.

"Tell me what you know about these guys."

Tate started to recite some stuff off the reports.

"Huh-uh. What do you know from looking at 'em, what they smell like."

"OK. Little guy's a bitch for the big guy, but he's crazy enough the big guy lets him have a vote. Not frightening in a physical way—you could slap the shit out of the kid with one hand—but for what he'd do to you in your sleep.

"Big guy, flat intimidating. Real cocky. I told Buddy to put him in the interrogation room and take the cuffs off. Just to let him know I didn't give a shit for his... whatever."

Jimmy interrupted.

"Get me one too, willya?"

"Mine's not empty."

"It's close."

Tate didn't sleep well that night. Lot of trips to the kitchen. Actually, he'd been hoping they might help him lose sight of that grin. It was as if the guy knew what was coming and knew he could handle it. He'd twist it into something malignant, something with a smell that wouldn't wash clean.

This was not the career the Drawdys had mapped out for their son. Growing up, there'd been someone to pour his orange juice. Someone to bring the car around, answer the phone.

It was ringing now.

"Clary's?"

"Char, this better be good. It's 6 a.m."

"Oh, it's good. I just got the stuff back on those two guys. Pennsylvania sent the warrants. And a whole bunch of other stuff."

"What kinda stuff?"

"You'll see. Come on now. I'm already sitting in the parking lot. How long's it gonna take? You could just throw on some clothes and come over."

Five minutes later, he was in the BMW. Char wasn't the only one who gave him shit for the car. Leather, electronics, wood trim, V-8. He'd had the sense to peel that Ivy League sticker off the back.

He drove around the corner, took Drayton to Abercorn, parked on the street. She was in a back booth, drinking tea, had a biscuit and some jam. She'd ordered for him. Spanish omelet, bacon, potatoes, bowl of fruit, coffee, orange juice. He started in.

"What? You tell em I hadn't eaten for a week?"

"Hey you remember what you said to the chief? About just seeing those guys made you wanna get a big dog? Your instincts were on the money, baby. These may just be the baddest creeps we've ever laid eyes on."

"We've both met some bad creeps."

"Read the file, tough guy. Then tell me."

She was right. The eggs got cold.

WHAT A STRANGE TOWN it was. Tons of tourists and a whole lot of mildewed money. You could be here for a couple of generations and still be considered a newcomer. One of those towns. Old furniture, old booze and old families. Great atmosphere. Some good food. Nice part of the country.

And here they were. Two guys so blistering mean Tate was having trouble thinking of a word that fit. Satanic, maybe. Savage... fucked up.

The big guy, Griffin, 17 years old the first time he killed somebody. He'd had a sawed-off shotgun and—if you believed his story—he was twirling it that day like a Texas six-shooter. Both barrels went off accidentally, right into his buddy's face. They couldn't prove it wasn't an accident. He got 18 months.

And there'd been that statutory rape charge, the one with the young lady who would later refuse to testify. The D.A. in Pittsburgh said she'd been unable to accept their assurances they could protect her.

She said he'd been real nice to her, polite, sugary sweet. He brought flowers, held her door. He had a sense of humor. But then she could still see his face, those gray eyes, suddenly dark, the hand around her neck, the voice so deep and menacing it was like it came from underground. The reverberation, enough to make her heart explode. Beyond that, the memory was faint, and for that she was grateful. She'd gone straight to the police and then she'd changed her mind.

She was sorry, actually, really sorry. But she'd felt quite sure he'd kill her dead if there were any trouble.

Little guy was a cousin. That's how they knew each other. Had a serious rap sheet by the ninth grade. Last time he'd been busted, he was drunk, tossing rocks through department store windows so he could steal the female mannequins. Had several of 'em back at the house.

Tate was telling Jimmy about it. Jimmy's place. Drinking a beer.

"Having a relationship with the dummies, if you know what I'm saying."

"Seen that before. So what've you got on these guys now."

"Escape... both of 'em. Statutory rape of the girls, which is weird because you'd swear both of 'em are old enough. Char's got some radar on 'em. Thinks they whacked that woman we found out toward the beach."

Sitting in the kitchen, big enough for a crowd of cooks to work, redone with Italian tile and copper and granite. Etched glass on the cabinets. They had their feet up on the table, some kind of heirloom piece.

"I can see that," Jimmy said. "I can see them being good for that. But you didn't pick up on it?"

"No, not exactly. I think they're way wrong, but I didn't just automatically put that together."

"Now that you've heard it...?"

"What I think is they're capable of anything. The guys both seem like total sadists, crazy fuckers."

"That's enough to start with," Jimmy said. "Your lady in the woods died nasty. You've got these guys in from outa town. Push 'em together and see what you come up with. It doesn't always have to be some kind of sixth sense. You can just ask yourself what's possible and then you see if you can work it out... how it happened."

"I did kinda road-test it with him when I saw him."

"You asked him about the missing lady?"

"Yeah. Denied it."

"So you got nothing."

"Mmmm."

Tate asked if Jimmy wanted to come in, see these guys for himself.

"I'll work on it with you. But I think... like this. You check stuff out. We'll talk about it later over a beer. I'm working that bank case right now. That's plenty."

"I hear you," said Tate. "I think you wanna coach me from the sidelines. That's OK. I'm glad to have it. You know what? No reason you couldn't coach a lot of people. Why don't you move up, take that new job? You gotta be getting tired of riding in that Crown Vic."

"Just between us... I am moving inside. They've been after me for years and I just didn't wanna nursemaid anybody. There's a job opening up now that I think I might actually like."

"What's that?"

"Head of a new detective team, special assignments. I'll get you in on it too, but not right away. And don't let that sweat you at all. You and I are gonna keep drinking beer."

"Good for you, compadre. Why'd you wait so long?"

"I dunno. I guess I just didn't want to report to people I didn't respect. Gonna be a couple of retirements next month. Keep that under your hat."

"Don't worry about it," Tate said. "Heard those rumors. Glad that clears the air for you."

Jimmy waved it off, as if he were brushing a spider's web from a doorway.

"Actually it doesn't quite clear the air. When you're here a little longer, you may find out some stuff."

"Like what?"

"Not now. So, how you gonna get these guys for the killing?"

"I work both ends. I push the girls. But I don't want it in my lap. I wanna know for myself, how and when and why. I wanna be able to put it together."

Jimmy got up and went to the fridge. He got a couple of beers. Tate held his aloft.

"Did this look empty to you?"

"Yeah it did."

3

RIGHT AWAY, Tate could see there was going to be a problem keeping the girls under lock and key. The younger one, Lisa Hillerman, hiding in a corner in stunned silence for most of her waking hours. The older girl, Jeanne Mabrey, passing the afternoons screwing a succession of corrections guys and deputies. By the time he'd gotten wind of it, she'd been moved to a separate hallway, away from prying eyes. Tate went to see the head jailer, said he'd heard there'd been some problems.

Ansley Newsome was his name. The Noose. Old guy, former regime, had a small desk he sat as if it were the only dry spot in the room. Said he didn't want to hear anybody tell him how to run his jail.

"Your call," said Tate. "I hear she's confiding a lot with one of the women on the force. Wouldn't want to see anything happen here."

Newsome, in his mid-60s, maybe more. He'd been a captain, a unit commander. Got caught doing something. Tate didn't know the story, knew there was one. Newsome had been quietly swept under, moved to pasture.

A jowly sort of guy. Pocked face. Thin hair. False teeth in the front, attached to the bone in years past, when close was good enough. Tate thought those teeth had to be trouble if there was steak on the table. Every so often, Newsome would run his tongue across the back of his top teeth, swallow and then go on. Gave his words a persistent texture of wet. The kind of thing that could make a man angry all day long.

That, and his nose. And a hard look at where he'd been.

"Anything happen, like what?"

"Like you've been around a lot of years, must be getting close to retirement. Wouldn't want to see anybody bad-mouth what you've done for the city."

"And if it was you?"

"Me, I'd put her in a big cell with a bunch of women, under a camera."

"Can't do it, smartass. She's under age, has to be in her own hallway, away from the rest. And the main hall's the only place that gets filmed."

"Sure. But you wouldn't want it to look like you weren't by the book. Maybe you could buy another camera. Or put the adults in the juvey wing and give her and her little buddy the big hall to themselves. That way, she gets to talking, nobody looks at you the wrong way. You're doing everything to protect her."

"Yeah, bullshit. I don't need advice."

"And I don't need my case to go down the tubes, old man. You might think about whether those cases of beer you're charging the boys are more important than your pension. Tell you what, though. I don't wanna tell you how to run your jail. So I'm not gonna do anything about this for another seven minutes or so, give you some time to make some changes."

And here was the nose, his tell, a juvenile flare-up, a signpost. It turned red when he got pissed. Nothing he could do. His cratered, ruddy face, like a character in a Dickens novel.

Doubt if Noose read much Dickens.

The Noose, glaring at the pictures on the wall, the grime behind them, the waxy spot on his desk where his forearms rested and the unblinking pressed shirt in front of him. A pressed shirt on a red hot kid with a purpose. Like a fucking vulture.

He hated him, young guy, college degree and nice easy hands-folded talk. Until you figured out what he was really up to. Hating him pretty bad now.

AT FIRST, Tate had thought about getting a bungalow out at the beach. Blend in. But that was a quick route to mildew. Beach bars weren't the way to move up in the organization. Get a place downtown, where you can get to the office quickly, be a part of what's going on. Not a part of the past.

This was not a landing point. It was a way station.

He'd spent four years at Princeton, pre-med. He'd done well. He was resigned to the next phase.

And then one summer, one of his dad's doctor friends had gotten Tate a job driving an ambulance for Candler Hospital in Savannah. The big hospital. The one where they brought the folks who'd been stabbed or shot. A few months around cops had taught him that what he really wanted was not an office full of runny-nosed kids and their equally snotty parents.

He wanted the street. He loved the movement, the pace, the mission, the energy. He worked hard, played hard. Basketball on his days off.

Tate wasn't anything spectacular. High school ball, college intramurals. Played some decent D, had a crisp pass underneath. Slow enough he needed to let somebody else bring the ball up court.

It was good balance. It was what he needed. Otherwise, he'd go to bed and lay there, staring at the ceiling.

That night he went on a date, the first in a long time. He'd been talked into it. A real estate saleswoman, drove a Mercedes.

He hadn't missed money. This girl had wavy hands, small jewelry, plenty of paint, perfect hair and could go for long stretches without a breath. The waiter had yet to come around to ask what they wanted. There was a good game on. Now he was learning the best places to shop.

She was the kind of female Tate's mom used to bring home to meet her son. Purses and shoes that matched. Tidy skirts and perfect posture. Girls who said *gosh*.

He got home early, woke up with the sun, made coffee. It was threatening heat, but on the sidewalk outside his window, it was still cool and damp in the shade. Patches of moss clinging to the edges of the bricks and on the slate just past his iron gate. He turned on some music. Big Bill Broonzy… "Key to the Highway."

Tate had developed into a major fan of the blues, and this was strong stuff to get you going in the morning. He stepped out the side door, the one with the little cowbell up top. A thin walkway of brick pavers, surrounded by beefy azaleas leading to the street.

Butterflies, already, and some carpenter bees, fat and searching. Under the kitchen window, a tiny mound of sawdust. He bent down to look. Along the sill, a hole about the size of a fountain pen, perfectly rounded. He sat on the steps to lace his shoes. And then he was over the fence, heading for the park.

It was nice to be running down tree-lined streets with sidewalks with good things to look at. There was atmosphere. And if you ran a route, there was a destination, not just the routine of circling something.

He liked to head north on Drayton, toward downtown, the park on the left, some great houses on the right. Wide sidewalks on both sides. Lots of people walking their dogs.

Some unfortunate "modern" buildings that could be ignored. Why would somebody put up a piece of crap made of concrete and steel and glass in the middle of a historic district?

Mostly, it was old stuff, houses with great porches on three floors, columns, windows with style. A nice canopy of trees.

Plenty of burglar bars, though.

Through the intersection at Gaston. Down to the Chamber of Commerce, one of his favorite buildings. Left on Bay Street, past the old Custom house, City Hall.

Up Montgomery, dogleg at Bryan Street, on past the Civic Center. Here, just a few blocks farther, the city had endured a notorious triple murder more than eight decades earlier. An open doorway, the body of a woman, her skull crushed in. Another woman, down the hall, crushed skull. A third, in a bedroom, her skull also crushed. A bloody ax nearby.

It had happened during the day, close to businesses. People wondered why no one had heard a thing, or admitted to hearing.

Past the Civic Center, the trees began to thin. He'd hang a left at Gaston, up to Barnard, some good houses there, left on Park Avenue and up to Drayton.

He got back to his place, tossed his wet clothes on top of the washing machine, showered, put on a tie. There was a preliminary hearing. A public defender would take a run at getting the boys out of jail.

In years past, it would have been held in a gorgeous old courthouse, right downtown. The old courthouse, the one built in 1881. Now that was a courthouse.

But this was a big, modern rectangle, the kind of thing people got paid to build back in the 70s. Designed to resemble a shoebox with windows. Nothing disturbed its smooth edges. Couple of feeble trees out front. A place so sterile you could hardly keep grass alive. In a city full of history, built on colonial themes, there wasn't a column to be seen.

Carpet on the floor, a half decent bench for the judge. Hard pews for the public.

Tate sat behind the bar. Shawn James, the prosecutor, arrived early. He was alone. This nonsense wouldn't take but five minutes.

John Robert Griffin came in looking energized. His lawyer had
gotten him some clothes for court. Khaki slacks, a blue shirt and
a tan sports coat. He'd shaved and his hair was cut.

He looked over at Tate, gave him a smile. And then it all came
back, that first meeting.

Tate had gotten there early. There was a table and a couple of
hard steel chairs. Tall ceiling, a window up high covered in mesh.
The sun casting oblique shadows across the floor and the walls.

They brought him in. Take the cuffs, Tate said. The officer
balked. Tate waved him off.

Griffin was facing the wall. The officer told him to lift his hands,
unlocked the cuffs, slipped the chain from around his waist.

Want me to stay in the room?

You can go, Tate said.

Still with his back turned. Still standing.

"Have a seat."

Griffin turned to face him. Standing motionless, a small grin,
showing his teeth. Nothing else changed. But in that instant,
Tate saw a piece of himself he'd never seen before, something
he had thought might not happen to him, not until he was old
and put up.

It made him dizzy, as if the ceiling had lifted back and now he
was staring into a burning sky, hoisted up, swaying in the breeze,
shadows fading in, fading out, slowly revolving, a vein throbbing
behind his eye. His scalp tingling, his face suddenly wet.

He wanted to turn away.

He reached for his coffee, took a sip, set it back down. He
kept that hand on the cup, feeling the heat. Told himself Griffin
couldn't read his mind, couldn't hear his heartbeat. He counted
to 10.

"Where'd you grow up?"

Griffin smiled. He was relaxed, in his living room, having an afternoon chat with a neighbor. He lifted a hand, waved from the elbow, like the pope.

"Pennsylvania, but of course you knew that."

The voice was deep, sonorous, with just a trace of the north.

"Pretty country?"

"Not bad."

"What made you head this way?"

"A chance to see the world. I didn't want to join the army."

His hands were flat on the table, the nails quite well cared for, which was something of a surprise. Each time he spoke, Griffin slid his hands forward. Now they were almost touching Tate's.

Tate pushed back, reached for his cup, but then Griffin was leaning forward. His head tilted just to the side. That grin again, with a narrowing of the eyes. The room, suddenly smaller.

"Do I make you uncomfortable detective?"

Griffin's voice low, almost conspiratorial. And in that instant, Tate knew Char was right. And he knew a lot more. He forced himself back in, their noses a hands-width apart.

"What? A pissant like you? Fucking some runaway sophomore with a couple screws loose? I'm sorry, no pun intended. You may think you're the most interesting character on the prowl. Sorry pal. Everyday stuff for us. Can I get you some coffee?"

Griffin chuckled, straightened up, smacked his hands together.

"Well done, my friend."

They talked awhile longer. And then Tate got up to leave.

Griffin stood with him.

"Tate? Do you mind if I call you Tate?"

He didn't reply. Griffin, buttery charming now, held out a hand.

"Thank you for coming to see me."

Tate wasn't much for shaking hands with bad guys. He made an exception. Griffin held on too long, staring as if lost in concentration at a spot on the floor.

Tate went to the door and knocked for the jailer. After Griffin's hands were cuffed again, Tate walked through. Griffin called out to him and he turned.

"Tate, my friend, you just be glad we're not everyday stuff."

"**YOUR HONOR**... we understand counsel for the prosecution intends to oppose bond for these defendants. That is entirely inappropriate. We're talking about a couple of young men who are charged with a crime of adolescence. And when the court comes to realize how readily these young men were deceived, it will come as a complete surprise to think there is this much anxiety in this case.

The judge looked over his glasses.... "Mr. James..."

"May we approach..."

Shawn James was a big man who almost always came to court in a suit, blue or gray, almost always with a striped tie. Black shoes, highly polished, glasses with silver frames. He let the public defender wait for him, rising from his chair as if he'd spent the weekend digging stumps out of the ground. When he reached the bench, he raised a hand in deference.

"Permission to speak freely, your honor."

"You're no longer in the military, Mr. James."

"I'd like to set the record straight."

"Please."

He turned to the defense attorney. Sighed deeply. Shook his head.

"Mr. Langford, there's a very good chance these men will be on trial for murder in the very near future, not just the statutory rapes. I intend to present a full history on your clients. For your own good, I suggest you don't toy with the court."

The lawyer's smile faded. His breakfast began a return call.

"What history is that, exactly?"

"If this is news to you, I expect you're not going to be very happy you were assigned this case, counselor. Perhaps you should have prepared."

"You may return to your seats gentlemen."

He started with Griffin. How, a couple of years before, the cops had come to his house to find a neighbor dead on the ground. At least they thought it was the neighbor. There was just the body, nothing left above the neck. Griffin had said they'd been playing cowboys and didn't realize the gun was loaded.

The gun in question, a sawed-off, double-barrel. Afterward, Griffin had stayed out of trouble for a long time. Traveled, worked. Then back in stir for a couple of armed robberies. And there was that guy in the cell with him, the guy who'd fallen off his bunk, hit the concrete floor, busted himself open pretty bad. A passing guard happened to see him. Griffin said he'd slept through it all.

Middle of the day.

Suspect number two... Richard Allen Wigle, who'd spent his life lashing back for the perverse genetics that had left him so mercilessly ill-equipped. As a youngster, 17 felony arrests... assault with a deadly weapon, grand theft. He'd been sent to Mercer and, for some bizarre reason, so had Griffin.

The prison had been built in back in the '80s. Lots of the cons spent their days working outside. Breaking out was easy.

There would be no bond. The boys would remain in jail.

The day after the hearing, Tate went back. He'd gone into the ring and lost. Now he was looking for redemption. They would meet in an interview room down the hall from Griffin's cell. Desk and a phone. Portrait of the president.

Tate was waiting. Griffin came in and sat down, benign. Not so many years ago, this was somebody's kid. Wore a little baseball cap, played with cars in the back seat.

"Tell me about the first day you got here," Tate said. "When was that?"

"What? No psychoanalysis today?"

"I asked you a question."

"All right. I have no objection. It was Tuesday. We got a room at a small hotel along the highway, two rooms actually. Richard and his little Lisa had their own. Jeanne likes her privacy, particularly when she's inflamed. Some days, she doesn't even want meals, just likes to stay in the room. It's like nothing satisfies her. You've met her? Of course you have. Tell you what she likes? No, you wouldn't want that, not right now. Perhaps a later session."

Tate didn't look up from his notepad. He wrote something down. He took his time.

"You stayed in."

"No. We wanted grits. Never had em. Thought we'd wait until we were way south before we tried. Kinda tasted like worn out corn meal to me, the sort of thing poor people might eat, or rich people might give to their poor people. How about you, Tate? Do you own anybody? Anybody you might refer to as 'my man?' What about 'boy?' Do you use the word at all? Of course I'm joking. Obvious to me from day one you were the ethical sort. You like to escort a woman right to the door, I suspect. You're not married. You've never had time for it."

Tate got up and moved to the other end of the table to get away from the sun. He wrote something down.

"You had grits."

"Yes we did."

"And then."

"Bacon, good bit of bacon, which I found a little suspect. Not that it wasn't fresh. It was just that thin, cheap bacon you find a lot in your rural areas. I can see you being fairly particular about that. You're kind of fastidious about some things, aren't you? It's not how you like to see yourself, but you do have that 'I like things just so..' kind of approach to certain aspects of your life. Probably have a messy desk, then again you like to put your suspects away for a great many years, isn't that right?"

Tate tore a piece of paper off the pad, folded it, put it in his pocket.

"It is and I'm quite successful with it. I've got a scorecard. Like to see it?"

"You really don't, but you'd put something together, just for me. That's one of the things I really like about you, that and your dark side."

"My dark side would hardly compare."

"You think? Nothing keeps you up at night? I can see you losing a fair amount of sleep, but it wouldn't be pissy stuff from work. It would be stuff like that slutty girl who wanted you down under the bleachers, but then she wouldn't let go. You didn't like remembering it later."

Another pause.

"And then what did you do?"

"We drove around a little, no place in particular. I don't like the tightness around your eyes. You haven't looked this bad since that first day we met."

Tate leaned back in his chair, drummed his fingers on the table. Then he nodded.

"You're a little puffed up today aren't you?" he said. "Make you feel important to blabber on like this? Actually, I've been meaning to ask you..."

Tate leaned across the desk. Hesitated. Almost whispering.

"The shrinks think you're probably a closet pedophile. You think that's true?"

Tate, tilting his head to the side, raising his eyebrows, waiting for an answer, a polite smile. Griffin lifted his hands slowly from the table. He stuffed them deep into his pockets. His eyes burning a hole.

"And what about the car?" Tate said.

"What car?"

"The car you were driving when you picked up the woman you murdered."

It was that afternoon that Tate's life changed.

GRIFFIN HAD only been back in his cell for a couple of hours. They'd brought some lunch. He ate. Then he said he needed to see a doctor. Something was wrong with that salami, he said. He was feeling flat awful.

The guy in charge of the wing wasn't sure. He went to the head jailer. He wasn't too sure either. There was no nurse on duty today. But then he started to think about Tate Drawdy, about how it was going to be such a big case and all. About his pension, about staying out of trouble. He took the officer aside.

"You take him. Take another guy with you. Get somebody with some beef on him. Keep him cuffed. Keep your eyes on him the whole time. No waiting outside the doc's door. Hear?"

Griffin had his pants around his ankles when they came for him. He was sitting on the john, his head in his hands. He didn't look so good.

"Come on mister. We're taking you to see the doc."

"You mean it?"

The way he looked up, you could tell he was grateful. Must be feeling pretty bad. They gave him a few minutes and then they walked slow. Griffin wasn't saying much, but he was compliant as all hell. None of that attitude. They drove gently, heading down Cartaret, past the old shopping center, the tire place. All the sudden, it seemed like everybody else was in a big hurry. Griffin, gazing out at the palms lining the street, wishing he could open a window.

They pulled into the clinic parking lot. The officer kept his hand on Griffin's head as he got out of the car.

He marched Griffin inside while his buddy went across the street.

"You can take those cuffs off," the doc said. "And then you can stay here with us while I examine him."

"My boss says the cuffs stay on."

Griffin just handled it, smooth as silk.

"It's all right, doctor. I don't mind. Let's keep the cuffs on. I just need to get something for my stomach. I don't think I've ever had a belly like this before."

And then, as if to demonstrate, he started to stand up from the table. But he was just wobbly and leaning forward and the officer stepped closer for some support and in that instant Griffin had that boy's 9mm out of the holster and jammed down his throat.

He shushed them as if he were quieting a restless toddler.

"No noise now or you're both gonna take one in the face," Griffin said.

"Now unlock these cuffs."

He got those hands loose, used his free hand to push the cop back against the table. His gun hand he lifted high in the air and then brought it down hard, crushing the barrel against the side of the doc's head. The doc went down. Blood began to cover the floor.

"Got kids?" Griffin said.

"Huh?"

"You got a family... wife, kids?"

"Yes sir. Yes sir I do."

"OK. Here's what we're gonna do. You're gonna walk behind me to the car. You drive. I'm keeping the cuffs loose on my wrists and the gun in the doc's little sack here, just like he gave me some pills to carry back. If there's any problem at all, I'm gonna hit you twice. Once right in the belly, so I hit your spine. You wanna guess about number two?"

"No sir I don't."

"Promising student."

They went out the back door. The cop eased the car out of the parking lot. Nobody saw a thing.

Griffin got comfy in the back seat, keeping his hands out of sight.

"See, your first mistake was letting that other guy run over to the barber shop. Three guys I had no chance. But you screwed up, didn't you?"

"Yes sir."

"OK. You trust me, right?"

"I don't know."

"Honesty. I like honesty. Tell you what we're gonna do. You're gonna advise me. If your advice sounds good enough, I'm gonna let you live. Work for you?"

He nodded.

"OK. I wanna know which way to go. A place to hide for a little while."

The jailer took off his hat and laid it on the seat next to him.

"I would stay inland. You head for the beach, you'll be too easy to corral. Only one road goes out that way."

"Good enough. Take us inland."

COUPLE DAYS went by. No sign of the car. No sign of Griffin. Guys working around the clock, on their days off. When the victim was a cop, the troops turned out. Looking everywhere, checking the roadsides. Tate and Char went by the hospital to see the doc. It didn't look good. Afterward, Tate dropped her off. His phone rang. It was Jimmy.

"Hey man, I got a couple beers need drinking."

Jimmy liked to drink beer, but only at home. He had a rule. You can't be a cop and drink in town, at least not a good cop. Bad things might happen.

Tate took Abercorn to Washington, parked on the street. Jimmy's pickup was still out front. He could hear the radio playing on the porch upstairs. Tate let himself in, headed across the marble floor, past the antiques and the ornate chandelier to the wide curving stairway. There were little lights along the edges of the risers.

Jimmy was in a rocker under a fan.

"Let's talk about your bad boy. Where would he go?"

"There's people looking all over the country now. I think they're wasting their time."

"Because...."

"He's not running," said Tate. "He's just chilling out someplace nearby. He doesn't want to get away. He wants to stick around, fuck with people."

"Who, especially?"

"I'm guessing me. Char busted him, but it doesn't pump him up to take Char on. Probably sees her more as a juvey officer anyway. I'm an adult and he needs somebody to beat."

"I like how you see it. So where do we go from here?"

"Not sure where else to look," Tate said. "We've got a full-court press on and no sign of him or the jailer, Russell... you know him?"

"Sure."

"I think it might be simpler to put me someplace where he can get at me, find a way to get that out. Pick him up when he goes for the bait."

"Strictly off the books."

"Yeah."

"You put something together?"

"What if I maybe get a TV interview or something? Say a few words for the camera that might piss him off. Mention where I'll be the next day or so, someplace he can get to."

Jimmy nodded. "Put you inside. Me outside."

"Yeah."

"That might work. Let's hope he's got a TV."

He knew Jimmy would want in. Jimmy liked to keep moving. He was one of those guys you could ask to help you fix a busted toilet or build a deck or run conduit and then you'd be embarrassed to realize he could have done it faster without you. Long, thin like a distance runner, corded veins on the insides of his forearms, hands with big knuckles. A broad forehead that clenched tightly in the presence of fools.

Jimmy could have done fine pretending to work in a bank. But Jimmy was too antsy for a desk. Besides, he'd been born a cop. Crewcut, wiry, eyes that moved in an instant from patience to fire.

The next morning, Tate gave a call to a local reporter. It was a guy who'd asked him for a favor one time, some inside scoop on a case. Tate had told him to fuck himself. They met over sausage and grits.

"I saw a piece you did the other night," Tate said. "Feature story, I guess. You had kind of a travelogue thing going there. We saw out the windshield, the road you were taking…"

"The piece about the old lady who paints out on the island?"

"That was it. Got a proposal for you. What if I asked you to do an interview with me that would be kinda similar?"

"Not sure I follow you, but I'd be glad to get you on camera. What do you want to talk about? Griffin, I hope."

"Yeah, it'll be Griffin. Look… I know you guys don't allow your subjects to set any terms or make up the rules. But there's something I need and it's important. You do this my way, and I'll make it worth your while. Beyond that, I don't want to explain. If you agree, I need you to make it happen the way we're talking about."

"You're asking a lot. What exactly are you after? And what's in it for me?

"Thanks at least for listening. I haven't been too easy on you and I wouldn't blame you for telling me to fuck off. But, like I say, this is real important."

So Tate laid it out for him. The interview would be at a fish camp, just this side of the causeway. The gist would be that Tate was going to spout off about what a scumbag Griffin was, and how he was going to rot in hell. As for the travelogue thing... that would be the reporter showing how he'd cleverly tracked Tate down while the detective was taking a few days off to fish. Catching him off guard.

The hook was they were going to keep advertising the interview during the day. Tune in tonight for an up close with the detective... shocking details. That sort of thing.

"Be up to you to get your folks to agree to pump this thing up," Tate said.

"I think I see where this is headed."

"You don't see and we're not going to talk about it. Not any time. But I will tell you this much. You do this my way and nobody else knows that the idea came from me, you and I will have a long and happy relationship."

"OK. I hear you. So what are the shocking details we're going to hear?"

"It'll be something good enough you don't get into any trouble with your bosses."

Tate and Jimmy got out there about mid-afternoon. Both of them taking vacation days. Tate parked out in front of the cabin he'd rented. Tate brought a couple of good books. Jimmy, some fishing rods.

"You want to get a couple of hooks wet while the sun's up?"

""Never got into fishing."

"I could teach you."

"You're teaching me enough already. Fishing's not my cup of tea."

"Suit yourself."

They'd only been there a couple of minutes when Char drove up. She came inside carrying a big bucket of chicken.

"Figured you guys would have already gotten the beer."

"What are you doing here? You can't stay here."

"Relax. He ain't coming before dark."

4

THEY SAT all night. Not a damn thing. When the sun began to
edge up over the horizon, Jimmy came inside.

"I've done a lot of stakeouts over the years. The more you do
'em, the more you don't wanna do 'em."

"You think we're done here? They won't show the thing on the
TV anymore."

"I can see one more night."

"Yeah. Let's get some sleep."

Jimmy was headed out the door when a car pulled up outside.
It was Char again.

Jimmy marched out and smacked his hand hard on the roof of
the car.

"Thought I told you to stay away from here."

She pushed the door open and stood as tall as 5'1" would let her.

"I did what you said. I went home. Now if he was gonna show
up, wouldn't he would have been here by now? So I came back
out. You saying you don't want these McMuffins?"

She was thinking that innocent grin was going to wipe the
slate. Jimmy wasn't having any part of it. He grabbed her arm and
pulled her inside.

It was starting to get muggy. Clouds drifting slowly above them
in a pale gray sky, teasing the sun. They were close to the water
and the skeeters were bad. A lot of insects making noise. There
was a wet, decaying smell of mud and fish and the river and centuries of birds sitting in the same place. You could grow to love

that smell, but it would make you want to take off your shoes and eat supper on the porch.

Tate was pissed off.

"It is completely ignorant for you to show up here. What if the guy was hanging out?"

"Geez, I dunno. It's daytime. Why would he take that chance?"

Jimmy was at the window, watching. He interrupted, still watching.

"When you're dealing with real bad guys, you want to admit to yourself right off the bat that you won't always know what they're going to do. They'll be a whole lot smarter than you think, or a whole lot dumber. They'll do something completely unpredictable, just because they felt like it. The guy could walk in here right now."

"So why are you two going it alone? Why don't you have six guys out here with you?"

Tate answered.

"Because this is a total shot in the dark. We're probably wasting our time. It was just something we felt like trying. But let's be perfectly clear here. From this point on, I don't want you anywhere around this case. No more surprise drop-ins."

Jimmy pulled a chair out for her, took her arm.

"If he was around, he might have seen you, Char. So you're staying at my house for the duration. You're not driving your car anymore."

She started to protest. He held up a hand. Then he took out his phone.

"Dispatch? Yeah. Jimmy Patterson here. Who's got the desk right now? OK. Can you patch me through? Thanks.

"Thomas? Hey it's Jimmy P. I guess you've heard I'm going to be made captain. Yeah, it's for real. Look, I'm gonna ask you for a couple things today, all right? OK. Thanks buddy. First, I want a guy detailed to sit at my house at night for the next week or so. I may or may not be there. And I need an extra squad car dropped off this morning at Scotty's. It'll be for Char Pinckney. Whoever drops it off can drive her car back to the shop, OK? Thank you, my friend. I will be by later and sign for this."

He turned to Char.

"You see where this is going? You won't be home. You won't be by yourself. You'll be in a very conspicuous car. And one other thing. Until he's caught, you're going to call in every stop you make, 24-7, clear?"

His voice, growing insistent, like water coming to a boil.

"Geez, Jimmy."

"Sorry. We're not taking chances here. You're on this case. You grabbed these guys. Griffin could decide he wants to hurt you. So… you stop at the store, you call in and give your location and how long you'll be outta the car. You call in what street you're driving on. All of it."

"I can live with staying at your house a couple days, but this…"

Jimmy stepped back from the window, pulled a chair up close. She flinched as he leaned toward her. He put a hand on her arm.

"Char, no more playing around. This is the kind of guy who wants to inflict pain and misery and God-awful fear. His history is just a preview. This guy thinks he's a legend in the making. He's building to something.

"And one other thing. You see him and you're by yourself, you get away easy. Quick."

"Sure, yeah. I understand. You want me to…"

He stopped her with a finger in the air. Speaking slowly now.

"Or else you kill him, right now. No arrest. No conversation. No glances. No second thoughts. I want him dead. Understood?"

She nodded, distracted by the veins in his neck and along his arms, wishing she'd stayed home.

"Char…?"

"What?"

Jimmy took her wrist and pulled it toward him. He took her other hand.

"I want a promise from you that you will kill this mother fucker before he gets anywhere close. You will shoot him like he was a target on the range."

She got a little teary. She looked at Tate, turned back to Jimmy, nodded.

"I promise."

She hoped Jimmy never had reason to look at her training proficiency scores. Barely passed. Char, the instructor had written, was minimally capable of firing "in the general direction of the threat."

That afternoon, Char was headed out to the dry cleaners when she got a call from a dispatcher downtown. It had been 10 minutes since they'd heard from her. Char laughed. Then the dispatcher told her about Jimmy Patterson stopping by. Jimmy had posted a note over the radio. It said if he called in and whoever was on duty couldn't tell him where Char was, they were out of work.

Jimmy's promotion had just been announced. He was a big cheese now.

THAT NIGHT, Tate and Jimmy hung out at the fish camp again, with the frogs and the insects and the thick, pungent air that hung over the marsh. Both of them lathered up with bug stuff. Tate had the air conditioning off and the windows down, listening. As for Jimmy, he was outside, about eight feet off the ground in a hunter's chair he'd strapped to a pine, black on his face and hands.

"Pretty hard to sneak up on a guy in a tree."

He'd need a chiropractor. Sitting in one place for a long time, not Jimmy's strong point. He got as comfortable as he could and settled in. Pretty soon he was itching, imagining something small and disease-ridden breaking a trail up the seams of his pants, heading for that pool of sweat collecting in his shorts. They'd make some kind of nest, move in.

Jimmy's watch had one of those buttons that illuminated the face. He'd put it into a pocket. He had a radio and a 9mm. Hanging from a strap above him, an M-16. Jimmy was wearing night vision goggles, "starlight" scopes. Vietnam era stuff, but the department got them cheap.

Tate had an unmarked cruiser. They'd parked it about 25 yards away from the house. There was a small clearing and a path made of flagstones, with pale nightlights across the front and down the lane.

The weather had cooled a bit, a blessing. There was a breeze that tossed the Spanish moss and rustled the leaves. You could hear the crickets and the night birds and, every so often, a guttural grunting that slapped the air and echoed across the water. Jimmy thought it might be a gator. There were guys who could hear that stuff and tell you just what it was.

Griffin showed up around dawn.

Jimmy heard him coming through the woods, moving slowly, taking his time. He was still a ways back, somewhere behind him. Jimmy had his phone set to Tate's cell. He hit send, turned it off. It would vibrate once in Tate's pocket.

Jimmy reached for the rifle, counting his breaths. A scuff, pine straw. Movement behind the car. Something metallic reflecting in the light.

The voice was almost sing-song, playful.

"Tate. That you, Tate?"

Tate, quickly, from inside the cottage.

"That you, John Robert?"

There was just the slightest hesitation, the moment, all stage-timing perfect.

"Just wanted to stop by."

For a few seconds, there was silence. And then the explosion lifted the car and set it back down hard. The windows of the cottage shattered. The birds and the bees all scattered. There was nothing to shoot at. Griffin was gone.

A couple of guys from the fire department gave them a ride back into town. Tate talked Jimmy into stopping by the house for some bacon and eggs. As they drove up, they could see an officer on his back, his head leaning against the front door. It was Russell, the jailer. Jimmy got to him first, saw he'd been shot. Wasn't bad.

"Dunno why he let me live. He said he thought you'd be home soon."

There was more searching to be done. Russell had a pretty good idea where they'd been holed up, although he'd been face down in the backseat for some of the driving. But he knew the area, knew they hadn't gone far.

Eventually, they found it, an abandoned cabin deep in the woods. A little TV with some rabbit ears, a pile of food wrappers in a corner, a sprinkling of roaches. And there was the note.

TATE,

HEADING HOME FOR A SPELL. (I KNOW WHAT YOU'RE THINKING... GIVE UP ALL THIS?)

YOU TAKE CARE.

YOUR FRIEND,
JOHN ROBERT.

CHARLENE PINCKNEY hadn't always wanted to be a cop. She'd just needed a job and they were hiring. At first, the guys tended to make fun of her. She had the freckly face of a Brownie scout, bowl-cut sandy-brown hair, strapping shoulders, muffin hands, a chest like a bag of sand. A desktop hit her almost waist high. She wore simple dresses with buttons down the front and the kind of shoes you see in the old movies, square-toed and black and not the slightest bit stylish. The little linebacker, they called her.

Char never let on that it bothered her and she could hold her own in the squad room. And once, when a cocky young patrol kid had made a remark that was clearly over the line, Char decked him good. Then she helped him up.

The chief put them in the same car for awhile. It wasn't much later that she became a juvenile officer. She was real good at talking with the parents and she was passionate as hell about the kids. Always down at the schools, working with the truant officers, just making sure.

She'd been all the way out to the island that morning, almost all the way to the hotels, out past the fort and the marsh and the river, the Crab Shack and the tourist places and the liquor store and the galleries.

Seat pulled up close. Both hands on the wheel.

It was tempting to head down a side street, maybe Johnny Mercer Boulevard. Out far enough to see those sweet lanes winding through wrought iron and brick and mounds of azaleas. Lush grass, cutting-board flat. Lightposts with beveled glass. Clusters of high-end weekenders set back from the road in dark wood and steel. Broad, mint julep porches. Discreet signs close to the ground, in Cambria. Sagos and windmill palms. Must be nice.

She'd go for the big kitchen, with the glistening appliances and the high-end cabinetry. There'd be one of those built-in wine racks. She'd have to go on a spree to fill it, let the bottles get dusty.

It was time to start working on the girls.

Char had gotten up early, fumbling around in the guest room on Jimmy Patterson's second floor. It wasn't her day off. Still, she'd put on a pair of shorts and a t-shirt and a baseball cap. Tate was waiting for her outside the chief's office.

"What's with the beach look?"

"I'm going to discombobulate 'em."

"Baseball caps bring confessions out of people?"

"This one will."

"Could revolutionize the police business."

The chief was equally curious, but Char set them straight.

"I'm going to meet with both of the girls outside in the yard. They haven't been out since they got picked up. I'm got some homemade chicken salad and some sweet tea and a couple of little pastries. We're going to hear the birds singing and see the sky and I'm going to remind them how nice it is to be free and unencumbered with sick bastards who like to kill people for kicks."

The chief wasn't buying.

"We talk to suspects separately, Char, for a reason."

"Sure, I know, but these kids are trapped in some kind of crazy world. It may be that they have to agree to turn together."

"And I suppose you'd like to put them back in the same cell so they can counsel each other."

She nodded.

"Sorry. Not a chance. You turn em, then a defense attorney gets hold of the fact that the girls have had time to doctor their stories. Their testimony's worthless. Not going to happen."

"OK. I hear you," and, seeing the look on the chief's face, "Look, I'm not going to screw this up, ok?"

A female jailer came for the girls at 11:30. She brought them some shorts and golf shirts and some flip-flops, told them to follow her outside. They passed through empty hallways out of the cellblock and down the stairs.

Char had put a flowery cloth on a picnic table under a tree, with real plates and silverware.

"I heard it was gonna be that mystery meat again today for lunch. Thought you girls might like a break."

Later, she described it, laughter in her eyes.

"It was like Christmas. They looked at each other. I thought the little one was going to cry. I chatted with them about where they went to school, did they have any boyfriends, did they have any favorite bands or clothes.

"And afterward we had some of my mom's homemade oatmeal cookies. I showed them a picture of my mom, with her gray hair and her wrinkles. And then I told them they'd look like my mom by the time they finally got out of prison. And that it might be the last time in their lives they ate lunch without somebody standing over them with a gun.

"I was just getting warmed up when Lisa started bawling."

That evening, she got a call from the chief. The lawyers had been in touch with Shawn James.

Both girls wanted to cut a deal.

TYREE LAMONICA'S girlfriend would tell people her name was Lolly. It wasn't. He guessed she just liked the sound. He didn't much care for it. He called her by her real name.

Laura.

Tyree had met her almost a year and a half ago at the Bayou, down on River Street, off Abercorn Alley. Blues club. Thick stone walls, window frames made of brick. One of the old riverfront warehouses. Good shrimp.

She'd been sitting at the bar drinking what looked like a vodka tonic. Medium-length light brown hair tied back in a ponytail with a rubber band. Pair of simple earrings, some pink polish on her fingernails.

She had a Navajo-looking silver wristband with a blue-green stone. Some parts of the stone looked rich, brilliant; others, murky and deep, like ocean water trapped between rocks. Later, she would tell him it was a blue gem turquoise from Nevada. And then he wanted to go there.

She had on snug blue jeans that finished partway down her calves and an oversized man's shirt that hung loose and looked so damn good Tyree figured every man in the place must have already been shot down. Otherwise, that seat next to her wouldn't have been open.

When he took off his coat, she could see the knots rippled above his shoulders, the way his arms hung wide, lats sweeping across this back. Forearms like he'd been a pipefitter who couldn't be troubled with wrenches. They talked a bit. He told her he was a cop.

"I know who you are," she said.

"How come?"

"One of the girls behind the bar pointed you out. She said, that big guy with the cowboy hat and the long black slicker... he's a cop. He comes in here because he likes the band."

"Yeah, that's me. And you? What do you do."

She was a dancer. He said he could tell she was in good shape. He wanted to know was there much money in that and was it hard to stand just on your toes. Tons of money, she told him. But no toes. And then he figured it out.

"Yeah," she said. "Exotic. My club's just a couple blocks from here. Stick around, you can see my show."

"Oh, that's ok. I gotta go pretty soon."

"Don't be such a baby."

In the brief silence that followed, he shrugged, tilted his head, thought about it for a minute. His mouth had turned dry, so he took a sip of beer before he answered. Rubbed his hands on his pants.

"OK."

And then he swallowed slowly, tilted his head again.

"Maybe I could buy you a drink after."

"Yeah."

She had the kind of hazelnut skin that seems to tan in early spring, high, round cheekbones, arching eyebrows that looked suspicious and amused at the same time and perfect teeth, as if she'd had just the right braces as a child. He liked it that she wasn't a blonde and that she didn't try to fill every gap in the conversation.

The sun was just beginning to set and, as it fell, it left a soft orange glow behind her shoulders and bounced like glitter from her earrings and her eyelashes. He finished his beer and went to coffee.

He'd followed her home that first night, just seeing she got there ok. Gave him a chance to run her plates, check out whether she had a jacket. She did. Couple of priors for misdemeanor assault. She'd bounced a beer bottle off a guy's head. She'd shoved a guy off a bar stool.

It was a couple of nights later that he asked her about it. She said the guys she'd smacked were getting a little on the gropey side. That's how she phrased it. After they'd met for a drink a couple more times, she told him he could get gropey his own self, if he wanted.

Then she moved in.

Laura, an art student at the Savannah College of Art and Design. Drove a brand new F150, extended cab, had one of those hard tonneau covers. Paid cash for it. She had bushels of money. And so did Tyree.

They liked to treat each other to a good dinner. Downtown, over to Hilton Head, some of the nice places now on the mainland side.

They went to Charleston, ended up going back a few times for the seafood at the Crab House. She got the crab cakes and the lobster every time. And a California Cabernet, because it was the priciest thing on the menu.

She got a tourist to take their picture standing out front. She liked the old sign.

He could talk big around Laura and she just laughed and slapped his arm. He could get all fancy and puffed up and act stupid and she just liked it.

After a time or two, Tyree quit going to her club. It was her business. But he tended to get pissed off at the guys there, staring at her, yelling things, wanting to tuck money into her g-string. Guys who wanted to reach up and touch her.

She thought it was a good idea, him staying away, especially after that guy came walking up to her in the parking lot after a show. He put his arm around her. Tyree broke it.

We were gonna be late for supper, he told her.

He'd rented a nice new Cadillac for the drive.

Part Two

5

THE PRIEST came in from the beach on President Street, turned south on Abercorn and headed for the Cathedral of St. John the Baptist. It was one of those architectural wonders built back when people put a lot into their houses of worship. It was a surprisingly cushy assignment for a guy just getting his start, but people liked him and he'd been blessed with an abundance of charisma.

He was young and he didn't make much. Drove a Volkswagen, hardtop. And when there was any chance he might be overheard, he listened to classical music. But whenever he got out of town for a few days, Father Palladino was far more likely to listen to some raunchy funk and leave his razor behind.

Dark curly hair, cut short, but hanging over his ears, a long, thin nose, five-o'clock shadow by 3, engaging smile.

He parked on a side street and dodged a crowd of tourists getting off the trolley tour. Black socks, Bermudas and sunburn. Palladino sidestepped a middle aged couple on the sidewalk and overheard them whispering loudly.

"Look at that gorgeous church, Eugene. Let's see if they'll let us go inside."

"Jesus, woman, now we have to look at churches?"

Palladino stopped and turned back toward them.

"You can go inside anytime, ma'am. And if your husband's tired of sightseeing, there's a great Irish pub right down the street."

The husband slapped his hands.

"Now that's what I'm talking about. You're right dear, the church looks spectacular. What say I meet you back here in an hour, hour and a half?"

She stammered, but turned quickly back to Palladino before he could make his escape.

"Young man... I think you should meet my daughter. That's her, the lovely brunette just getting off the bus."

"The man's a priest, dear."

"A priest? Is that right?"

Palladino nodded.

"Oh dear. Forgive me."

"That's quite all right. Sometimes it shows, I guess, even without the collar."

Eugene laughed.

"It's 12 o'clock and you're walking into a church with a stack of books. It wasn't too hard a guess."

"A fine-looking young man like you. You seem far too young to be the priest of this enormous church."

"We have quite a number of priests here, ma'am. And I am by no means *the* priest. I'm just a priest."

"I hope I haven't said the wrong thing."

"Not at all. My name is Vincent Palladino. How are you liking Savannah?"

They shook hands. Eugene reached out and clasped Palladino's shoulder.

"Geez, Father. I don't think I've ever met a body-builder priest before. That's a heck of a set of guns you got there."

"Eugene?"

And now both men laughed. Her husband explained:

"It's slang, dear. It means... big arms."

Eugene struck a pose, crunching his shoulders forward, fists clenched at the waist, stuck out his lower jaw. Palladino roared, slapped him on the back.

"Looking pretty good yourself there, young man."

"Stop right there. Let me get a picture. You don't mind, Father?"

"Naw, that would be great."

He put his arm around Eugene and the two of them hammed for the camera. Introductions all around. The mother, Emily, and daughter, Dina.

Eugene could see both the Jorgenson women were smitten.

"Father, I wonder if I could ask a favor."

"Of course."

"We're leaving tomorrow and we'd really like some good sea-food tonight. Could I persuade you to join us—and choose a restaurant?"

Palladino hesitated. Dina took a step toward him, took his hand.

"We'd really love for you to come."

Quite the looker, mid-length curly hair, tall, almost as tall as he. Very fit. Dark eyes with elegant lashes. The cheekbones, high and strong. Her nose, very precise. A simple cotton shirt over a pair of loose-fitting shorts that tied at her waist with a string. He decided quickly.

"That's very nice of you. Why don't we meet downstairs at the Pink House. There's a great old bar on the bottom floor. Big fireplace, heavy beams, very old, lots of atmosphere. Good place to get a glass of wine and the waiter will let you know when your table's ready upstairs."

She let his hand go now and nodded.

"That's awfully nice of you."

"It might be a good idea to get a reservation. Can I leave that up to you?"

They agreed to meet at 7, shook hands once more and Palladino walked inside, heading down a long marble hallway toward the back of the church and his small office. He set down his things to rummage for his keys.

Bookcases on three walls. A small fireplace. On the wall above it, the Sword of God, with a headpiece engraving of Michael, the archangel.

He'd been working at his desk for more than an hour when he heard a light knock at the door. He opened it. A young girl, not more than 16. White pleated skirt and a blue button-down shirt. On the pocket, her school insignia. Through her clear backpack, he could see textbooks and binders.

"What brings you here at this hour, young lady? You should be in school."

She tilted her head to one side and gave up a shy smile.

"Teacher's work day, Father. We're supposed to be in the library or spending the afternoon working on our team projects. My team leader has a cold."

He stuck his head out into the hallway and satisfied himself no one had seen her. He held open the door. She walked slowly past him, swaying her skirt from side to side.

Palladino was curt.

"You're not supposed to be here. You remember our agreement."

"If I promise not to come here again, will you let me stay?"

She was pacing slowly now, studying the titles on his shelves, but keeping her body angled slightly toward him, so that he could admire her figure. She had blonde hair and big blue eyes and her lips held a thick coat of purplish gloss. They were fiercely pursed, in a way the young boys at school found irresistible.

Palladino put his hands on his hips.

"No you may not stay. And if you don't go, then you and I won't be able to meet anymore."

She turned quickly, tears forming in her eyes. And then she nodded.

"Yes, Father."

She walked slowly past him to the door.

"I won't do this again. I promise. I remember what you said. I remember everything you told me."

"People would not understand. I would lose my job and then I would have to go away."

She was facing him now, staring into his eyes.

"Yes, Father."

She waited. He reached out, put his hands under her arms and slowly lifted her off the ground. Her face flushed. He held her off the ground effortlessly, then slowly lowered her until their mouths were close. He kissed her. She walked quickly down the hallway and out the back.

THE RESTAURANT was the perfect end to their vacation. Eugene wore a tie, his hair slicked back hard and straight. Both women wore light sweaters over their dresses. Palladino arrived a few minutes late, a dark sport coat over a thin collarless shirt.

They had Pinot Grigio in the bar downstairs on a big sofa in front of the fire. Brick walls and a low ceiling. Brahms and clever conversation. And then they were escorted up two flights, grooved wooden stairs showing 220 years of wear. Bedrooms turned into dining areas, marvelous chandeliers and fancy table settings, mirrors in heavy gilded frames, knotty wood on the walls.

They ordered crab cakes and fried green tomatoes, fried shrimp, chicken and garlicky spinach. Eugene asked for two more bottles of Pinot. Emily was dying to know why Palladino had decided to become a priest.

"My father was caretaker of a big church in upstate New York. He'd been doing it since before I was born and the three of us—my parents and me—lived in a carriage house the church owned on the property next door. When I was seven years old, my father fell off a ladder and was badly hurt. He died about a month later.

"The diocese was really generous about it. They said the two of us could continue to live there until I graduated from high school, or college, and my mom could then move in to one of the church's nursing homes. My parents were older, in their 50s when I was born.

"And so I lived on the church grounds my whole life and the priests were sort of my surrogate parents. They taught me Latin, boxing, how to dance."

He could see the curious looks... the sympathy and the concern.

"You can put your minds at ease. Nothing bad happened. None of the fathers took advantage of little Vincent."

Emily sputtered a reply.

"Oh, we weren't thinking anything."

"Of course you were. Don't apologize. This is the world we live in. The church would be a lot better off if we could all speak openly about this stuff. There were some who saw the church as a way to take advantage of impressionable kids. Unfortunately, the hierarchy thought it was a good idea to try to sweep that under the carpet.

"Look, there are 110,000 priests in this country. The vast majority of them are truly fine people who are dedicated to the church."

Dina reached across and refilled his glass.

"And being around them is what persuaded you?' she asked.

"Yes, that and gratitude. It was a wonderful place to grow up. I had opportunities other young men would die for. So far, it's been a good choice."

"You're not sure?"

"No. Can't say for sure that I'll stay. There are some parts of the work that I find truly rewarding. But I still don't know if I'm cut out to be a man of the cloth, pledged only to God for the duration."

It was getting late. Emily and Eugene were struggling to stifle yawns. Dina suggested heading back downstairs for one more drink at the bar.

"I'm afraid I've had plenty," Eugene said. "Perhaps you two young people can go on. Father, if you don't mind, can you run Dina back to our B&B after?"

They walked outside and said their goodbyes. The air, losing the day's warmth. She walked to the curb and stood for a moment. There was just the sliver of a moon. They could see several couples on benches in the square opposite the restaurant, sitting close.

"Where do you live, Father? Here in the old downtown district?"

"I've got a place at the beach. It's about 30 minutes from here."

"I'd love to see it."

He smiled. They started for his car, which was parked on the other side of the square. Then she stopped, asked him to wait, and ducked back into the bar. When she came back out, she was carrying a bottle of wine.

"I couldn't get any glasses."

As they walked toward the car, she took his hand.

He started the car, took the beach road. There weren't many cars. She put her shoes on the floor, pulled off her underwear, reached over and unclasped his belt. He pulled into the slow lane.

6

WHEN THEY arrived at the bungalow, Palladino pulled the bug under the branches of a great oak along the side of the house. She took off her dress.

The VW was a little too cramped for anything ambitious. Dina looked back to the road, then jogged to the door, leaving him to gather up her clothes. She tried the door. It was unlocked.

She was already in the bedroom when he got inside. She'd turned on a bathroom light and pulled the door half closed.

"We don't have a lot of time, your eminence."

And then she was pulling off his pants. He started to speak, but she put a finger to his lips.

In the car on the way back, he asked her: "You're thinking of staying?'

"Maybe for a little while. Just to soak up some atmosphere. Any good places to rent?"

"You might find something in the old town, be a nice way to get a feel. Most of em don't have much in the way of fancy bathrooms or kitchens, but they've got tall ceilings and big windows, great personality. You'd like it here."

"Might be fun. But you don't need to worry about me, Father. I won't crimp your style."

"Worry was not what I had in mind. I'd love to see you again."

He smiled. So did she.

"I am the soul of discretion."

"Are you Catholic?"

"No. I'm sorry."

"No matter. What do you believe in?"

"I'd like to find something. Right now, the only thing that really seems to get me going is Harry Connick Jr."

"Me too. Got a bunch of his CDs."

"Which way do you lean? The old stuff or the new stuff?"

He laughed.

"Actually I really like the very early stuff."

"I saw him on TV one time," she said. "Somebody asked him to describe how he was different from Sinatra. He says, 'Well Frank would sing it this way.' And he sang a few bars. And then, 'I sing it this way.' And I really couldn't tell much difference."

"Wonder how that happened. Give him time, I guess."

They were both laughing now.

"How do you support yourself?"

"I'm a paralegal and I'm charming. I can find work pretty easily."

"You are charming."

"I thought you thought so."

It was late when Palladino dropped her off. He parked behind the church, came in through a side entrance and went into the nave. He loved seeing the church at this time of night, when he had it all to himself. He liked the little spotlights reflecting off the altar, the marble, the engravings of the evangelists, the serenity.

He unlocked the door to his office and saw the note on the floor. A tiny sheet of paper, crisply folded.

Looked for you earlier.

He smiled and stepped back into the hallway. There was no one there, only darkness.

He sat down at the desk and began reading. And now, a scratching at his window. He went over to look. A face. He unlocked the window and cranked it open.

"This doesn't look like team project work to me," he said.

She held up her arms to be lifted inside.

"I'm spending the night at a girlfriend's. She made me promise not to tell her parents she was sneaking out for a couple of hours. It's off Liberty, a couple of blocks over. I saw your light on. I can only stay a minute."

She went to the door, locked it, turned out the light. He sat, watching while she tossed her clothes in the corner. There was just enough light from the street. In a moment they were on the floor. Palladino had to keep reminding her to keep her voice down. And then he was asleep on top of her. Soon she, too, was asleep, snoring lightly.

And then a key turned in the lock, slowly, noiselessly.

Bare feet hesitated on the marble floor. The door, gently pushed back into place. The feet came closer. They were almost on top of the sleeping pair.

For a time, the intruder stood without moving. Then there were two small pops, like children's firecrackers in an alley. The feet stepped away. They retreated, tiptoeing toward the wall, then the fireplace. More slowly now.

Two hands reached high, lifting that defender's sword from its hook.

The feet moved boldly now, quickly back to the window, where they stopped, the stance wide. Then, a horrifying sound as the blade raced through the air.

7

8 A.M. SATURDAY. It was two months since Griffin had disappeared. Tate had the day off, for a change. Reading the paper, drinking some coffee.

The phone rang. It was Jimmy.

"Hey. You remember I told you I was gonna get you on my team…"

"Yeah."

"Today's the day."

"What's up?'

"Got a priest, young guy, dead."

"Somebody whacked a priest?"

"In his office, middle of the night."

"Holy shit."

"Actually there's a lot more to it. We'll talk when you get here. Come on over to St. John's. And lay real low. Before long we're gonna see a bunch of cameras out here."

"I can imagine. You want me to shower or come now?"

"Shower's OK. Just be here in five."

He skipped the shower. Got there just in time see Jimmy standing in the hallway, surrounded, calmly telling a gaggle of church fathers no, they could not keep the crime hushed up.

"I understand how you feel. But we cannot order the girl's parents to keep quiet. What do you want me to tell them? Somebody murdered your child, but we need to keep it under control for the sake of the church? I don't see how we can do that."

Tate waited off to the side. Jimmy saw him, excused himself.

"Hey. Robert Landis is here, looking over the bodies," Jimmy said. "The photographs are done, but they're still wrapping up inside. Look, I know this sucks, but I need you to make a visit here to the parents."

"What parents?"

"Little girl who was with the priest."

"What?"

"They were doing it in his office," Jimmy said. "Somebody walked in on em. Shot em both. Looks like a .22. Then they stuck a big sword in his back. His head's practically severed."

"You sort of neglected to mention that part of it on the phone."

"I was gonna see if you could put it together. Two people, naked… blood."

"Good clues."

"Yeah. Anyhow, we have the girl's wallet. I feel real bad about how we don't know squat here, so you're going to have to be kinda careful with it."

"The girl reported missing?"

"I'm not sure, but it doesn't look like it. It's gonna be tough. You'll have to tell em you don't know a damn thing, except their little girl was having sex with a priest in the middle of the night and they got attacked."

"Landis has been in looking at the bodies, says there's no indication of resistance. Looks like they didn't see it coming."

"Are we gonna let the parents have a look?"

"Don't know how we can stop them. Do what you can. Try telling em the crime scene is full of cops and we expect the parking lot's gonna be full of media. Probably won't work. But if you keep em long enough we can at least get the bodies to the coroner and they'll have to go there."

Tate had done this before, a couple of times. Worst part of the job. He stuck a blue light on the roof, put it away when he got close. He parked in the driveway. Looked in the mirror long enough to smash down his hair.

They both came to the door, Mike and Liz Chalmers. They were nice people. A nice house. Nice cars. Somebody had put a lot of work into the lawn. He asked if he could come inside. He could see them weighing it, figuring the daughter had gotten into trouble.

They gave him just enough room to get inside the door. He got right to it, as gently as he could. As soon as they knew, they were out the door.

Seeing their faces was going to make it impossible to get much sleep for a couple of days, but he knew why Jimmy had asked him to go.

He told them he'd leave a policeman out front to keep people from bothering them.

THAT AFTERNOON, late, they were in Jimmy's new office on the second floor. He'd just moved in, still a lot of boxes around. A mid-sized room with an old oak desk and a couple of filing cabinets. Jimmy had brought some reproductions for the wall... a Rembrandt, a Modigliani. Not your typical cop fare.

There was a heavy door, a couple of chairs. Acoustic tile on the ceiling. In the offices, cheap carpet. In the hallways, crappy tile floors. The walls were brick, painted a milky white, with paneling on the lower half. The fluorescents gave the whole place a kind of faded yellow tint.

The old police barracks overlooked Oglethorpe, at the corner of Habersham on the east, the west side facing Abercorn, with the cemetery in between. Decent view of the headstones.

There was a call from the front desk. A young woman downstairs wanted to talk with the detectives. It was about the case.

An officer brought her up, a tall young woman, athletic, con-servatively dressed in a gray pants suit. The suit looked new. She stood, shifting her weight from one foot to the other.

"My name is Dina Jorgenson. I saw the TV news about Father Palladino. I don't think I know anything that will help you, but I thought it was my responsibility to come in.

"You see, I may have been the last person to see Vincent... before the young girl of course."

She explained about her family's trip down from Maryland, that they'd met Palladino outside the church, had dinner. She didn't leave anything out.

"Look, Miss Jorgenson," Jimmy said. "I apologize for this, but if you don't mind, I need to know a little more. Obviously, the father had a pretty active sex life. It looks like that will be a factor."

"I understand," she said. "Sex with two women in the space of a couple of hours. And he was a priest. You have to wonder if maybe that's why he was killed."

"Mmm. Well, let me do this. I'll ask you to tell the whole story, and I'll ask you some questions. I'll record it. And then I'll ask you to sign a statement . Would that be all right?"

"Yes."

She knew what she was getting into, knew what it could cost her. She was resigned to it. She started over. Told them what they had to eat, what they talked about, told them about her parents, told them about the drive out to the beach, his place, his bedroom.

"You seem ok talking about all this," Jimmy said.

"Yes. Well, I wish I didn't have to. It's embarrassing. I hardly knew him. But I'm a big girl."

"You said you initiated the sex. And he was a priest. What made you think to do that? Why'd you think it would be ok?"

"He stayed after my parents left. He had no hesitation when I suggested we drive out to his house. When we were outside, I held his hand. I stood next to him. He wasn't the slightest bit

uncomfortable. I felt pretty sure he had normal adult relation-
ships with women.

"And there was something he said at dinner. I don't remember exactly. Something about whether he'd always be a priest. He
didn't think so."

Tate asked a question.

"Beyond his lack of nervousness, did you think being with a
woman was something he was used to?"

"He knew his way around the bedroom."

"No apparent discomfort with the contradiction?"

"No, Mr. Drawdy, he seemed genuinely at ease in both worlds.
He spoke very sincerely, very appreciatively, about the church. At
the same time he was... very confident."

She said he had dropped her off about 11:30. She'd left without
her room key and had to call the manager, so he would be able to
verify what time she came in. She'd gone upstairs and looked in
on her folks, adjoining rooms. Her dad was asleep, but her mom
had been sitting at the desk playing solitaire. They went into
Dina's room, talked for an hour or so, about whether she wanted
to stay in Savannah awhile. She'd been looking for a change.

They'd gotten a wild hair and had gone down to sneak a fancy
dessert from the kitchen. She'd seen one of the overnight staffers
there.

Her parents were home now. They'd had a long talk. Dina
thought she might stay on for awhile, look for work. She was
thinking Savannah might grow on her. Her mom had seen that
coming.

Eugene and Emily didn't know anything about what had happened, unless of course they were watching it on television, which
could easily be the case.

So Dina had a pretty good alibi, based on Robert Landis' esti-
mate of the time of death.

Jimmy was going to ask her to write out a statement. First, he wanted to know what she made of it.

"I think he was a complicated man. If you think about it, he'd spent the last few hours with me. And not an hour later he was with a little girl. Why? Was he insecure? Was it a Clinton thing? I certainly wouldn't have spent any time with him if I'd had any sense this was a conquest.

"And now I have a question. The TV said violent murder. You haven't said the cause of death."

Jimmy shook his head.

"No."

She hesitated. He wasn't going to say any more.

"Well, captain, what I make of it is there was *another* woman. I suppose the girl's parents could have wanted to kill him. But their own daughter?"

"Mmm."

"All right. What are the chances of my leaving here with my reputation intact? Or am I going to be tabloid fodder?'

"Thank you for your frankness, your cooperation," Jimmy said. "Right now, it's pretty hard to say. There's no reason for you to worry right this minute. But at some point, we're going to arrest somebody for this. It could come out at trial."

"Terrific. Do I need a lawyer?"

Tate answered.

"We'll need to verify what you've told us with the hotel. You ought to stay in town. If you like, you can call back tomorrow and we can tell you as best we can about how things stand.

"I guess he didn't mention any concerns, no one mad at him, no one he'd argued with, had an issue with."

"No, nothing like that."

She stood, shook their hands, turned to go. She seemed tired now. She looked down at her jacket.

"There aren't any price tags on me, are there? I had to stop on my way over, pick up something for my little confession today."

She walked to the door and turned to look at them. Then she nodded and walked down the hall.

"Bad luck," Jimmy said.

"Yeah."

TATE HAD PLANNED to shoot some hoops that night. He didn't much feel like it. He called Char.

"How about a beer?"

"Wow, I bet you could use one. What a nasty day."

They were going to meet at an old place on the south side of town. Tate said he'd pick her up.

They talked about baseball. Tate wanted to know about some guy who'd asked her out. She went and, for the first in a long time, he wasn't a complete nerd. Weren't a whole lot of really cool guys standing at her door, she said. But she did feel like it was important to meet people. She belonged to a group from church that went bowling.

"I'd rather hunt for men at the symphony or even a baseball game. But, of all the things they do, bowling is the only one I can stand. They do a museum walk. Tried that. I was the only one there under 70."

As for Tate, he said he went in spurts these days. Sometimes he felt real social, had a lot of energy, wanted to meet people, have some fun. Sometimes he just wanted to hang out, try to recover from the intensity of the work. In the relatively short time since he'd become a cop, he'd learned there were days when dealing with low-lifes and tragedy just washed off your back. And there were days when it was a pretty good load. It was best to stay disciplined, not get too far out of shape, not to string together too many beer nights in a row. He could see where it would age you. Jimmy'd held up pretty well, though.

No doubts. He'd found the career he wanted, at least for now.

Char thought it was easier for the women. They tended to prop each other up, their friendships were easier, more supportive. But she'd noticed, you didn't see too many older women staying on the job. Mostly it was the ones who desperately needed that income and the pension. Women who had some options tended to want to move on to something else before it took away their youth.

There were women with kids on the force. More nowadays. But it was hard to accept, letting so much evil come that close to you. You were afraid it might rub off on the kids.

Tate's phone rang. It was the office, forwarding a call.

"That you Tate?"

He could almost see the face.

"John Robert?"

"Hey. Geez, I was watching TV and saw that thing at the church. Saw you walking across in front of a camera. You working on this one? How'd you rate?"

"Where are you, John Robert?"

"No place special, my friend. I just wanted to see how you were."

"Thoughtful of you."

"I'm a sensitive guy. Hey, from the looks of it, this is one of those crimes where the cops aren't telling very much. Give me the scoop from the locker room."

"Only thing you need to worry about is looking for me over your shoulder."

"Do you dream about me at night, Tate?"

"Actually I'd forgotten all about you, until right now."

"Good thing I called, I guess. Hey this could be a tough one. Young priest, the girl... in that town. Got your hands full don't you? Say, why don't you just give me your home number."

"Rather talk face to face, John Robert."

"Bet you would indeed, old buddy. Tell me, Tate, are you with anybody these days? Somebody you can talk to? 'Cause I can be there for you, you know that. I'll always be there, my friend."

And then he hung up. Tate ordered another round. He told Char what Griffin had to say.

"That bastard. I hope we find him soon."

And then she hesitated.

"Actually, I hope somebody else finds him soon."

8

TATE HAD AN IDEA where Griffin was. He'd have to go
through the drill to confirm it. Frustrating, but inevitable. Tracing
a phone call wasn't like what you saw on TV. The whole thing
about keeping the guy on the line for minutes while some guy
wearing headphones spun knobs, that all went out with manual
switchboards and black and white movies. Electronic switching
systems had been around for years, along with automatic location
indicators.

Even cell phones. Every call left a record.

You got a court order. The phone company pulled up the data.
It wasn't complicated. Cell phones sent out a signal to search
for the best tower around them. The phone company's billing
records would show what cell towers handled the signal, which
would give you an approximate location of the phone when the
call originated. The records would also show which towers were
used while the call was connected, and would also give an approximate location of the phone when the call ended. Even if Griffin
used a burner, a prepaid throwaway phone, you'd know where it
came from. It wouldn't tell you where he was after he made the
call. Griffin wasn't stupid, but it wouldn't be hard to find out
where he'd been. It was a place and a time.

The next morning, there was a long piece in the New York
Times about Palladino. Tate was glad to see there weren't any
leaks from the department, but the paper knew all about Palladino's childhood, his less-than-perfect adolescence. Palladino,

a rowdy kid who'd been rescued by the local priests. The paper knew about his time in old Savannah. They knew about his sophomore squeeze.

Tate got a call from Dina Jorgenson. She'd seen the story. And now she was wondering just how long she might remain anonymous. She asked Tate if they could meet for coffee.

"Come by here if you like, although the coffee's pretty bad. If you're afraid it might be a little public in this building, I don't mind answering any questions you have over the telephone."

"I was hoping we could meet somewhere else."

Tate was hearing something in her voice. He stood up so he could pace. He thought better when he was moving.

"Can I be blunt with you?"

"Of course."

"I think you're looking for a friend. You're new in town, don't know anybody and you've had a really bad experience. I'm sympathetic as hell, but I'm not gonna be that person for you. You ought to call a family member or somebody to come down and stay with you for awhile if you're bent on staying.

"When you and I talk, it's going to be about the case. Understand?"

"Yes, you're right. I'm sorry if I was being inappropriate. It's just that you and Captain Patterson are the only people who really know about all this and I'm pretty scared."

"I know."

There was resignation in her voice now. She'd been tough when she needed to be. Now it was starting to wear her down and the reality of what might come from that mob of television and newspaper coverage was starting to sink in.

"All right," she said. "Is there anything we need to discuss?"

"Not right now."

"Thank you detective."

Jimmy knew the manager of the B&B where the Jorgensons had stayed. Dina was still there. He'd called and asked if anyone had seen her the night of the killing. The manager backed up her story. He'd seen Dina Jorgenson return that night and then later for that double chocolate layer cake.

If the medical examiner was right about the time of death, she was in the clear. Be nice to be able to tell her that, but that wasn't going to happen.

JIMMY PATTERSON had a theory. The killer was someone who worked at the church, a nun or a staffer, someone with a key. Palladino would not have taken his clothes off without the door locked. Aside from the girl, it wasn't likely anyone else was going to be visiting there that late. Of course, Palladino could have given a key to someone. Pretty risky though.

Then again, what wasn't risky about any of these scenarios? Wasn't like there was any simple way the guy could run around. Even an average guy's social life would ruin a priest and anybody with him.

Had to be somebody close by. And that theory was only reinforced when they got a good look at the crime scene photographs. Right next to the body, blood all over the floor, telling a story.

Jimmy and Tate were in the lab, looking at the pics on the tech computer. Tommy O'Shaughnessy had enlarged the area around the body.

"Take a look right here, bout a foot away from their heads. That's where somebody's gonna be standing to swing that thing. OK, now, lemme enhance it, enlarge it. OK, see right there? Look at the spatter coverage. It's not complete. It's hard to see, but I'm gonna show you with this little tool. We call it a lasso, gonna create a shape of a foot. See what happens when I overlay it? Covers up some of the spatter. See it? Right there at the edge.

"Now I made another shape, this time a bare foot. Overlay that... doesn't cover as much but still... right there at the top, blurs a tad. And now, the piece de resistance. Proportion. Let's make this foot smaller, about a size 6. See, now it fits right up against the spatter perimeter. I'm guessing you got a child or a small woman, barefooted. And whoever it was left with some blood specks on their feet."

O'Shaughnessy rolled back his chair, crossed his arms. Jimmy put him in a headlock.

"That is some fine work there mister. I'm gonna want you to tell me the exact size and shape of that foot. If you can make me some kinda representation of the foot that would help a lot.

"Now we just need to think through what this might be telling us. Tate?"

Tate bent over the screen. He reached for the mouse.

"All right. Lemme just make a couple of tweaks here."

O'Shaughnessy leaped up.

"Don't touch that!"

"Just kidding." said Tate, "OK. I think we're probably looking for a woman because this guy likes to fool around. We could be looking for a kid cause he's a priest, but right now we've got nothing in that direction. As for the bare feet, you'd think it's somebody trying to be quiet. Or maybe it's somebody who's already not wearing very much in the way of clothes."

Jimmy turned to O'Shaughnessey.

"How about you?"

"He had a date. What he forgot was he made two dates for the same time. Shoulda used a crackberry."

"Yeah, could be." Jimmy said. "We got a crime of passion. She comes in, expecting to see him, not expecting to see him on top of anybody else. So she whacks him, both of em. Couple of ways this could have gone in the shooter's head. She—assuming it's a she—wants to take him out, kills the kid cause it's murder and you don't leave anybody else alive. She takes them both out cause she hates em both right now. Jealous out of her mind.

"But the real obvious thing… he gets it twice. She shoots em both, then sticks him with the big sword. He's on top, sure, but there's no second hit on the girl. Just him. He's the one who betrayed her.

"And the other thing is the weapons themselves. Gun gets it done right now. Impersonal. Sword is real personal. Real up close. You can be under control and blast the two of em. The sword is real anger. She shot em. Then she either pulled that sword off the wall because she knew it was there, or because she walked around a bit and worked herself up into even more of a rage."

O'Shaughnessy jumped in.

"She carried some bloodstains over to the wall. We found em with the ultraviolet. She carried the blood across the room, so she'd already shot em and then went to the wall, stepped around the little fireplace and got down the sword. Then she finished him. Kaboom. Keep in mind, we've got two sets of blood spatter. The gunshots and the sword. Lot of blood from both, but the sword gets credit for a bunch. We figured out the timing of the thing when we walked the room."

"Yeah. And the anger thing makes a ton of sense," said Tate. "But here's one other thought. What if the sword is more than just a way to get extreme with the guy? What if it means something? There's some symbolic thing with it, either between them, or just by itself. Maybe it's a church thing. We need to know what that sword is, what it means, why he had it hanging up. Where he got it. Is it like a priest trophy, merit badge? Sounds stupid mebbe, but I think the sword's another actor here."

Jimmy smiled.

"I think you're catching on to this business kid."

THE BIG MAN was walking down the hallway, in early for his shift.

"Tyree... hang on."

A young woman from patrol. She was carrying an envelope.

"My kid had some extras, duplicates. I told him you were looking for old U.S. stamps."

He opened the envelope and poured them out into his hand. Some flags, some airmails, a couple of presidential.

"Hey, these are great. Can I give you a couple of bucks for your kid?"

"No, that's OK. He said he had more than one of these. You think there's something there you don't have?"

"Yeah. I don't have but a few airmail stamps. I have some flag stamps and last week I got a few that show a porch in the background. Flag over Porch, they're called. Very cool stamps. But, you know, I'm just getting started, really, and I only spend five bucks a week. Sometimes you have to go 10. That's my limit. Small payroll for us 'serve-and-protect' types."

"My kid loves it. Glad to see him get into something that has him off the computer, at least some of the time. And he's learning some stuff."

Tyree grinned, pointed a finger at her.

"OK. Here's one for him. Who was the first postmaster general of the United States?"

"I think he's gonna know that one. Ben Franklin, yes?"

"Nope. Trick question. Tell him he has to look it up."

"Wow. OK. So, anyhow, there you go. Gotta run."

He'd enlisted the neighbors, the guy in the mailroom, told people to ask their parents. He'd bought some stamps online and found he'd been suckered into getting bunches of the same stamp. But he was doing all right now. He'd gotten a really good stamp from the mother of one of his buddies. She had an old letter she'd saved, didn't need the stamp.

He made a phone call to a guy he'd seen in a web listing for a local group of collectors, asking if they'd pass along any throwaways. He didn't shoot for anything too ambitious.

Tyree Lamonica, with a cute history lesson for the kid. Who knew? If you'd asked around, people would say Tyree probably spent his Sunday afternoons cutting the grass, tossing some iron at the YMCA, taking a nap in front of a game. Here he was, huge mitts sticking bitty stamps in a book. The Big Guy, saving tiny pictures of flags.

The hardest part was handling the little stamps. It was almost impossible to get your finger underneath.

Tweezers. No problem. Once you had a good hold of em, you could get the stamp, you could put it where it needed to go. Picking up the tweezers, that was the trick.

He spent a few minutes at it every night. Laura didn't seem to mind.

She'd sit and read a book, might watch a British drama on the public channel. If it was close to sundown, she liked to light a bunch of mosquito candles, sit in an Adirondack out back and stare at the marsh. Their place, out by Isle of Palms, along the river.

It was some of the priciest real estate in town. The neighbors were curious, to say the least. But they kept their mouths shut and their curtains closed. Nice thing about the neighborhood, nobody was really that close by.

There was a long sandy lane leading up to a crushed-shell drive, a big stretch of marsh out back, massive oak trees in the yard. Empty lots on either side. Straight out behind the back door were cabbage palms, red cedar, plenty of pine trees and palmetto scrub. In a live oak about 40 yards away from the house, she would sometimes spot a statuesque owl. She'd been hearing it for a long time, finally spotted it.

She had walked down toward the tree, got pretty close, stood there, staring at the bird.

As time went on, it became more of a ritual. Toward sunset, she'd walk down toward that tree and there he was. She'd speak to him. Simon, she named him. Later on, when she'd sit in a chair with a drink in her hand, Simon would fly toward her. Just coasting really, wings outspread. He'd fly a few feet over her head, then park on a pine tree branch that overlooked her spot. Later, he'd fly back to his oak tree and she'd walk inside.

She'd call out to Tyree when Simon came by, or if there were egrets, or ibis or herons. They were far enough away from people that you'd see deer and possum. Lots of coons. Tyree said there were bobcats. He'd sit with her. Then he'd finish looking at the mail.

Laura, the squeeze. She had figured out pretty quickly that Tyree had more money than you'd figure for a cop. A good bit more. It was the house. And those statements from his broker. That first time he'd started opening the mail in front of her, he looked a little sheepish. Actually, real sheepish. He waved the investment paperwork and hemmed and hawed, started to explain. She stuck her fingers in her ears and walked down the hall, saying *lalalalala*.

So he took her on a ride out to Port Wentworth, past the house where he grew up. Wasn't quite what you'd call a house. It was a single-wide at the end of a dead-end street, set back in a pine tree stand. Siding peeling, a discolored patchwork of corrugated PVC covering a homemade front porch, torn plastic stapled to the window frames. The whole thing, listing to one side on top of stacked cinder blocks in each corner.

He'd slept on the couch in the living room, two feet from the front door. They ate hot dogs from the infra-red machine at the convenience store. And peanut butter sandwiches.

His dad drove a truck, came home one afternoon to find his oversized son excitedly telling his mom the football coach was interested in him. Daddy said if his boy Tyree set one foot on that football field, instead of chopping wood in the back, he'd slap him upside into next week. Firewood sales were daddy's drinking money.

Tyree allowed as to how he could whip his daddy's ass every morning before coffee and never break a sweat.

That night, after dinner, Tyree said he was going out to see some friends, some guys on the team. His daddy said no. Tyree kept going. And later, when he got home, he was just about to the door when a 2x4 came swirling out of the darkness. He awoke hours later, face-down in the dirt. And he waited.

The sun rose early that day. He could hear his daddy moving around the trailer, telling his mom he hadn't seen the boy. He had coffee, breakfast. And then he came out the door, into the sunshine, into his young son's gargantuan fist. One punch. Broken nose. Two front teeth, lying in the doorway, like the bars of a prison that had decayed and fallen aside.

A teammate's family had a garage with an apartment overhead. Tyree lived up there his last two years of school.

His little sister was still at home, Annette. Tyree wanted Annette out of there as soon as he could make it happen. At least that's what he kept telling himself.

As if you could spend all the money and then the guilt would be gone.

Laura still didn't want to know. Whenever the mail came, if there was a Wells Fargo envelope in there, she'd say lalalalalala. He got the message.

There was one thing she needed to hear, though.

If anything ever happens to me, you get out of here and don't come back. And take this with you.

With that, he knelt on the floor and brushed his hands along the baseboard underneath a bookcase. He showed her what looked like a dry crack in the paint. Just above it was a clear plastic tab. He had her tug on it. A section of baseboard pulled loose.

She would never have seen it. Neither would anyone else. Inside, a briefcase. He opened it. There were statements from his investments, a slip of paper with the directions to a safety deposit box and a key.

There was also an envelope. He showed her... it was empty.

"Later, I'm gonna put some records in this here envelope. If all else fails, you take that, if nothing else. Stuff it in your pants or something if you have to sneak out."

He kissed her.

"Don't nobody but you know about this."

9

JIMMY PATTERSON could have followed in his parents' footsteps, put on evening clothes when the sun went down. His father, a Telfair Museum trustee, a Georgia Historical Society director, custom drawers in his closet for his bowties. His mom, Tour of Homes, first vice president of the Savannah Women's Club.

Wisdom, Justice and Moderation.

Jimmy was 45, lean, broad-shouldered, brown hair, slightly graying at the sides, a no-nonsense crewcut. The forehead, deeply furrowed, eyes that blazed with intelligence. The nose, broken early on during a 20-year career.

Lived in a big house, drove a classic '55 Thunderbird. Black. Nicely restored. He'd married once, young. But she had hitched herself to the man she thought went with the mansion and the car and it hadn't lasted.

Tate had asked whether he was happy with the choice.

"Yes I am. Let me tell you something, bro. You see the nice house, the furniture, the paintings, the big ceilings. I inherited all this stuff. I'm a cop because that's what I care about.

"I love the house, my friend. And here I'll stay. But I don't require the lifestyle."

Tate understood, better than most.

"So you'll stay? Retire from the force?"

"Maybe," said Jimmy. "If I don't, it won't be to go to some other police force. I'll do this until I get tired of it, then head south for the fishing, get something on the Gulf side. I've got enough money in this house I could do what I want. But what about you? Looks to me like money ain't your problem either."

"Nah. Money is not my problem."

Jimmy had talked with every person who had access to a key to Palladino's office. The rector, the office assistant, the bookkeeper, the head of maintenance, four housekeepers.

He'd filled up a couple of legal pads with notes. And now it would be a question of adding in the nuns. There were nearly a hundred in the diocese, although many were stationed outside Savannah. In the city, there was a Catholic hospital and eight other Catholic churches. Some of the nuns lived on their own. Some lived in buildings donated to the church. Rich people getting a tax break.

Tate started building a chart. This was going to get cumbersome. Finally, they called it a day.

He was worn out, heading home, taking his time, looking both ways, letting people cut in from the side streets. Freddie King cranked up on the player. Tate thought he could hear traces of Freddie in a lot of the newer guys, the good ones anyway.

He circled the park. A few runners were out. Some parents with strollers, some kids. He thought about washing the car, taking a run, wasn't sure he had the juice for it.

He came to a decision. He'd turn on the TV. If there was a good game on, he'd put his feet up. Didn't have to be that good of a game. Then a call came. It was dispatch, routing it to his cell.

"Tate. It's your buddy from Jersey."

The voice was slow, full of care. He pulled to the side of the road.

"John Robert. Are you serious? You went back north?"

"And you've been combing the bushes in South Georgia? Spare yourself the energy. Anyhow, I called to help you out a little bit."

"Uh huh…"

"I thought I might give you an assist with the case, help you get it solved."

He pulled to the side, shut off the engine, lit a smoke, dragged on it, thought about hanging up. Griffin waited. Finally, Tate broke the silence.

"And why would you do that?"

"Do not take that tone with me. Tate, I need to know something right now. I need to know that you think this is real."

"What's real?"

"What is between us, the bond, that special feeling. I know you felt it."

Tate laughed.

"That's a good one, John Robert. What kinda love are we talking about here? Cause I thought you were a guy who liked women. And killing."

"Here's what I want, detective. I want some kind of sign. I know, we should get tattoos. Let's change our names. We can be Frankie and Johnny. Or Thelma and Louise. Would you do that for me?"

"I'm not doing squat for you. But I thought you were going to help with the case."

"To the chase, then. One hundred bucks your young priest was not just fucking with a prom girl."

"And what else would he be doing?"

Disdain in Griffin's voice.

"You haven't got it yet. I thought you were clever. You're chasing two people. Actually, three, if you count me."

Tate threw the butt out the window.

"I quit worrying about you, John Robert. Somebody else will have to pick up the slack. But this is really touching. You've been spending all your free time at the library, reading spy novels."

"Actually, my friend, I think the good Father had a hunger. And hunger is something I understand. So here's today's clue. A guy with that kinda jones needs to run, and he ain't running at home."

"Tell me again why you would want to help me, John Robert. I'm having a hard time understanding your motivation here?"

The voice was deep and slow, no effort to hide.

"Don't want you getting too much stress on this new case. Then you'd have nothing left for me. And while you're at it, my friend, you might watch your back down there. Word to the wise."

Tate started the car, drove home. It was close to sundown. He went into the kitchen, grabbed a couple of beers and a box with some leftover pizza, carried everything onto his screened porch. He put the beer on the floor. Something was chirping over his head, raspy sounding. Could be a squirrel. Seemed like it had about 40 different calls. Mocking bird.

He could hear truck traffic in the distance and, maybe a half mile away, somebody opening up a Harley. Might be down on Gaston.

He sat for a minute. Then he stuck the beers back in the fridge and carried the pizza box out to the car, headed for the beach road.

Griffin's voice, like he knew things.

It wasn't such a big leap. It made sense and Tate would have gotten there by himself. The man just had more confidence than you could stand, like a brightly lit corridor that led to a door you'd rather not open.

Palladino's house was still taped off. Tate let himself in. He'd already been through everything in his office at the church, a cursory look out here, waiting for the evidence guys to get through.

He started with a small desk in the study. Tate pulled everything out of the center drawer. There was a printout from a CD he'd ordered. Mozart. Some old photographs, looked like Palladino as a teenager with a woman in front of a stone cottage. There was a small pickup truck in the background, with tulips and roses on either side of the door and under the windows.

In a checkbook, the amounts, dates and the balance, everything neatly tied up. Only a few checks were missing. There was a payment for a subscription to Travel & Leisure and a donation to the local Catholic Social Services office. He'd paid $600 to DLB Carpentry. The notation read "fix shingles." Membership to the Y.

There was a pad with dates and titles. He'd been keeping track of the books he'd read.

Buncha stamps. A letter from a grade-school class he'd visited. At the bottom of the pile, a letter, written in hand, on letterhead from a parish in upstate New York.

> *Vincent,*
>
> *It's going to be awfully hard for us to see you go. But this is a wonderful opportunity and a great assignment. You will do truly marvelous work and you will see God's hand in all that you attempt. I know that this task will bring the answers that you have been seeking. Whenever you encounter any doubt, ask Him for guidance and it will be given. And you can always call an old friend. Remember that we are all truly blessed. And you are one of God's special creatures.*
>
> *Do good work. Make sure and get plenty of exercise. I know it means so much to you. And you know how much I always admired that about you.*
>
> *Never forget how pleased we all are about your decision. Your mother would be very proud. And don't forget to pack the sunscreen. Please let us know how you are faring. Our little community has lost a son. But all birds must grow and leave the nest.*
>
> *My beloved son....*
>
> *Uncle Carl,*
> *Blessed Sacrament*

Tate put the letter on the floor. In the other drawers, a box of unused checks, paper clips, staples, a pad of post-it notes, a couple of chap sticks.

Tate went into the bedroom. He'd been here before and looked around. This time he was more patient. He turned on the lights. On the wall, old prints... a zeppelin flying over a German cathedral, a pair of airborne skiers at Chamonix, a couple in evening wear drinking vermouth.

The TV was tuned to ESPN. There were a few videos in a small bookcase... some old movies. Nothing remarkable. He turned on the VCR and fast-fowarded through the first few minutes of each one.

Audrey Hepburn in "Breakfast at Tiffany's." Cary Grant's "An Affair to Remember." Clark Gable in "It Started in Naples."

Old romances.

There was a dresser. Underwear, socks, T-shirts—one pile of nice ones, one pile for working out, looked like.

On the floor in the closet, two pairs of those soft-sided faux dress shoes, two pairs of running shoes, two pairs of basketball shoes, some flip-flops. He pulled out each hanger and looked at the clothes. There were dark pants and white dress shirts, some khakis, some long-sleeved casual shirts, short-sleeved casual shirts.

On the far wall, a priest's cassock, several sets of black shirts and pants.

On a wire rack, a box of detachable collars, sweaters, mostly thin turtlenecks, couple of heavy winter pullovers. A black raincoat.

Nothing.

He walked back into the study. There was another, smaller closet next to the bathroom. It was locked. He smashed the knob with his heel. It came loose.

This one was more interesting. A winter coat of shearling and leather, another light leather jacket, a handful of sport jackets, and suits, a light blue pinstripe, a Zegna, another Zegna, gray, a tan Hart Schaffner Marx, a black three-piece.

Nothing in any of the pockets.

The suits were a couple of grand apiece. Tate had a few of his own. Then, Tate was a rich kid. Palladino wasn't. There was a long overcoat, Italian. In boxes underneath, dress shoes. Cole Hahn, Allen Edmonds.

There were boxes on the shelf above. Tate carried them over to the bed. Inside, fine dress shirts and belts, a couple of light wool sweaters, underwear, fancy beach clothes. And one box held the passport, driver's license and credit cards for Vincent A. Parker. A big pile of paperwork underneath, tucked into manila folders. Piles paper-clipped together, all the edges matched up with great care.

And a photograph.

She was young, thin, blonde, a very nice body. She was holding a camera with her right hand. It was stretched out to the side. She'd been facing a full-length mirror to take the picture. She was naked. Her face, half- covered with a scarf, tied in the back like a bank robber in a western.

The other hand, on her hip.

TATE SWUNG BY Jimmy's on the way home. He could see the back porch light on. He walked around to the side of the house and yelled. Jimmy told him to come on up. He was listening to a game on the radio. Jimmy liked the radio announcers better than the TV guys. Bluejeans, a T-shirt, bare feet on an overturned washtub.

Tate told him about the suits.

"I'm thinking back to something Dina said," Tate said. "You remember? She was embarrassed about it all, about having hooked up with a guy who had that much going on. She said something about how she wouldn't have messed with him if she'd thought it was... what did she call it? A conquest?

"Yeah, that was it."

"That tells us something about her. Mebbe it tells us something about him too. He's pretty good at this. Comes across real genuine. Has a great story. Getting laid is the game. And he brings home a shirt. I was wondering why he'd have some underwear in the drawer in the room, and some more in the closet. Most all that stuff in the closet is hardly worn."

"Trophy collector."

"Yeah. Now I'm thinking I need to check his credit card bills, look for hotels, bar tabs."

"Trips out of town."

Tate told Jimmy about Griffin's call.

"He's a smart boy. Good guess the priest is doing his Vincent Parker thing somewhere else. But let's look at why Griffin wants to feel like he's helping you. This is all building up to the return engagement. Either he comes back and hopes to get to you on his own terms, or he gets you up to where he is.

"You need to be real sensitive here to where he's going with it. Right now, sounds like he's still playing with you. Obviously you want to go after him whenever you have a sense of where, cause the mother fucker plans to whack your ass when he's tired of fooling around."

"I'm counting on it. Meanwhile, the phone company lawyer is jacking me around about tracing the call, saying it may take some time. Asshole."

"I know a guy who can make a call for you. So whaddya got right now?"

"Fragments, a bunch of relentless fuckin' fragments."

10

TATE WAS STANDING at the urinal, zipper down, when the Noose came in.

"Well if it ain't Clark Gable. I woulda figured you'd have your own private bathroom, big boy like you. Something fancy like that girly car you drive."

"Noose. Still collecting beer for letting scumbags fuck that teenager?"

"None of your fucking business, college boy."

Tate stepped back from the wall, turned to face Newsome.

"Let me give you a tip, old man. Those girls and their boyfriends are going down for murder. It's going to be a long, nasty case and all this shit is likely to come out. Wouldn't be surprised if the girls, or at least one of em, try to roll over on you to get some leniency. So, not only are you gonna be in the shit, you're going to embarrass the department."

Newsome zipped his fly, spun toward Drawdy, his face reddening fiercely. For a brief second, a clenched fist in the air. And then he backed off.

"One of these days, college boy. One of these days..."

He flung the door open, slamming the handle against the wall.

THE GIRLS were talking now.

They'd been hitchhiking. That's how they met. John Robert and Wigle had picked them up and they were well stocked. Money

and drugs. The girls wanted both. They wanted a good time. They
started running around. They went to bars. They hung out at the
strip club where Jeanne worked. And then one night Wigle disappeared for awhile, came back with a pile of money. He'd rolled a
drunk staggering out of the club.

It seemed like a good way to go.

It wasn't long before they developed a more elaborate scam.
Jeanne took a guy up on an offer to meet later at a hotel, a married guy. It was just a couple of blocks from the club where she
worked. He'd been one of the guys stuffing bills into the strap she
wore around her waist.

It was an older hotel, had a little refrigerator in each room.

She was undressed and so was he. The guy was starting to drool
when Griffin burst into the room, the outraged boyfriend, ready to
cause a ruckus, ready to ruin the guy's life, ready to call the wife.

Griffin was scary persuasive. He had a gun.

And a camera.

Jeanne sat back on the bed. They made the guy sit next to her.
She pulled her knees up. She frolicked. The poor sucker was happy
to drop a chunk of change to make it go away. They ran it a couple
more times, put together about 10 grand.

Enough for that southern holiday.

That day they saw the woman carrying the groceries, it had all
been harmless fun. They'd gotten good at the psychological bait
and switch. Nice, until it wasn't time to be nice anymore. Why
she was a target, they had no clue. Griffin stopped the car. Griffin
picked her out. Griffin was the one. When John Robert got angry,
you did whatever. You did it right now.

They were pretty stoned. It was all John Robert's fault.

At this point, the girls were trying to cut a deal. Things were
still in the early stages. But the gist was, the girls would have to
tell everything and then see what kind of mercy the prosecutor
wanted to bestow.

They asked Shawn James, the prosecutor, for a meeting. A small conference room, oak table, cushioned chairs, historic photos of the city in dark, heavy frames. Forsyth Park; a line drawing from the Battle of Savannah, the old Chart House, shots of River Street, with wrought iron balconies and brick lintels over the windows, an old paddlewheeler on the river, the Gerken Family Grocery Store, which later would become the Crystal Beer Parlor. The cannon at Fort Jackson.

Shawn James wasn't playing along. He said so.

"My interpretation of these events is not quite so benign. Taking drugs and running around with bad boys and even robbing dumb tourists is a far cry from murder. You want me to believe this was the first time these young ladies ventured into violent crime? I don't think so."

The lawyers said the girls were insisting they'd just been along for the ride.

"Bring your clients to my office for lie detector tests, one girl in the morning, one in the afternoon."

Their lawyers counseled against it. Both girls said yes. In the area of previous acts of violence, both flunked miserably. Shawn James told them both the same thing. One more chance. After that, no deals. And so the stories changed somewhat. The girls admitted to being involved when some johns got robbed. It was more than simple extortion. Some of them got robbed at gunpoint, some got whacked over the head. Some got roughed up pretty bad. The girls were part of it.

James wanted details, names and dates. Didn't mean much. The johns would not have gone to the cops, although there was a guy who'd taken himself to a hospital then made up a story. The cops didn't believe it.

James met first with little Lisa Hillerman, the 15-year-old. They sat around a conference table, Lisa, her lawyer. Char Pinckney was there.

Char spoke first.

"How are they treating you over at the jail honey?"

The girl started to answer. James interrupted her.

"Miss Hillerman, you understand the decision about whether to proceed here with any kind of plea arrangement is solely up to me. If I don't like the deal, I will walk away and you can take your chances at court. Or you can cooperate and hope that I feel like being lenient. Do you understand?"

She nodded. She knew what was coming.

"Once we start down this path, it will be up to you to answer every single question I ask, whether you like the question or not. If I think you're lying or you're holding something back, I will walk out the door and we're done. Do you understand?"

"What's going to happen with Jeanne?"

Sing-song, swaying from side to side, pouting.

"That will be up to Jeanne.

The girl was hesitating. James stood and walked around behind her.

"You're past worrying about your friend. Those days are over. At this point, you are simply trying to get your life back.

"Tell you what. We're not going to talk about anything today. Whatever you're going to do, you're going to do of your own free will. I'm going to leave now and I'm going to let your lawyer talk to you a little bit about what we've said here. Then you can decide if you're ready to move forward."

James took Char by the arm and headed out the door. The girl put her head on the table and began to cry.

TATE TOOK the stairs down to the first floor, went outside for a smoke, out by the cemetery, on the west side of the building. By himself. The side door opened. Tyree LaMonica stepped through the opening, tipping his shoulders as he slid around the jamb. Graceful for a big man.

He bummed a light.

"How long you been with us now, Mr. Drawdy?" he said. "Going on about a year, something?"

"Something like that."

"Getting to know your way around, I suspect. City been good to you?"

"I like Savannah. I was ready for a change."

Tyree tilted his head back, blew smoke toward the clouds.

"Anything you need help with?" he asked.

"What'd you have in mind?" Tate said.

"Oh, I don't know. Some of us been here longer, we know where to find things. You might like to meet a nice girl for a Friday night. You might want some entertainment of some kind."

"Thanks. I think I'm good. I've met some folks."

"All right then. Not a big deal. Reason I ask, and you probably know this, is things can be good here for guys who know their way around."

"Don't I know it," Tate said. "I can't go much anywhere without somebody offering to buy me a cup of coffee, tell me lunch is on the house."

Tyree laughed and kicked a toe against the walk, turned to look squarely at him.

"That is for darn sure. Sometimes I have to flat insist. I tell them I can't keep coming in if you won't let me pay."

Huge grin on his face.

"Yeah," Tate said. "Small town, in a lot of ways."

Tyree nodding. Still making eye contact.

"But I'm really thinking long-term. You know, how you fit in…"

"Sure," Tate, nodding back. "I think I know what you mean. Why don't I keep that in mind?"

"Good enough. You keep that in mind. And thanks for the light."

11

THE VAN headed east on Bay Street, away from the river. There was no moon. A blustery wind tossing the Spanish moss. A few cars in the other direction. It was late. A chill in the air. The driver wore a baseball cap, pulled down snug. Otherwise it would have rubbed against the ceiling. Still, he crouched over the wheel, the seat pulled up closer than it needed to be.

The van belonged to a painting contractor. Satisfaction guaranteed. Ladders strapped tight to the roof, the owner's name stenciled onto the back and across the sides. He was listening to a game, window open, heat on. Gloves, a fancy watch, the dial casting a pale green image against the windshield.

Then he was on President Street, paralleling the train tracks and, just on the other side, the sand traps and fairways at the golf club.

He chanced to look in his side view mirror. A tenth of a mile back, he spotted the low-profile lights of a patrol car, keeping its distance.

They rode together for a time, down Pennsylvania, past cottages set close to the road, the high school, some houses with attached garages, from a time when cars were long and low. Slowing almost to a stop for the cut-through to Bonaventure. He was careful to use his blinkers. Almost there.

Standing on a corner, a yipping lapdog and his bodyguard, a stocky shepherd. As he eased through the turn, the big dog snarled, threw himself at the car, then chased him for half a block.

He ignored the dog, drove slowly. It wasn't far.

The van pulled up before the two stone pillars guarding the cemetery. The driver turned off the headlights, stepped out, carrying a long set of bolt cutters. He sliced through the lock, swung open the gates and drove under a canopy of live oaks, Spanish moss hanging like shrouds, continuing down an avenue that felt like the entrance to a cave.

Behind him, back at the gate, the police car eased quietly to a stop. The driver, a big man who drove with one finger wrapped over the top of the steering wheel. He put the cruiser in park and slid the seat back.

The van kept straight for a time, past statues of angels and children, mausoleums and crosses. It stopped when it came to a dirt lane bordered by a flock of headstones.

Out stepped the tall man, very thin, with big hands that hung half a pencil's length past the end of his sleeves. The pants, equally short, with a pair of ancient white Converse that seemed ill-suited to his surroundings. Still wearing the gloves. He paused, turned to look back up the lane, then walked to a gravesite. An archway covering a large stone urn. Behind it, he found two large suitcases. Held one by the handle, put the other on top of it, under his arm, and stuffed them in the back of the van.

He drove quickly back to the gates and passed through, ignoring the patrol car parked there. After a moment, the cruiser, too, pulled away and headed south.

JOHN ROBERT was glad to be back home. It was colder here, colder than Georgia. But that was ok. He didn't care much for the heat.

He spread a map of Savannah across the bed, studying the downtown, adjusted the pillows at his back. He had a scrap of paper where he was making some notes. On the nightstand beside him, a bottle of Russian vodka, today's New York Times.

He set the map aside and walked to the window, watched the street for a few minutes, then took a book from the shelf. In an old duffel in the closet, he'd found some sweat pants and a couple of shirts, some socks. He'd had to stop in a pharmacy for toothpaste, soap, a hairbrush, only to discover there was no longer any water on at the place.

Easy fix. There was a crescent wrench under the sink. After dark, he went out to the street and turned on the valve. There was no gas, though, which meant a cold shower.

There was no carpeting, so he pulled a blanket off the bed. Spent half an hour doing pushups and situps.

Slept like a baby.

He'd taken a Greyhound out of Savannah, all the way to Fayetteville, then Amtrak into Pennsylvania. Though he hadn't been there long, it felt especially good to be out of jail. He'd had enough of meatloaf and tight spaces and clanging bars.

TATE WAS SHOOTING some hoops at the Y after work.

A couple of guys invited him for a beer after. They went to Spanky's, old place down on the river in the bottom of what once had been a grand cotton warehouse back when folks rode horses to work. Weathered wood and stone, some stained glass, hanging plants. A good crowd. Tate got a couple of slices with mozzarella. Steve Miller was playing, some Allman Brothers. Good to listen to, but Tate wished they'd bust out some Musselwhite, mebbe a little Freddie King.

They talked about the price of gasoline, the waitress, heroic moments in their athletic careers. When the waitress came back with the second pitcher, one of the guys, a point guard with delusions of a 10-foot jumper, began to talk about her, with an arm locked around her waist.

Tate leaned over, put a brotherly hand around the back of the guy's neck, clamped down until the guy began to wince.

"If you need company that bad, I'll come sit in your lap."

The guy let her go. Tate nursed a beer for a few, put $20 on the table and headed out. He'd just gotten onto the street when he felt a hand on his arm. She wanted to thank him for the rescue.

Name was Barksdale Newman. Middle name, since he asked, was Wofford.

"Your daddy got the stars and bars over the fireplace?"

"Fraid so, but not many guys make the connection."

"Where I come from," Tate said, "we know most of the Gettysburg generals."

She put her phone number on a slip of paper. Said he'd call her.

He stood, watching her walk back inside, realizing it wasn't just chivalry when he'd told the guy to let her go. It was funny the way things happened sometimes.

He made his way up the cobblestone lane toward the top of the bluff, walking underneath a high ivy-covered wall made of stone. Rusted iron railings up top, a strong scent of magnolia. The buildings here were all brick, with windows as tall as the streetlights. The rocks underfoot, ballast from the old ships. Everybody knew the story.

The crowd was sparse and he was feeling just tired enough to take it slow going home but then he could see the BMW was leaning to the side, a screwdriver sticking out the right rear tire.

Somebody had pasted a bumper sticker across his back windshield. I LOVE PITTSBURGH.

He shoved a hand in his pocket. What an idiot he was. Right there, middle of the night, in the open. T-shirt, shorts, pair of high-toppers, wallet, keys.

No gun.

He kept walking, like it wasn't his car. He had Jimmy on speed dial, told him where he was. He rounded the corner just short of the bluff. He was moving quickly now. The sun was mostly down but it was still hot.

Still enough light for shooting.

Laughter and muffled reggae from the club down the street, tinkling glass from a restaurant below. He reached the top, listening for a footstep. Time to make a decision. Then a couple of bikes ground to life, one out in front, another off to the side, maybe 50 feet back. They'd decided for him.

This wouldn't take long, too many people, too many cars. He broke into a run, hard, aiming for Bay Street beyond the park, his shoes squeaking, slipping on the cobblestones, feeling his collar scratching his neck, a stiffness in his ankles, the clarity that comes when the odds aren't good.

Weaving through the trees, Spanish moss whipping at his face, trying not to trip over the roots of a big live oak. The guy on the right was closer. Four quick shots splashed on the ground behind him. Tate dived, rolled between two parked cars, glass shattering around him. The second guy was firing now, some kind of machine pistol, and cars were slamming on their brakes.

The guy on his right throttled up, must have his gun on a strap around his neck. He was getting outside of him. There was no time. The other guy was close, spraying shots, working him out from behind his cover. Tires exploding. Screams from tourists on the other side of the street. The pizza strong in his throat.

He got set to sprint for it. Then a big Crown Vic slid sideways into the intersection and the driver came out shooting. Jimmy Patterson never looked so good. He was down behind the door, resting a hand on the hood as he fired. Both guys were shooting at Jimmy now. Sirens in the distance.

"Glove compartment," Jimmy shouted.

Tate almost made it to the car.

JIMMY WAS TELLING the story later in the hospital. Char was there, and the chief. Tate was saying his leg hurt like a bitch and Char had a hand on his shoulder and another hand on top of his head. She was biting her lip and Jimmy was saying do you want to hear this story or not.

He'd taken out the first biker with his fourth or fifth shot. The second guy decided to boogie, fortunately, because Jimmy'd used up all he had without rummaging around back in the car and there wasn't a whole helluva lot of time for that. The second biker got about four blocks before he ran into a police roadblock, tried to jump one of the patrol cars and had taken three shots in the chest before he touched down. It was already on the TV news.

Shootout in the tourist corridor.

They were going to keep Tate for a day or so. The bullet had passed through the hamstring, right leg, no hoops for awhile. The chief put a uniform on the door, just to be on the safe side. Jimmy wanted to know did he want him to smuggle up a few brews. Maybe later.

He didn't get much sleep. The next morning he was tearing through breakfast when the door opened. It was a patrolman, said he was just coming on for the day.

"Captain Patterson was here overnight. He sent the guy on the door home."

"Jimmy was here? All night? That asshole."

"You think the captain's an asshole?"

"No. No. Never mind. I didn't mean it that way."

Just then the cop's radio squawked. There was a girl downstairs, wanted to come up. Said her name was Barks. Wait a minute. The officer listened for a second to his radio. Sorry. Barksdale. Says her name is Barksdale. Tate said ask her if she can pick up a couple of large coffees.

She looked good in jeans.

"We were all watching the TV over the bar and then they had your picture. I got somebody to cover for me, and came over but they wouldn't let me come up last night. It was past visiting hours and they said nobody could see you anyhow."

Tate said it was damned nice of her to swing by, but he would have preferred not to entertain her in the little gown thing. Don't be silly, she said.

She had short hair, a man's cut. It was just slightly red, and killer cheekbones. Green eyes. Good veins in her forearms and across the back of her hands. She looked to be in her mid-20s, not so young she couldn't be an adult. No purse.

She had running shoes with purple stripes. Tate noticed they had plenty of wear. He was wishing he could see her feet, any calluses. She sat down and put the stripes up on the side of the bed.

"Now why is somebody trying to kill you?"

"I notice you're using the present tense. Both of those guys got killed last night."

"Well, did you know those guys or did somebody hire them? Because your chief told the newspaper this morning they were hired killers from somewhere out of town and nobody here knew them."

"I dunno. We don't need to talk about that."

She drummed her fingers on her knee. Her hands looked strong. No polish. She thought a minute, drummed her fingers some more.

"OK, you seem like a really nice guy and I'd love to get to know you better, even though it's only just a quick first impression. But I can tell you right now if you're gonna be one of those stoic, non-communicative males, I could not be less interested."

Tate laughed, took a sip of his coffee.

"Well," she said? "Clock's ticking."

"Oh. You mean I need to pony up some details now."

"Fraid so."

"Or you'll categorize me as a typical dumb-ass and move along."

"About the size of it."

"You're already thinking the cop thing is big hurdle. You don't want to have any romances with cro-magnon types."

It was her turn to laugh.

"I'm just trying to decide if I want you for a friend. Romance would be another subject."

He told her he'd talk about it, at least enough to deal with the stoic, non-communicative thing. But he hoped she'd understand there would also be some issues about confidentiality. He wouldn't be spilling the beans about an investigation. She tilted her head to one side and drummed her fingers some more. He hadn't stopped the clock.

So he told her there was a guy in Pennslvania who might have it in for him.

Just then the phone rang. She handed it to him.

"That you Tate?"

"John Robert."

"Holy shit my friend. Are you all right?"

"Word travels fast."

"There's been quite a bit of media coverage. How are you feeling?"

"Not bad. I was wondering if I might have run into some of your associates last night. We didn't have much of a chance to get acquainted. They're not saying much now."

"No friends of mine. Sounds to me like those guys were trying to perform over their pay grade. The reports say you were injured. This is not good my friend."

Griffin was modulating his voice, softening it, raising the pitch just so. Sing-song. The voice you used with your great aunt when you turned down the third helping, or when you read stories to very small children. A pure little voice.

Tate said he was touched by the concern.

"Don't be silly, mon ami," Griffin said. "If I were not otherwise involved, I'd want to be there by your bedside, holding your hand."

"Sorry you can't make it down. I've been waiting to finish our last conversation, talk about you and homicide and statutory rape. Escape... Shrinks..."

"You'll see me soon enough. Not just now, though."

"Shame. You could at least send me a current picture, John Robert. Are you growing facial hair? Getting a tan?"

"Sleep well, Tate."

Griffin hung up. Tate handed the phone back to her.

She stood.

"Did I just see you playing some sort of psychological game? I did, didn't I? That was your guy from Pennsylvania..."

Tate looked away.

She put a hand on his face.

"Jesus, Tate."

She swung the door closed behind her.

12

"MY SENSE is that he was sending me a message. Those guys were part of the game. They were supposed to miss."

"You could take it that way. But that would make you a complete idiot."

"Jimmy, look, maybe I messed up their plan, not getting into the car. Running."

"Got this figured out have you? You are a fucking dick. I have a simple rule about murderers. It is complete bullshit to try to figure them out. Think about this for a minute. What would it take for you to kill somebody? Not just kill them... want to kill them. What would it take?

"You can't imagine it, am I right? Bottom line... Murderers are insane. And you think you have a guy figured out who not only does this shit, he enjoys it. Let me tell you this, compadre. When cops play that game, it's pure bullshit. It's an affectation. Be honest enough, be man enough, to say 'I have no fucking idea what this head case is up to.'"

They were at Tate's house. Jimmy and a couple of guys had ferried him out of the white room. Tate, propped up on a pillow with a beer. And now Jimmy was showering him with love.

"I thought you were a smart guy. That's why I wanted to work with you. Tell you right now, get off this infantile speculation or I'm gonna decide you're just another asshole."

Tate held up his hands in surrender.

"All right. OK. I have no idea whether Griffin sent those guys to kill me or just shake me up. All I'm saying is it feels like he wants to play some more. That's my instinct."

"That's a possibility. So is you being dead. For all you know, the guy could have a hit out on you and right now you're as hot as Satan's ass after a bad burrito."

Tate drained a beer. He started another. He made a fist, tucked it under his nose, nodded.

"Sure. You win. So lemme ask you this: You ever get so personal with it that you wanted to wipe the guy off the face of the fucking map?"

"We all do, my friend. Then you have to decide whether it's right or not. And whether you can."

Tate was going to be off for the week. He had a good excuse. He looked for that scrap of paper, couldn't find it and called down to Spanky's. They wouldn't tell him how to reach Barksdale. They wouldn't pass along a message.

Tate had a brand spanking new pair of crutches. He drove down to the river, parked illegally out in front of the place, hobbled in. Spoke to the bartender. The guy was not interested in making 20 bucks.

He was back home when the phone rang.

"Heard you were looking for me."

"Yeah, but they're not going to help me out. Nobody's willing to tell me how to get in touch with you. So I guess we're not going to be able to talk."

"Paulie took pity on you. I think it was crutches and the limp and the pale face."

"You gotta use what you have."

"So I'm off today. Can I get some food and bring it to you, or do you need groceries or anything?"

"Actually," he said, "I was hoping we could just talk some."

"What's the matter? Are you bashful cause you're still in that cute gown?"

"No, fortunately. And I can eat out of my own refrigerator. Look, can I make you a proposition?"

"What's that?"

"I'd like to get to know you better, but I'd like to do it over the phone, if that would be all right. I don't want to see you right now."

"Why?"

"If anybody's following me, they'd see you. They could follow you. I can't take that chance."

He could picture the fingers, drumming.

"I understand. How long do you think this will be? Or is this just how your life is?"

"Probably not long. My life is pretty normal except for this one thing right now. My friend in Pennsylvania doesn't appear to be a patient man. So… I've been meaning to ask you. Where are you from? And do you run in those running shoes?"

She was quiet for a moment.

"OK," she said. "Let's talk."

They went through some of the preliminaries. Tate asked her if she'd like to talk some more. She was ok with it. He thought she was smart and quick and they'd laughed some and he was extra sure he'd like to do this face to face. But this was not a good time.

"So," she asked, "are you sitting there with a gun beside the bed?"

"Yeah. But ordinarily I don't. This is just for right now."

Long pause.

"Why don't I call you next?" she said.

He thought that sounded like early progress. They agreed on a time. Couple of days. Nothing too eager, but promising. Tate thought he'd like to wrap things up with Mr. Griffin. But he couldn't see how he was going to make that happen. Not right away.

So he found something else to do. Called the office. Got in touch with one of the guys on the team. Tate had brought home the stuff from Palladino's closet, the one with the locked door. He had a handful of receipts.

Hotels, gift shops. An investigator would call, ask for their records. They'd find out who bought the item, reach out, find out how they met Palladino. Shouldn't be too hard, as long as his guy approached it just right and the shop owner was feeling generous.

They got their first sliver of information the next day. A Dallas gift shop, just small enough they hung onto a paper copy of the transaction. Elizabeth King had paid for a pair of linen trousers and a silk shirt. That, plus a belt, almost $750. They'd had to tailor the waistline. They delivered the pants, had the address.

Tate called her.

"Did you know a man named Vincent A. Parker?"

"Yes and I saw his photograph in the newspaper, the New York Times I believe it was. Of course, they said his name was something else, Palladino. He was a priest. I knew it was the same man the moment I saw that picture. And they described him as a body builder. Then I knew for sure."

"So it's the same man you saw last November in Dallas?"

"Yes. Am I in any kind of trouble here? I certainly have never been to Georgia and I can find all sorts of people who can tell you I've been right here all along. I do quite a few activities. And I would certainly never physically harm anyone."

Tate wanted to reassure her. He wanted her to talk. So he laughed.

"No trouble. We're doing some backtracking to learn more about his trips out of town. And you've obviously had some contact with him. I'd like to hear details."

She didn't answer for a moment. Then she came back, very businesslike.

"Are you the man in charge of the investigation, Mr. Drawdy?"

"Yes."

"Then here's what I'm prepared to do. I will provide you with a full accounting of my whereabouts during the time that the young man was killed, along with people who can vouch for me. If that information satisfies you, I want a letter from you, signed by your lead prosecutor, that I am in no way a suspect in the case and that I am cooperating with authorities of my own free will. At that point, you may interview me in complete detail and I will answer all questions. The interview is to be here, in Dallas, face to face, with my attorney present and it will be videotaped by us, to be retained by us.

"Are my conditions clear to you?"

He sighed.

"Are you an attorney, Ms. King?"

"I am."

"Let's talk about what it is we're going to talk about. I think…."

She interrupted.

"Let's assume for the sake of this discussion that my alibi is airtight, Mr. Drawdy. What you really want to know is whether all this rigmarole is worth the effort. I will tell you now that the young man was a service provider and I can put you in touch with his organization; that is, if it hasn't packed up shop."

"You're saying you hired Palladino?"

"The man was an escort, detective. It suits my image to have an attractive date for certain functions. That being said, I assume that represents the possibility of a break in the case for you and that you now recognize there is a certain time value to the information."

"I see some possibilities. How soon can you have your information to me for verification?"

"I have it now. I prepared it after I saw that story. There is contact information for all of the people I encountered throughout the weekend in question. I have not spoken to any of them about the possibility of being interviewed. I'll ship it to you this instant."

"One last thing, Ms. King."

"Yes."

"I've been looking at your website while we spoke. Looks like you've got quite a practice. I assume that part of your motivation here is to prevent any negative publicity."

"You would be correct."

"Then here's what I'm prepared to do. Send me your alibi. I'll have it checked out. If the district attorney agrees, you'll get your letter, but it will include the appropriate qualifiers. And then we'll talk, by phone, on a conference call if you wish. I'll have my prosecutor in the room. You can have your person.

"If at any time between now and then, or later, you do not take my call or you are for any reason hard to find I will have you brought in for questioning by a good friend of mine on the Dallas force. He's a very showy guy. Likes to run his siren."

Two could play that game. She complied.

The young father, it turned out, could be hired for a long weekend, sometimes longer. Tate asked her for the names of any of her friends who'd used the service. Elizabeth King traveled in a ritzy crowd. And she had one other nugget. The woman who ran the agency, The Baldwin Group, it was called, had called her one day from someplace close to a river.

What river?

Same question she'd asked, after hearing that big ship's horn over the telephone. It was the Savannah River. The woman said she had a place close by.

Elizabeth King had the phone number for Palladino's agency. It was a cellphone. A dead cellphone.

13

THE GIRLS were talking now and their stories were kinda matching up, but not with precision, which was a good sign. It had the ring of truth. And now they were racing to be cooperative.

The body had been found shortly after the killing by some dirt bikers. It was lying in the tall weeds, back from the side of the road. The girls told the officers where to look for Wigle's little knife. The dogs found a hose there too. Items that would play well in court.

On the other hand, Richard Allen Wigle had no interest in talking to the cops. The girls were the ones. He'd never done nothing.

Like what?

Nothing. Whatever it is you're chasing.

Wigle thought the girls were scum. He just wanted that understood. Whatever they had to say was bullshit. His lawyer told him to tone it down.

Bullshit. The girls are bullshit.

Wigle had on a clean orange jumpsuit. He hadn't washed his hair. His fingernails were dirty. The look of a man who spent the day soaking in his own juices.

The prosecutor, Shawn James, crisp in a button-down polo, a tie of alternating diagonal red and blue, those fat stripes that people had been wearing since the war. He'd brought a little something extra for the meeting. He put his briefcase up on the table. It wasn't one of those expandable lawyer's things on wheels. This was pricey cowhide, slender, with gold clasps.

They were in the little conference room adjoining the jail. No security issues.

James snapped open the case, one side at a time. He reached in, pulled out an envelope, slid it across. Wigle opened it. That strawberry birthmark turned a deep purple and a slight moan escaped his lips. He pushed the envelope away.

His lawyer folded his hands.

"What do you have there, Mr. James?"

"It's a photograph. See for yourself."

The lawyer reached over, lifted the envelope apart with his thumb, just enough to see the close-up of that little knife. Stan James had another envelope. He slid it over. Wigle's hands were shaking. He looked. Another little moan. He pulled down the sleeve of his shirt, began rubbing his face with it. The lawyer looked too. Close-up of a moldy garden hose.

Shawn James rapped his knuckles on the table.

"Do you know what I like to call moments like this, counselor?"

"Tell me."

"Bon voyage."

Wigle snuffled. What's that mean?

"It means," James said, "this boat is about to sail."

And then he laughed.

"You're not forgetting, are you Mr. Wigle?"

"Forgetting what?"

The voice, tinny, from a scrunched-up face. Wigle wasn't going to make it to Disney World.

"Coker vs. Georgia, young man. The death penalty applies regardless of whether you held the murder weapon. We have a kidnapping victim who expired in the perpetrator's custody."

He rapped his knuckles once again.

"Back to the issue. Leaving the harbor, gentlemen. So let's understand each other, shall we? As you know, I will be prosecuting you for the murder of the woman, for the statutory rape of one or both of the girls. And then there's the pièce de résistance."

He pointed to the photographs, gave Wigle a little wink.

"I don't have to prove you did the killing. I just need to show the woman died in your custody. So any negotiating you have to do goes directly to this core question, young man: Am I going to have an overweight, tobacco-spitting country boy in a crew cut strap you down and stick a needle in your arm? Or do you want to throw yourself on the mercy of the court?"

The lawyer lifted his hands from the table, cleared his throat. He was ready to get philosophical.

Wigle, flip-side, was popping his eyes out.

"John Robert made me do it. He made all of us do it. The mother fucker is psycho. He woulda killed me."

The lawyer told him to stop. Wigle kept blabbering.

"Shut up," the lawyer said.

Wigle wasn't listening.

"He's the one. Him and his fancy little warehouse loft and his fancy little elevator and his Starbucks and his fucked up little toys."

Wigle was getting all worked up. Shawn James thought blood might start pouring from between his lips.

TATE WAS walking now. He'd go for short stretches into the kitchen and back, up and down the hall, trying to speed up the process. He'd gone to the doctor. Take your time, the doc said. Don't push it.

What happens, Char wanted to know, if he goes at it too fast? She'd taken him there, thought somebody needed to ask the question. Doc said he'd be tired and sore or end up right back in bed, slow down the recovery.

Tate was gracious enough, offered to have the doc arrested. But now, a couple of days later, he'd been cleared to walk a little for real. Char offered to get him, drive to Forsyth Park, bring a couple sandwiches. Tate took her up.

She made him bring the cane they'd loaned him at the hospital. If nothing else, she said, it would keep people from bumping into him. He brought a CD, Robert Johnson. "Come on in my Kitchen."

Turned it up loud. She jumped.

"The doc says it's good for my leg to turn up some loud music."

"Did he say it was good if I make you walk home?"

She turned it down, drove slowly, as if she were trying to keep the car from bouncing too hard over the bumps in the road. Gave him time to observe his surroundings.

They got a shady spot along Gaston Street, away from the fountain. Strollers, joggers, a pair of women leading gray-headed blind men. There were kids running in and out. A couple of benches down, a woman with an old lapdog that wouldn't quit its wheezy barking.

"Sounds like somebody throttling a little Chinaman," Tate said.

"Hush."

"Got a call from my mom last night, says she wants to come down."

"That's nice. When's she coming?"

"Hell, I don't want her down here. Too dangerous. The only reason they haven't already been crawling around is they were out of the country and missed the news."

"So what are you going to do?"

"I dunno. Maybe go up there for a quick drive-by. At least that way they're not seen with me if anybody's keeping an eye on me down here."

"If it was my mom, she'd have me off to the doctor's."

"I'm hoping I'm just gonna have to sit in a big chair the whole time I'm there."

"What about the girl with the funny name?"

"What girl?"

"The one who came to your hospital room the next day, who left pissed off about five minutes later. She must like you or she wouldn't have been pissed off and I hear she was quite the knockout."

"They tell you any other secrets?"

"It's a cop shop. You think we don't know what you got in the fridge?"

They finished their sandwiches and stood. Tate, rising slowly as he stretched the leg. And then, across the street, the car parked in front of the Oglethorpe Club, a big man inside.

"Wait for me a second," Tate said.

Cars slowed to a stop as he reached the sidewalk. Across the street, Tyree LaMonica was sitting in a cruiser, smoking a big cigar, his hat on the seat beside him. The car windows were open.

Tate crossed over.

"That you, Tyree? I thought I spotted you over here."

"And I thought I spotted you. How's the recovery going?"

"Pretty good. Doing a little bit of walking, as you can see."

"Good thing. I'm glad it wasn't something worse. We don't get guys shot up much around here. Like to keep it that way."

"You and me both. Were you looking for me?"

"Nah. Just glad to see you're doing well."

Tyree stepped out of the car, reached a hand out to Tate's shoulder. "But you'll let me know if you need anything?" he said. "You remember, we were talking before…"

"Yeah. Thanks. I'm good. Be back in the saddle shortly. Say hey to the troops for me."

"Will do."

They shook hands. Tyree reached out, gave Tate's shoulder another squeeze.

"Get some rest," he said.

Tate walked back across the street. Char was waiting there.

"Tyree? What's he doing here?"

He turned back to look. The cruiser was moving slowly down the street.

"I think he's keeping an eye on me."

That afternoon, Tate got on a plane for Atlanta. He'd reached the point where he almost hated to fly. No legroom. Kids yelling. That relentless pestering about safety regs.

His folks met him at the airport. His mom started to cry when she saw the limp. He told her it was no big deal. He had a story. She wasn't having it.

"You think because you're a big shot police officer I don't know when you're lying? I can see it in your eyes. And you're look-ing very tired. Why can't you finish medical school or go into the law like your father and forget this little escapade, this police business?"

Tate laughed, put an arm around her. His dad grabbed his bag.

They went home. It was one of those houses the tourists slow down for... a long winding drive past burly outcroppings of aza-leas, clusters of stone terraces spread like fortifications across a rolling lawn that rose up to a regal colonial on top of the rise. A deep porch with rockers fronted by two-story columns too big to get your arms around, French doors everywhere, lintels over the windows. The grass, cut in such straight rows the guy must have had a laser pointing device on his mower.

It wasn't hard to come home. His mom made shrimp and grits. For supper, there'd be fried chicken. All his favorites. They wanted to know what he was working on. He told them about the priest. They'd seen it on TV. His dad pushed for details. Tate told him he wasn't going to be able to pony up. First thing he'd tell them and then his dad would start telling the story to his buddies at the club and then it would be all over town.

"Tate Drawdy, you apologize to your father."

THAT NIGHT Tate called Jimmy. Said he still couldn't figure out why John Robert kept one of the officers tied up in that cabin for days.

"Could be a lotta reasons," Jimmy said. "Might need a hostage. Might want to keep a source of information around."

"Wouldn't he have felt more in control if he was on his own?"

"Mebbe not. He does seem to like an audience. More likely he thought he might need a chip if things got sketchy."

"And he's a nasty son of a bitch," Tate said. "He mighta been holding onto him until the brainstorm kicked in."

"Yeah. He's real creative. How the folks?"

"You'd be pretty jealous if you saw what I had to eat."

"So you're not just gonna be slow when you come back. You'll be fat and slow."

"Bout the size of it."

Tate watched an old World War II movie with his dad. After his folks had gone to bed, he went out back by the pool. A cabana made of stone, with a slate roof, surrounded by tall pines. There was a small refrigerator there, and a grill. He got a beer and eased into a rocker. Handmade, by the husband of the woman who had cared for him as a child.

"You best be careful… don't make me come after you," she'd say.

And the opportunities to say it had been plentiful.

Young Tate Drawdy liked to run and hide and set little traps for Lena. He was a God's truth handful, but she had something the other Druid Hills maids could only envy. Lena had his daddy's blessing to tan little Tate's hide up one side and down the other whenever and wherever it was deserved.

It was muggy that day, full of the scent of magnolia. A wet, spring morning. Tate, crewcut, jeans too short for his legs, mud on his face.

She'd taken him to the school fair. The crowd, full of moms and their kids. They were standing at the edge of the playground to see a police dog demonstration. These dogs, the officer had told the crowd, were precisely trained to do only what they were instructed to do. It had begun to rain. No matter, the officer said. They would sit without stirring through a thunderstorm if need be.

And then, for a moment, the clouds parted. The sky, suddenly a deeper blue, the sun beating down, no movement in the air, moms turning listless, kids losing patience. Tate tugged on Lena's skirt. She bent down. He whispered. I bet I can make those dogs jump. And with that she snatched him up quick and shook a finger in his face. You be smart now, she said, and don't let *nobody* tell you dem dogs don't bite.

Such temptation was too good to resist. As the rain returned, Tate found a rock and fired it straight at one of the dogs. It may have been his decision to run that set the drama in motion, but moments later a jet-black German shepherd with teeth as big as anything was staring him in the face and he was crying his eyes out.

And for that, as he stood in the downpour, he got a spanking and a lesson: Tempt the devil and the devil will have his due.

Now, decades later, the air again very still, winter-crisped hydrangeas hanging heavy against the fence, a siren in the distance. He heard it, but it didn't matter. It wasn't his town anymore. He finished his beer and limped back inside.

It was good to be away, to sleep in the room where he'd grown up, his bed, his stuff. Familiar turf, almost like a holiday. Actually, it was. He read a book, watched a couple of movies. The following night, he went out with a couple of buddies. Like his dad, they wanted to hear some inside scoop.

Weird how things changed. Growing up, they'd had so much in common. Rich, smart kids, good on the field of battle. But for them, the battle was still the gridiron. Now, just a storehouse of memories, stories to inflate over time. Tate's world, not the same anymore.

His buddy the surgeon, in practice now with his father. Second buddy, a banker. Another, building shopping centers. They'd had catered parties as kids. They'd driven BMWs and Corvettes to school. It was another life.

Good to see old friends, but there was a distance now, because of his job. And his salary.

On the third day, it was time to go home. It was a good break. It had given him a chance to come to some decisions.

It was time to get Griffin off his back.

He called the jailers, asked if they'd heard any nuggets, Char, Shawn James. Nothing. That night he went to see Jimmy, brought a 12-pack.

Jimmy was standing at the door when he got out of the car.

"Saw you coming. Whaddya got? Bunch of em? Come on, let's sit in the dining room."

It had fuzzy wallpaper and little nooks in the walls for knick-knacks. There was an impressive chandelier. All the furniture was upholstered in bright flowers and there was cut glass on the coffee table, more on the piano, with a healthy coating of dust.

"I've never been in this room."

"Me neither."

Tate tossed Jimmy a beer, opened one for himself, set two on the floor. He took the rest into the kitchen. Jimmy hadn't opened his, but there was a pillow on the coffee table.

"Put your foot up, get comfy. So what's your plan?"

Tate sat down and started to stretch out the leg. Then he stood and pulled his shirt out of his pants, shrugged his shoulders. He picked up the beer, held it up to the light.

"What are you daydreaming about now?"

"Just noticing what good color this beer has. We should all count our blessings, particularly for this beverage. You know the colonials made beer because they couldn't always find clean water. So they drank it all day."

"Rugged."

"Can we smoke in here?"

"Fuck no. Light me one too."

Tate lit the smokes. He held onto the match, looking.

"There's no place…"

"Put it in that little dish there."

"Be the only time this thing ever gets used."

"My mom used it."

"For what?"

"How should I know?"

Tate killed his first beer, opened the second.

"What?"

"I'm just waiting for you to get to it."

"All right. It's time to chase Griffin down and I haven't got squat to work with."

"Yeah."

"What would you do?"

"Not much you can do. Talk to everybody again. Make sure nobody forgot anything."

"Great."

"Or you could come up with some new ideas. You're a smart guy, right?"

14

JEANNE WAS in her bunk, the blanket pulled up to her chin. But she was dressed, had her shoes on. The Noose had come by. He had a proposition. She was going to get a night on the town.

Well, not exactly on the town. She was getting out for a night, so she could screw a guy in a hotel. The Noose had told her to do it. He'd make it right for her. Money, some nice things to eat. Good treatment.

And if things went well...

Tyree came for her about 11. She didn't hear him come up the stairs. Crepe soles. He brought a big raincoat and a slouchy hat. He tapped lightly on the bars. She was awake, lying on the bed. She swung her legs around to the floor. Her toes were curled and small, like a child's.

"We're taking my car. Don't want anyone to recognize you."

She smiled. He unlocked the cell door. Held the coat for her. She stepped into it and they started down the stairs.

"You OK with this?"

"Sure. The Noose told me it was good for me to do this."

"You understand, right? You can't talk about this. But the Noose, he knows people. He might be able to help you at trial, you know?"

"That's right. That's what he said. But who's the John, the guy tonight?"

They were at the car now. She got in, kept the hat on. It was a big Chevy sedan, with a bench seat. Tyree had slid it all the way back.

"He runs a big biker bar. Some of the guys on the force drop in there sometimes. He's a friend of the department, a good friend of the Noose. And me."

"OK. Then you're gonna bring me back later?"

"I'm gonna bring you back. And there's one more thing. This is real important, understand?"

He reached out, took her wrist. He didn't squeeze. He just held it and turned to look at her.

"What?"

"He wants a picture of you. He asked about it twice. He wants a picture of you naked."

"Sure. That's OK…"

Now he squeezed. She collapsed into the seat.

"It's not OK. No pictures. None. If there's a camera, you avoid it. And then when you leave, you bring it with you. Are we clear?"

"Yeah. Absolutely, Tyree. Now, can you not break my fucking arm?"

He started the car.

"I'm sorry. Did I hurt you?"

"No, it's not… It's OK."

"OK. I'm sorry."

It wasn't a hotel. It was a motel. Tyree pulled over to the side of the road and pointed.

"Number 5."

It was 4 am when she called Tyree to come get her. She was waiting outside when he drove up. She saw him pull up across the street. When he turned his lights out, she ran across.

He pushed the door open for her.

"Everything OK?"

"Yeah."

He looked at her. Then he put the car in gear.

"Put your lights on."

He nodded.

"Look, Tyree. I need a favor. I know this is not part of the plan, but I need a favor."

"Don't even think about it. We're going back. We're going back right now."

She punched his arm.

"Don't get all excited. I just want you to stop at a Burger King or something. There's got to be someplace open all night. I am fucking starving. Can you do that?"

"Yeah, OK."

In the drive-through line, he was staring at her.

"I don't know what you want. But you got this kinda big brother look on your face. If that's it, the guy was fine, OK?"

"No problems?"

"No. He's just an old married idiot and he has some fantasies about a young babe who can still move. And he did ask about pictures, but I said no. And that was it. Piece of cake."

"Piece of ass, you mean."

"Yeah."

CHAR RAN up the stairs to the second floor, turned a hard right. Jimmy was at his desk.

"Take a walk?"

"Sure."

"I saw something I don't like this morning. And there's plenty I don't like in that jail. But this is a little too squirrely."

And so she told him. She'd decided to pop in on the girls, talk a little, see if they needed anything, see if they needed to talk.

Jeanne was sound asleep in her bunk.

On the chair in front of the toilet was a big raincoat, a very big coat. She called out. Jeanne woke up. Char said she'd asked about the coat. Jeanne had stammered a bit, said one of the jailers brought it up when she called out that she was cold.

"That's what blankets are for."

"So, what's your gut on it," Jimmy asked.

"This is weird, but I thought she was a little scared when I asked about it. You know what I think? And this is crazy. But I think she was outside. I think she left the building. Why else would she need a coat?"

"Wouldn't be surprised if she made a house call. Newsome maybe. He runs that place like his little kingdom."

"Yes and I hear she fucks anybody who walks by. I didn't act like it was any big deal. I said OK and talked about other stuff. But I'm watching now. I'm watching real close."

15

IT WAS COLD and the rain was coming down, enough rain that you wouldn't see the sky all day. They'd borrowed an office in the back of the church. It was a big room with tall windows.

The old cathedral had been started in the late 1700s. French Catholics fleeing from Haiti had come in, along with other French, people with money and titles to hang onto. With all the stained glass and the Italian marble, it looked like it belonged in the center of a European city.

It was the not a place where you would expect to find someone feeling closed in and betrayed and hysterical, someone full of lust and anger. Someone who could look straight at something and not see it. Someone who wanted to exert so much force the earth moved, and then disappear in the middle of it all.

Somebody had lost their head here.

It was a nun. Had to be. Palladino had been killed in his office, late at night when the church was locked up. And his office door had to have been locked. Who doesn't lock the door when they're screwing a child? It was someone with a key. Someone in bare feet. And there was that sword.

Jimmy wanted to rule out any staffers. They'd interviewed them all. It wasn't likely one of the men... the yard guys or the maintenance guys. There were a few female employees. They had families. They had alibis. They didn't fit. It was a nun.

One by one they talked with them. Sister Mary. Sister Kate. Sister Antoinette. Sister Louisa. Sister Ellen. Sister Eva.

Sister Cacia was one of those women who look attractive from a distance, and then you get close enough to see the set of her face. Five-foot six, 125 pounds, with blond hair, blue eyes and heels that punished the floor, she pulled a chair from the table, sat down and pulled on the end of each sleeve until it was tight on her wrist. She had yet to make eye contact with either of them.

Tate looked over at Jimmy. He was tapping a finger on his nose. Tate looked at her. He waited.

She wore plain, square-toed shoes. Her habit was heavily starched, worn often. The creases were shiny with age. Her hair was pulled back hard, with a fat rubber band holding it behind her head. She wore no jewelry. On each thumb, at the inside edge of the nail, the skin had been chewed raw.

She was staring at a place behind them.

"Cacia," said Tate. "Is that Greek?"

"Certainly."

"What does it mean?"

"It is a blossoming tree that symbolizes the resurrection."

"And what is your last name?"

"Magdalini."

Jimmy spoke.

"Any relation to Magdalene, as in Mary?"

"Mary came from the village of Magdala, on the sea of Galilee."

"It must be nice to have a name with so much history."

She straightened her back. She crossed her legs, uncrossed them and folded her hands. She gave her chin a harsh tilt, as if she were practicing for the day she'd wear bifocals. There was no makeup.

Jimmy pointed to the desk.

"We have some water here. Would you like some water?"

Her lips, set wrench-tight in a place they never left. Her eyes began to flit from one to the other.

"What do you want from me?"

Tate answered.

"We're investigating the death of Father Palladino, but you must know that."

"Of course. So why aren't you out doing... whatever?"

Jimmy answered.

"We think it's possible someone connected with the church may have killed the Father."

"That is utterly ridiculous. Father Palladino was beloved throughout the church. He was loved throughout the community. Whoever attacked him must have been some kind of crazy person. Someone broke in here and tried to rob him."

"It doesn't appear that anything was taken," said Tate. "Perhaps it was some kind of hate crime, or maybe it was a crime of passion."

"You mean someone who had something against the church?"

"Perhaps."

"That's preposterous. Why would someone have something against the church?"

"Why does anybody shoot somebody else? We're just trying to put the pieces together."

She snapped her head from side to side. Any moment now, she would spit on them.

"Isn't that what you people always say? You need to be out arresting someone. It was someone who wanted money, or silver. Someone who wanted the money people give to the church."

"That's a good theory for us to look at," said Tate. "Then again, you know that Mister Palladino was with a woman at the time he was killed. A very young woman. You knew that? You knew they were naked?"

Her eyes reddened. She thrust forward in the chair. Her chin, like a rock.

"Why would you use that word?"

"What word?"

"Mister. It's Father Palladino. Have you no respect?"

"Forgive me."

She crossed her arms.

"You did know that…"

"Know what?"

"About the young woman. She was murdered too, the girl."

Her hand crept toward her mouth. She set it down. She laced her fingers once again.

"Is there anything else?"

Jimmy told her: "We haven't covered much ground just yet."

"Well you asked me my name and whether I knew things about the crime. I really cannot imagine how I can possibly help you. If I'm free to go…"

Tate stood. He held out his hand.

Sister Cacia arose quickly, turned and walked out the door.

"Thank you sister," he said as she disappeared. "You've been most helpful."

He walked to the door, closed it. Jimmy was shaking his head, laughing.

"That was too easy."

"Yeah."

"When did you know?"

"When she crossed her legs. I swear I thought she was gonna light a cigarette for a minute there. Or maybe set us on fire."

"Wrapped pretty tight."

"Yeah," Tate said. "Let's get her back in."

"Wait on it. Call her at home tonight, late. Have a guy outside."

"Think she's a runner?"

"Nah. I think she wants to do some more killin'."

"Couple of guys she just met?"

Jimmy laughed. "Big time. Wonder why Palladino was messing with her? She looks like she could blow up in about half a second."

Tate leaned his head to one side, hoping his neck would pop. Finally, he heard it. He smiled.

"I dated a girl in high school once. She asked me. I thought she was great until I got a better look at her. Then I didn't want to have much to do with her, but she wouldn't take no. I went along with it for awhile, hoping she'd get fed up with me. I tried real hard to be disagreeable, 'cause I wanted it to be her idea. All the other kids having a great time and I am locked down with this wacko. I finally had to just tell her off and I thought she was gonna strangle me. I swear I was looking over my shoulder for a month."

"And then you realized you really fucked up when you said yes the first time."

"No kidding."

"So how bad was it? You sleep with this gem?"

"Not a chance, and I had to scramble to keep it from happening. But that woulda been a death sentence. I knew that, even as a kid."

That night, they were sitting on Jimmy's porch. It got to be 9 o'clock. Tate called Sister Cacia. He got her machine.

He left a message, told her he had some more questions, asked her if she'd come in. He said please.

THE NEXT morning, the message light was blinking on Tate's desk phone. Jimmy was there.

"You gonna get that?"

"Yeah. In a minute. Just talked with the church administrator. Interesting."

"So?"

"There is no Cacia Magdalini. It's the name she chose for herself maybe five years ago. The checks are made out to Amber Harvey, late of Birmingham, Alabama. Accepted into the convent there through the intervention of the director of a homeless shelter.

Amber Harvey spent a good portion of her teenage years living on the streets. Before she found the church.

"She does her work, she's well-respected and nobody knows a thing about her. Except she owns an old house on the west side. Lives alone. I got a stack of money says we'll find out she's the one who cut the deal for Palladino's weekend with our lawyer from Dallas."

"And she's one pissed off lady."

"Well, we know that."

Jimmy crossed his arms. Patience, not a strong suit.

"You gonna get that?"

Tate reached over and punched the button. For a second, there was no sound. Then, a needle on a scratchy record. It was Mussorgsky. The music began softly. And then it grew loud. And then a click.

Jimmy punched the button again.

"What the fuck...?"

"It's a message," Tate said.

"What's it mean?"

"Means she's not coming in."

IT WAS SCARCELY the conventional appeal, for Laura. Tyree was a hulking, good-looking charmer, a bit country in his ways, somewhat affected, with his cowboy hat and his knee-length rain slicker and that bushy head of hair and a certain aw shucks conversation.

What struck her was something that seemed to come from inside of him, a quiet authority. Perhaps the piercing eyes, a deep blue, almost incongruous with his rough exterior. The eyes looked like they belonged to someone who was accustomed to getting his way, someone with a future. He seemed to relish the cop thing, the sense of order, the abundance of rules and the brethren bond and the hierarchy. He spoke of his fellow officers as if they had weathered battles together. She wondered how severe the stress could be when their trenches seemed no farther than a block from the corner donut shop.

But she respected the loyalty and the commitment and the cause. She was no rule-breaker herself, other than the discomfort that might arise in some quarters from a young woman who profited from the leering gaze of countless drunks several times a week. But she'd worked in a donut shop herself, and made more money now in five minutes than she'd made in a week there.

What had caused her to change course was happenstance. One evening, late, she drove down Abercorn. There, coming out of a strip club heading toward a parked car was a young woman she recognized from one of her art design classes. She was wearing a matching skirt and sweater set that looked like it came straight from Burdine's, something her mom must have picked out for school. In her hands, a roll of bills so large she was having trouble jamming it into her purse. If that was an evening's take, Laura needed a new occupation.

Two days later, she was onstage, dressed in a G-string and high heels. That next morning, she paid three months rent in advance.

She'd explained all that to Tyree. He understood, but had real discomfort with it. As they pushed a grocery cart down the aisle one evening, she caught him staring, jaw clenched, as a pudgy produce worker ogled her.

That guy must have recognized her, he said later.

That could be, she told him. Then again, guys had been staring at her long before she ever started taking off her clothes around a dancer's pole.

As the time between them stretched on, he broached… gently… the subject of her retirement from the stage. She must have made enough money by now.

Her reply was equally gentle. She would quit, at some point, but not yet.

134

16

SHE LOVED photographs. She loved to take them out and look at them. It was all that she had, really. Pictures from her childhood. Pictures of men and women and a little blonde girl. The girl, older in each photo, with different sets of men and women. Her foster parents, the people who kept her, one after another.

Pictures of houses. Pictures of schools.

She had taken the name Cacia in the eighth grade. The name of a character she loved in a children's novel. Books were her escape. She could retreat into a book.

And there was much to forget.

The time she'd been sent home with head lice. The year she'd slept on the floor of a bathroom with stopped up plumbing and metal doors she couldn't open on a bed made of rolled up newspapers. The foster dads who promised her things and bought her ice cream.

The day at Children's Services when they told her she'd gotten too old to be adopted.

They'd come for her in a van, honked the horn outside the trailer where her latest fosters lived. Couple of old drunks who wanted the state's monthly allotment.

"Hop in, Amber."

Not anymore, she told the driver. I'm Cacia now.

"OK. We'll call you Cacia."

Escorted to a back room where they tried on pink dresses and white Keds, the cute Pollyanna outfits they wore when people came to look. And then she walked out, out into the hallway. Into the incandescent smiles of three child care workers she had learned to hate over the last two years.

Someday she would be a child no longer. She'd dig a hole and fill it with poisonous spiders and cover it with branches. And she'd call to them, trick them into falling, deep, down.

Control.

"Look who's here Amber, I mean, Cacia. Look who's here!"

There, standing just off to the side, another little blonde girl, perhaps a year younger. She had a pretty smile, a bit tentative.

"Don't you recognize her? Amber don't you recognize Kathleen? Don't you recognize your sister?"

They'd been separated for so long, victims of a foster system that found it easier to divide the girls up, place them one at a time. And then they'd told her she was too old now to be wanted by anyone.

And then they'd taken her back to the old trailer and the old drunks.

Eventually she found the church. Or the church found her. And she accepted that life. It gave her time to read, time to be alone. She had settled on Savannah and the cathedral.

And the withered house she had come to call her own.

Tate parked in the driveway between rows of azaleas so thick he had to back up to open the door.

It was old Savannah... brick, wrought iron, enough Spanish moss to hide a cemetery. Dark and wet in the shade, slate covered in green mold. Layers of paint peeling off a front door besieged with wood rot. The damp hung like sweat.

He rang the chime, put an ear against the door and waited. There was no sound. Then, over his head, a frantic chattering. A squirrel sprinting along a branch leaped out, landing just above the gutter, scraping its way to the peak of the roof, its momentum carrying it across to the other side where it rolled and tumbled down the steep pitch.

He unholstered his gun and put a shoulder into it. The jamb splintered so easily he almost fell into the foyer. The place was bloated with antiques. A moldered chandelier hanging over two armoires, with two floor lamps side by side between them. A couple of trunks standing on their sides. A bookcase, shelves stacked with boxes wrapped in shipping tape. Carpet that hardly muffled the creak of the floorboards. With every step, it sounded like a nail working loose. She had lived here alone. For how long?

He did a lap through a kitchen stacked with empty bowls, a sitting room decked out in brittle flowers, tottery end tables and grimy lace, brass knickknacks turned to black and tiny porcelain figures of women with parasols. He put the gun away. The stench of ammonia, so strong he suspected it was the story of her life.

He started up the back stairs from the kitchen. They were narrow and steep and cluttered with gardening tools, empty flower boxes and case after case of Moet. He reached down and lifted back a lid. The empty bottles had been put back in place, upside down. He pushed through a door at the top. It closed behind him. A small motion light in a floor socket clicked on as he moved along the hallway.

He'd only taken a few steps from the door when the power went out.

There was no illumination. There was nothing coming from underneath the doors along the hallway. There were no windows, no light. He was partway down the hall and it was so black he couldn't tell which way he was facing. He felt his way back to the door and found it locked. He hadn't noticed it was steel.

The smell was powerful here.

The music began gently at first. Mussorgsky again... Pictures at an Exhibition, toward the end of the piece. The volume began to increase, ever so slowly. He stood, still, waiting. A minute passed, agonizingly slow. Maybe two.

He could picture her standing there, on the first floor, one hand on the stereo. She'd have a look on her face, jaw set, shoulders pulled back, her hands clammy, her heart hammering. She'd be staring at the ceiling, sending a message upstairs.

It was louder now, building more quickly. Then, a burst of impatience, the music suddenly blasting out in a torrent. The house vibrated with it.

His reception was about to begin.

He moved along the hallway, hand over hand against the wall. He was hurrying now. He found another door. Locked. He made a full circuit. There was no way out.

Don't let nobody tell you dem dogs won't bite.

He squeezed into a corner. What if she came in another door? She'd shine a light in his face and take him out. Or she'd approach in the blackness. Could he count on light coming through the door when she came up the stairs?

Assuming she wasn't already in there with him.

The music was deafening, like a rumbling in his bones. He sat on the floor, his back into the corner, legs splayed out in front of him, took out his gun. He felt for his cellphone. He had Jimmy on speed dial.

Then it came to him. He pulled the phone out of his pocket, held it high and punched the volume button on the side.

The light was faint, but in the blackness, it was enough.

She was at the end of the hallway, crouching, coming toward him, up on her toes, her hair hanging loose. She was naked. He remembered the photograph she'd taken in the mirror and the scarf she wore, the look of a woman who'd spent a lifetime out of place.

She came at him, running hard, the light reflecting off the polished steel of the archangel's sword as she leaped forward, hair flying, her bare feet clenched like talons, her face contorted in a scream he never heard, coming at him like a centurion, flexed hard, the sword held out in front of her, two hands, pointing at his chest.

As the light from his cellphone went out, he fired once and rolled away, then vaulted back on top of her. She lay motionless underneath him. There was no pulse.

IT'S KINDA like having bugs crawl up your ass.

"You've had bugs up your ass?"

"Well, what I imagine it might feel like."

"So you were scared."

"Shitless."

"Ever occur to you to take some guys along? We have a term for it. It's called backup. This seems to be something you have trouble with."

"I guess so."

"You're a fucking idiot. Bitch was working way over her pay grade. She'd had enough and she decided to cash it in, nowhere to turn. And you go by yourself. You think you woulda been embarrassed if your Lone Ranger thing got you messed up by some head case?

"She knew she couldn't go after you. But she did. Just like she knew she couldn't have a thing with the stud father. But she did. She worked at it. She probably spent a lotta time rehearsing her laugh and some light chit-chat. Then she'd analyze it later. How it went that day. And you came close to getting pin-cushioned, just like Palladino."

Tate finished his beer. He got a newspaper and put it on Jimmy's coffee table, and put his feet up on it.

"Son of a bitch. Put that paper down. You make me into some kinda what's her name."

"Who?"

"The woman who sells the pillows and shit."

"I'm supposed to know who sells pillows?"

"Woman has a TV show. You know what I'm saying. Don't make me into some kinda freak."

"Right. You're a self-respecting male. You got no furniture issues."

"So put the fucking newspaper on the floor and put your feet on the table. And get me a beer. Asshole. And, by the way, did your doctor tell you it helps gunshot wounds heal if you smoke like a fucking pack a day?"

"What are you talking about?"

"You're smoking like a fucking chimney. I just thought I'd mention it."

"Fuck you about the cigarettes."

In the morning, they sat down with the team that combed the nun's house. The guys had opened all the doors and windows while they worked. Some neighbors came over. They'd never seen the inside of the place. Didn't know the sister too well. She waved, said hello, checked her mail.

The guys had found a diary. Actually, a stack of them. There were lots of passages about Palladino. About how she loved him, how she'd sent him her picture. About the little escort business they'd started. How jealous she was. How they'd spend the money together. Soon.

She'd taken off her clothes for him, lots of times. There were lots more pictures. She'd pored over them, sent him only the best ones. Candlelight. Legs in the air.

And one shot of the two of them, dressed for church, standing out on the sidewalk in front of the cathedral. It was a perfectly normal picture. They would have asked one of their brethren to take it one day after church. A pretty day when the sun was shining.

She would have pretended it was just a spur of the moment thing, a whim. She would have planned for it, carrying the camera, always looking for the opportunity. She would have gotten more pictures with others, thrown them away.

She'd given him that sword, her weapon against serpents and the forces of evil. And used it to pierce his filthy heart. He could have loved her. He could have loved only her. They could have hidden away together in her wood-rotted, bug-infested, urine-soaked hovel. He could have drowned himself in champagne and felt the security that comes with metal doors and darkness. God wanted it that way.

17

"I'M PUTTING together a list of who to talk with about Griffin."

"Everybody is a pretty short list."

"So who would you put on there?"

"The other three in jail, really. Spend some time on the phone with folks up north. What you really want is somebody he hung out with. Let's work on associates. You may not turn up much, but you get in a spot like this, you need to be doing something."

They were sitting in Jimmy's kitchen, watching a ballgame on a little set on the counter. They killed a 12-pack, with Tate doing most of the work. Jimmy packed him into a guest room for the night.

The next morning, he went to Shawn James' office. He wanted to listen to the recordings of James' sessions with the girls, and Wigle. Then he went to see his boss.

"I've still got some time off, after that gunshot. OK if I take it now?"

"You've got plenty coming. You OK?"

"Yeah. Thought I might head up north, read the files, find some people who know Griffin, see if anything sticks out."

"How long you wanna take up there?"

"Week... 10 days."

"Do it. I'll put you on the clock. Expense the trip. I want you to keep it on the cheap, though. No fancy hotels or lobster. He's a suspect and he's a threat. I can justify doing this the one time. If you bust out and wanna try again down the road, we're gonna have to have something concrete."

Tate called a couple of detectives and a guy at the prison so they'd know he was coming. And he called Barksdale. They'd been talking. He knew something about her now, where she'd grown up, the things she cared about, the way she liked to cut to the chase with a tough question.

"I'm getting ready to head up north, see if I can chase down this guy that escaped."

"That sounds pretty dangerous."

"Not really. I'll see what I can find out, and turn it to the local cops, let them arrest him. I'll just help them out with information."

"I think you're bullshitting me. You know where he is?"

"No, nothing like that. I'm just doing some looking around."

"Fishing expedition."

"Exactly."

"OK. I'm off today. Let's meet someplace for dinner."

"Nah, I can't…"

"Cut it out. You are just being a stickler. I can tell, today is a day nobody is following you around."

"All right. Tell you what I'm gonna do. I'll meet you at the place and then when we go, I'm gonna have somebody follow you home, just to make sure nobody's tagging along."

"OK fine."

They met at 17Hundred90, between Oglethorpe and Columbia squares. Tate went in pretty regularly. A good place for southern fare. Slate slabs on the floor, brick on the walls, colonial portraits, a rustic bar in the back.

Tate wore a sport jacket and tie. Barksdale had on some pearls and a little black dress. It fit nicely. It was the first time he'd seen her in something like that, the first time he'd realized she was lean and hard and tight in some places, but not everyplace. It had the effect of softening some of his rough edges, which was a surprise to both of them.

SOUTH OF TOWN. The Noose's place, an old brick ranchstyle. Tyree was the last to arrive. He came in without knocking, wiped his shoes on a welcome mat, scanned the room.

Yellowing linoleum under a knock-off grandfather clock in the hallway. It opened onto a small sitting room, separated from an even smaller den, where one wall was covered with an entertainment center with a fat TV in the center. Veneer scuffed and peeling. The Noose had his money set aside.

Tyree took off his hat and hung it on a coat rack by the door.

"I thought we weren't going to meet like this anymore."

The Noose was standing in front of the picture window. The shades were closed. On three walls, dusty prints of golfers wearing knickers, knee-high argyles, pullovers and Gatsby caps. A couple of family portraits. Wooded scenes with packs of English spaniels giving chase.

Three deputies, all of 'em white, shoulder to shoulder on a rump-sprung sofa in a faded brown and white herringbone. Another in a wingback chair. There was a bowl of peanuts on a coffee table. The Noose began to pace. He was still in uniform.

"I heard some talk this afternoon about that scumfuck Drawdy. He's going north, try to find Griffin."

"So let him." It was the jailer, Russell. He'd mixed a drink. "Maybe John Robert fixes our problem."

"You in touch with our Pittsburgh boy?" Tyree asked.

"Been a couple days."

"This from a guy who's too cheap to buy a good holster, so cons can't grab your gun when you're not looking," Noose said. "Give him a heads-up, asshole."

"Can do," Russell said.

Tyree shook his head.

"What difference does that make to us?"

The Noose wiped his mouth with the back of his hand, left to right, right to left.

"It might be something Griffin would like to know. He can help us out here. Face facts, boys. We're in the catbird seat and we've been here for a long time. There's been no real heat, until lately. Drawdy is the fucking problem."

Tyree said: "I made a run at Drawdy. Just to be sure. He ain't interested."

"What'd you say to him," said Newsome.

"I said enough."

"What was it?"

"You don't wanna know."

"Yeah, fucker, I do."

"No you don't. Move on."

One of the deputies put his feet on the coffee table. The Noose leaned over and smacked his boot.

"Get off there."

The deputy pointed.

"I don't like where this is headed."

"It ain't just Drawdy," Russell said.

Noose snarled.

"Shut the fuck up. I know how to handle this."

Tyree spoke again.

"I think it's time you proved that to us."

And then the Noose made a fist, held it up for everyone to see.

"I'll handle it."

TATE GOT the message first thing in the morning. There was a guy who had some information about John Robert Griffin. Where he was. How he might be found.

From a friend, it said.

It was a biker bar south of town. Tate left Jimmy a message, then headed out.

Big lunch crowd. Bikes in rows out front. A few pickups with rebel flags on the fenders and the rear windows. Some guys had a flag on each side.

Bumper stickers about the difference between women and liquor, how liquor lasted longer. Women and dogs; dogs being more loyal.

I'd rather eat worms than ride a Japanese motorcycle

No fat chicks

My other ride is your mother

Honk if you've never seen a .357 fired from a moving Harley

Tate parked in the shade, walked inside, waited for his eyes to adjust. The coolness felt good. There were fans the size of airplane propellers cutting the air overhead. The scent of old beer, greasy fries and onions, generations of smoke, strong enough it would cling to his clothes.

Lynyrd Skynyrd's "Swamp Music" blasting through speakers suspended by chains from a popcorn ceiling sprayed black. It was a good tune he'd heard so many times he could hardly stomach it any longer. A good band relegated to tedium. He wondered how long they'd prayed for success before realizing what a monotonous legacy it carried.

The bartender was the closest thing to someone in authority he could spot. He began to make his way across the room. Sticky floor. He put his hand on the shoulder of a man in front him, hoping to ease by.

The man turned. Big guy, tattoos, gloves without fingers. He spewed beery breath into Tate's face, looked long and hard.

"You don't belong here, friend. The door is behind you."

Tate said nothing, tried to push past him. The man stepped in his way.

"Excuse me," Tate said. "I need to get by."

He was Tate's height, perhaps 30 pounds heavier. A longish beard, speckled with gray. His hair was curly and parted in the middle. Flat nose, heavily sunburned. Bushy eyebrows, yellow teeth. In his right ear, a feather hanging from some kind of miniature silver medallion. Jeans, a fringed leather vest over a t-shirt. Pack of Marlboro in the pocket. Monster belt buckle. Somewhere close by there'd be a Softtail.

He pulled the gloves from his hands, stuck a finger in Tate's chest, came onto him, chin to chin, an angry redneck spoiling for a fight.

"You and I are going outside, my friend."

Tate had been expecting trouble. The only surprise was how quickly it came. He smiled, leaned into the man's face.

"I'm not afraid of you, and I'm not going to fight you, so I'm really not afraid of you."

But now the guy was grabbing his tie, yanking him up short, forcing him backward toward the door.

There were times when being a cop meant nothing, especially when the cop was alone. Tate had hoped for more choice about when that might happen. Clearly he was wrong. It was something Jimmy would have understood. Jimmy would have had something to say.

For Tate, the realization itself was enough. For as long as this was going to take, he was no longer a cop. What he needed to be was the baddest guy in the room.

He pushed clear and, without turning his back, went to the door. The others in the bar, staring. But no one moved.

In a moment they were behind the building. The guy was tall. Looked to be strong. Fit but fat. And he looked like he should have been a better fighter. His balance was poor, his form laughable. He threw a punch and Tate sidestepped it easily. He threw another, lunging awkwardly and Tate gave him a hard right to the eye that dropped him to the ground.

Tate stepped close. Suddenly, the awkwardness disappeared, a stunt. In its place, speed, finesse and a long knife. Tate reeled back, ducking to the side as the blade swung toward his throat. No more fun and games.

He danced backward to gain time, stripped off his belt as the biker got to his feet, began peppering the man's face with the buckle as if he were snapping a wet towel in the locker room. The man lunged forward, whipping the knife through the air, chest high. Tate surprised him, stepped into the blow, using his forearm to block the attack, sent a vicious side kick into his right knee and, as the leg snapped and turned inward, he spun, off the ground, coiling in the air, kicking this time at the jaw of his collapsing opponent.

It was hard contact and he could feel the neck twist, a dry-twig snap drowned out by the music seeping from inside. A legendary fight, if there'd been anyone to see it. The sudden kick was something his doctor would have advised against, for good reason. That hole in his hamstring was calling his name.

He crouched over the man and searched his pockets. Empty. They'd known he was coming.

He stood, looked around slowly. The rear windows to the bar had been replaced with plywood, covered with steel bars. The door itself was flimsy, but a heavy burglar door hung open beside it. A dumpster, piles of cardboard boxes, a couple of broken bar stools and then a small vacant lot, weeds waist high, more trash. Just beyond, woods.

And now he had the overpowering sensation of being watched. He scanned the woods, had turned back to take another look at the body when he heard five shots, quickly. He dropped to the ground, saw a body crash down from behind a tree. Jimmy walked out, holstering his gun.

"I watched you go inside. This guy comes out the back right after, heads into the trees. The next thing I knew, we were watching your little drama. He was the backup and he was about to finish the job."

Tate walked toward the body. Another vest, another biker. On the ground beside him, a Smith and Wesson .357, the compact model, two-inch barrel, wooden grip. The kind of gun a biker might carry, wouldn't take up much space. Revolver, eight rounds. An expensive gun.

"I guess all this is no surprise, eh?"

Jimmy grabbed him by the arm.

"You're a piece of work, my friend. So... if somebody tells you the stove is hot, you put your hand on it real quick, am I right?"

THE STREET out front was lined with Harleys when Tate went back that night.

He parked off the highway. A young woman tending drinks squinted over the cash register, started toward him. Then she looked across at a guy sitting at the far end of the bar. He waved her off. She turned and walked away.

He wore a jacket and a dark sweater over a white shirt, expensive watch. He sat next to Tate. A couple of guys along the bar grabbed their drinks and walked over to watch pool. The man in the jacket picked up his stool and turned it to face him.

"Haven't I seen you in here before?"

"I was here this afternoon, briefly."

"That's what I'm thinking. Interesting afternoon."

"You figure on making it an interesting evening?"

"No."

"Good thinking."

"You're Drawdy? The cop?"

"I'm Drawdy. And, as far as you're concerned, I'm the new sheriff."

He waved to the bartender. She walked toward them, waited.

"You're welcome any time Mr. Drawdy."

And to her, he said, "Anything Mr. Drawdy wants."

He walked toward the back of the bar and through a door marked "Private."

The bartender was short and had blue jeans stretched tight over a butt shaped like a truck tire. Curls like she'd slept with her hair tied around salt and pepper shakers, wearing one of those off-the shoulder pirate shirts. She had feathered earrings that matched the one he'd seen on the biker that afternoon. And she had a tattoo just under the collar bone that stretched from one arm to the other that read: "No Ragrets."

She leaned over the bar.

"You wanna hear about the specials?"

He got a beer. Two red-headed fat women in tank tops and tight bluejeans were dancing close on the concrete floor under the blue lights and the stares and the smoke. An acoustic guitar player, bass, and an old hippie using a thin wooden box he'd turned into a surprisingly effective snare drum, had a set of ram's horns and a tiny metal ashtray bolted on top that he used for cymbals.

Fighting the music: scraping chairs, quaking beer and the resinous crack of pool balls echoing off the hard floor.

The old hippie, missing teeth up front, with a stringy western vest. A woman came up to whisper in his ear. He nodded, began to finesse some early blues, grimacing like a revelation was about to burst forth from the ceiling.

Since my ever loving baby left town
Ain't got no rest in my slumbers
Ain't got no feelings to bruise

Ain't got no telephone numbers
Ain't got nothing but the blues.

Grinning, posing, he squeezed out a falsetto and the crowd began to sing along. That's when they eased into "Rainy Night in Georgia."

Couple of rough bikers at the bar, staring at Tate. He ignored them.

The Irish girls, getting all worked up now, and the old guy, singing the verse, eyebrows clenched, and then they brought it down to a whisper and then it was just the voices and it dawned on the room that this was some sweet harmony and they started to yell and clap, gently and then more. And then they eased the instruments back in, brought it up, the old hippie spinning his sticks over his head.

A tired guy with varnished hair from a bottle stood, staggered two steps toward the stage, hesitated, swaying, put out a hand to hold onto his chair. Lifted his beer high. Rendered speechless.

They punched it for a time, driving the rhythm, toying with the crowd, and then, with that toothless smile, the old bum threw a little flourish on the rim of his ashtray cymbal, threw his hands out in front of him and the band stopped.

They sang the last verse a cappella.

Tate finished his beer, climbed into his car, drove home. In the morning, he would tell Jimmy: This was his new favorite bar.

Part Three

18

PITTSBURGH, Griffin's home town. Good place to start.

Tate got up early, had to fly through Baltimore. As soon as he landed, he headed out to talk to the cops who'd busted Griffin the first time, the time he blew a guy's head off.

Jonathan Bozeman, detective who worked the case, might have been a cop in waiting by the sixth grade. The kind of guy who liked things to be orderly. He had a row of plastic figures on his desk, from the Star Wars movies. They were all lined up and carefully spaced. Had a watermelon for a belly and a handshake that could bring you to your knees. Big eyebrows. Long nose. Pasta eater. Good sense of humor.

Not about this.

"Thought he was guilty as a son of a bitch. But he had a pretty good lawyer. I figure it was only the fact that they put me in front of the grand jury that got him whatever time he did get.

"But you can tell. This guy was bubbling up underneath. Blowing a guy's head off was a home run, know what I mean? He got juiced on it."

Bozeman had looked into Griffin's associates, hadn't found much. Didn't see where John Robert was up to much of anything else.

"Woulda helped if we'd had some decent priors. He had a juvey file. Physical stuff mostly. He wasn't robbing or doping. He got into lots of fights. I couldn't bring any of that into court."

And then Tate went on to Mercer, the prison where John Robert had spent time. Driving out over the Allegheny River, north on 79. Hills, scattered houses, subdivisions, and then countryside, farms. Not much more than an hour out of town.

Bunch of brick buildings from the 80s, a wooden fence. Minimum security.

Now they knew better.

He'd called ahead so somebody could pull the file. That's the thing about prisons. Nothing ever gets thrown away. Griffin's psych workups from day one were there.

Somebody had interviewed teachers he'd had along the way. No surprises there.

Predisposition to bullying, rebellion against authority.

One teacher had taken a liking to him. And even he had said Griffin was a smart kid who just seemed to enjoy shocking the hell out of people. There was no predicting what might happen, or what might cause him to push the limits. John Robert might react with aggression if he thought someone was threatening him.

He might do the same thing if somebody was nice.

The prison shrinks found no real tendency toward drug or alcohol abuse. They thought he was smart, and devious as hell. The shooting of a neighbor for no apparent reason didn't seem to startle the experts much.

One psychiatrist had added a note at the bottom. The inmate, he said, could be congenial one minute, remote and hostile the next. Latent hostility to spare. Then again, he'd written, Griffin might just be smart enough to fool all of us, and our testing regimes. One thing he felt sure about: Griffin had absolutely no concern for personal risk.

Flip side, it seemed. Personal risk, for John Robert, was downright enchanting.

There wasn't a lot Tate hadn't already seen, or figured out. But there were addresses, names. He thought he'd go by the place where Griffin used to live, knock on some doors, see if he could get a feel for the place.

See mom and dad.

But first, a trip down the hallway.

The sign on the door read "Frederick Washburn, Prison psychiatrist."

It was open. Inside, a guy who looked perhaps a year or two fresh from college. Strawberry hair, ruddy cheeks, a trace of a moustache. Eyes that suggested he was still pretty excited about the opportunity.

"You must be the Georgia detective, Mr. Drawdy."

"I am. I'm here looking into John Robert Griffin's case. You knew he's wanted for suspicion of murder in Savannah."

"Well aware of the latest drama involving JRG. He's pretty famous around here."

"I've been looking through his file. I brought it along in case you might be able to refresh your memory and, perhaps, give me a few insights."

"Thanks, but I could probably quote you chapter and verse from that file. No need to look at it. Happy to answer any questions."

His desk chair, the kind that swivels, no arms. Outside the window, a look at the prison yard. Heavy fencing between the office window and the grounds.

Washburn had good posture and a clean desk.

Tate took a seat.

"I've been through it all just now and there's really nothing there that surprises me. But your take would be helpful."

Washburn held out both hands like he was putting a cake in the oven.

"John Robert Griffin is what we professionals like to call OSM."

"What's that?"

"One scary mutha."

Tate played along. Big grin. Settled into his chair.

"Go on."

"You're familiar with the term 'narcissistic?'"

"Sure, but it's daily jargon, so we've probably bastardized the meaning. Break it down for me?"

"You're right. People do throw 'narcissism' around a good bit. Think of a narcissistic personality disorder as an extreme form. Let me skip the clinical stuff for the most part and talk about the characteristics. One of my professors in med school had specialized in the study. And the thing he said that stayed with me, especially when I encountered Griffin, was this: More pure evil comes out of narcissism than anything.

"Driven personality, relationally toxic, an expert at transforming some serious psychological wound into something that postures as a strength. The guy could be in counseling three times a week for a decade and never give it up. Amazingly complex web of defenses."

"So... bottom line?"

"In his case, it's a way of functioning without any semblance of a conscience. Very bold. Prone to real rage. He frankly does not give a shit about anyone. He may pretend. He may act like he cares. He could have a girlfriend, a buddy of some kind, but simply because it suited him."

He stopped to rearrange some papers on his desk, pointed a finger at Tate.

"Whatever that wound might be, it's left him with a hole in his soul, a black hole, sucking in everyone around him. He can't see beyond himself—his wants, his needs, his pleasures. The hole needs to be filled with ever greater, ever darker, experiences."

"And so..."

"Not just yet, detective. To really sum up this guy, you'd have to say there's probably more to it. There's another condition, something called 'borderline.' He looks good for that too, and, put them together, you've got more troubling aspects."

"Such as…"

"Huge instability. One remarkable thing that happens with someone like this, the textbooks will tell you, is that they can really admire someone, elevate them to a lofty position in their minds, and then suddenly… poof. Done."

"They lose interest?"

"They lose respect, admiration. One second, that person, a friend, a lover, anyone, is terrific. The next second, they're shit. The trigger could be anything… a sound, a word, a smell. And then they snap. You can see it happen."

"Not hard to see him that way. Is he troubled at all? Is this what you'd call a conflicted sort of guy?"

"Not a chance. Griffin absolutely loves who he is. And in his case, the condition is not some sort of fantasy, where he imagines himself as the president or a Super Bowl champion. He's already living the dream. He can do what he damn well pleases and other people ought to love him for it."

"How much contact did you have with him?"

"Very little. He clearly thought he was smarter than I was. Just between you and me, I thought that was a real possibility. And, can I tell you something in confidence? You won't repeat it?"

"Of course."

"There wasn't much point in my talking with Griffin. He wasn't going to play ball. I thought the question of how he ended up this way didn't really matter. And the bottom line is, he scared the bejesus out of me. I didn't want to be in the same room with him."

IT WAS a two-story bungalow, a small yard. The house was yellow, with a roof worn down by the wind and the rain and colored by years of leaves. Many of those leaves, still up there. A Mazda of some kind in the driveway. A car so small a teenager could pick it up to look underneath. The curtains in the windows were lace and there were puppies carved out of varnished pine sitting on the windowsills.

"We ain't seen him. He calls every so often, maybe once a year, maybe twice."

There was an air conditioner in the window and they talked as if it stayed on all day. Griffin's mom looked like anybody else's mom. She had a broad forehead, doughy cheeks, short, grayish hair and it was curly. She looked real comfortable in her own skin, and in that apron that said Best Cook You'll Ever Meet. Voice like a reformed smoker.

She had furry bedroom shoes on and a shirt and pants combo that looked like it came from Kmart. Shirt was light blue. Pants were darker blue. Some kinda stretchy material.

There was an occasional yapping from the back of the house. They'd locked the animal into the bedroom, probably for Tate's safety. Sounded like a vicious one-pounder.

And this was clearly the chair reserved for guests. It was the best-looking chair in the room, great big arms, fat cushions, green and yellow stripes. A tall, curved back, a pillow shaped like a loaf of bread in a matching cloth. It was off to the side, not the primo chair in front of the TV. He wondered if it was rarely used, to keep it nice for company.

The only problem with the chair was the stuffing. It was not just deep and soft. So now Tate, a good-sized guy, was staring up at everybody in the room. And once he decided to get out of this chair, he was in for some serious trouble. He'd have to push hard on the arms, scooch his butt forward, inch by inch. Some people liked a chair you could disappear into.

Mebbe Griffin really was here, hiding in the furniture.

The dad's name was Earl. A smaller version of his son, but without the strength. Or the hostility. Pink shirt, plaid shorts, held together with a braided belt, pulled tight underneath a potbelly the size of a small tv. Rings on the third finger of both hands, smallish hands. Hair that stuck straight up on top, like a kid from a 50s surfer movie. A face that had seen its share. His glasses were tied with a string and hung over the end of his nose. Lenses so thick his eyes looked like wet golf balls.

A guy who wanted to be liked.

"We went to the courthouse, when he got in trouble for shooting his friend. 'Course, we was pretty sure it was an accident, just like he said. But the police, they brought up a shrink, a guy who said Johnnie was not, you know, solid. Not solid upstairs.

"I don't know about that. But I can tell you, you don't want to make him mad. He got that from his mother, not me."

Earl stole a glance at the missus, sitting next to him on the sofa. She gave him a coy punch on the arm.

Bernadette was her name.

"It was like he didn't need us," she said. "He left home pretty early on, and he fended for himself. He had jobs. And then every once in awhile, he'd call up and take us to dinner. A little Italian place, usually, or Greek. He liked a salad.

"Now this last time, he brought that girl. We could tell she was trouble."

She leaned forward, lowered her voice.

"I think, while we were at dinner, she had her hand on his privates. I really do. Earl and I don't care for that kind of girl."

And then their only child had said he was going on a trip, heading south, see the country. The parents wanted to know where he got the money. He'd told them he had enough. And then he said his cousin, Wigle, was going along.

"He was trouble too, that boy."

They wanted Tate to understand, they'd had little to do with their youngster once he was full grown. He'd been at home through high school. That was almost 10 years ago. Since then, he'd been out west logging, he'd taken a job leading vacationers

down the Colorado River, he'd put roofs on apartment buildings, he'd driven a delivery truck. Always on the move, always
changing.

Tate felt sure the parents didn't know much. But he didn't want
to miss the opportunity.

"It sounds like your son was never one to shy away from hard
work. But it's obvious that you think he's been involved in some
illegal activity from time to time. Let me make something clear...
and I know this is difficult for you... but, right now, he's wanted
in connection with a killing, assault on a police officer, escape
and a few other things. This could turn out very badly if he's not
arrested quietly and brought back to Georgia.

"What I'd like is if you could tell me what you know about
what he's been involved in, when it started and who else was
involved. Anything you know, because I need to find him. If I do,
I'm going to try to persuade him to come back. If someone else
finds him, things might get difficult. You understand?"

Mom and Dad had questions. It was upsetting to them. But
they knew. They knew their boy was rough trade. They knew he
paid no attention to boundaries... "what good folks do"... is how
his mom described it.

Tate got some names. Some kids he'd played ball with in school.
A family down the road that had a boy the same age, with similar
tendencies. Some dope smoking, some stealing, fights.

Earl, head down, face to the floor, slumped, feeling responsible.
And yet, not. What could you do? Running his hands over his
hair, back and forth.

He spoke as if he were giving testimony.

"One thing, pretty early on. Just how you see somebody. Johnnie was a big strong kid and he liked to push other kids around. I
saw it. I was the same way, his age. But the thing... he'd get into a
fight and he'd push it way past a fight, you know? Like, he'd grab
a board on the ground and hit the kid in the head with it. He was

big enough... quick, strong... he coulda won that fight easy. But it was like he didn't wanna wait.

"It was like he enjoyed the rough stuff. We were down at the hospital a few times, sitting up with some neighbor family, after Johnnie knocked a kid into a wall or tossed him into a car. One time, he grabbed a kid. On a hill. Grabbed the kid, tossed him into a grocery cart and shoved it down the hill. The kid's stuck in there, racing down the hill. He got flying, right into an intersection, got hit by a couple of cars. Nobody got hurt. But it was real dangerous, you know what I mean? Johnnie, he thought that was pretty funny."

Tate got some more names.

"If I find him," he asked, "do you want to know? Do you want to get involved? Would he listen to you, if it came to that? If you called him on the phone, would he listen?"

Earl started to answer, paused, pressed his fist against his mouth, shaking. Bernadette took his arm.

"You call me. You don't call my Earl. We'll decide."

Earl began to sniffle.

"You see," she said. And now Earl had his head on her shoulder. She was holding his head and he was crying.

"I don't want my Earl getting upset. He never got over Johnnie leaving, him turning out that way. Me, I understand. It's not our fault he's that way. But Johnnie... we knew. At least we knew maybe that it could turn bad. I'll give you my number. Don't you call Earl."

Earl cleared his throat. He stood, stepped toward Tate, held out a hand.

"You don't need to leave, sir. Be comfortable. I'm just going to go lie down for a minute.

And then he started to cry some more.

Tate got out of the chair as gracefully as he could, took the man's hand.

"Thank you, Mr. Griffin."

Earl shuffled down the hall, turned into the last room at the end. Tate watched as the door closed. The dog stopped its yapping.

She reached over and patted the back of his hand.

"This is what happens when you have a bad son."

Tate was still standing. He took a step toward the door.

"I think I should go. Thank you for seeing me."

She took his arm, led him across the room. Then she stepped close to him and gently placed a finger on his chest.

"Mr. Detective, it was polite of you to see us about this. Me and Earl, we can see for ourselves what it means, a Georgia man up here, looking for Johnnie.

"I'm going to tell you something now, I didn't wanna say in front of Earl. You be careful. That thing with Johnnie and that boy, when that shotgun went off. That was no accident.

"A mother knows."

19

THE ROADS looked different up here. There was trash in clumps along the roadsides, something you didn't see quite as much in the south, and the overpasses were made of stone. Things looked old, in a different way. Atlanta and Savannah had their stories. This place had a history too. And the air was different, crisper. It was April and the humidity was already starting to build. There were butterflies in clusters around the hawthorn. The light, shallower, softer.

And the smells were different. When he got closer to the neighborhood where John Robert Griffin first killed a man there were shops close to the street and a smell of onions and garlic and something tangy. A slow breeze ruffled the umbrellas on wide sidewalks in front of small shops, awnings over the windows. Narrow row houses with iron benches and bike racks, narrow front doors over short concrete steps, narrow side streets.

There was a delicatessen with an awning of green, white and red and a list of specials printed in white shoe polish on the window. Tate had slowed to a stop for traffic in front. He rolled his window down all the way. It was too good to pass up.

He pulled into a parking space, left the car unlocked and walked toward the deli. There were a couple of small tables on the sidewalk with plastic flowers in painted vases. Tate grabbed a free City Paper out of a box by the front door and set it on the table. He put his baseball cap on top of the paper and walked inside.

An old song was playing on a small radio on a case behind the shopkeeper, a dark-headed woman with her hair tied back. She looked to be in her 50s. From behind you could tell she'd been making good food most of that time.

She had on a man's shirt, white, and a skirt, one of those wraparound types. Pink sneakers. She stood behind a glass case full of cheeses, breads, sliced tomatoes, pasta salad. On the shelf over her head, oversize cans of tomato paste and packages of linguini, fettuccine and spaghetti. A big clock and a cluster of straw baskets.

"One of my mom's favorite songs," Tate said. "Dean Martin, right?"

"You betcha. This station… nothing but Dino all lunchtime. All we listen to. So whatcha gonna have?"

"I dunno. Something smells really good outside. "

"We got meatballs cooking. How about I put some on a roll for you with a nice salad."

"That sounds real good."

"OK? You sit down. I bring it to you. How bout a beer?"

"Can I drink a beer outside?"

"I'm gonna put it in a nice cup for you. You wanna hear that 'Volare' man outside?"

"You betcha."

He sat down, then moved his chair so he was in the direct sunlight. She brought out a plate. She had bushy eyebrows, the faintest glimmer of pink on her cheeks and a head full of curls. Broad shoulders and smart hands.

"Now you have a nice lunch."

"Hey, can I talk to you a minute? You got time?"

"Sure. What's on your mind? You're kinda cute, but I'm married, I gotta tell you. I know a lotta you boys from down south, you lose your heads, you find a woman who cooks good."

"How'd you know I was from down south."

She sat down, slapped his forearm.

"That's a good one. Now what you want to talk about with Rose?"

"What do you call this neighborhood?"

"You serious? You're not joking? This is Little Italy. Bloomfield."

"That's why everything smells so good. Has it changed much over the years?"

"Oh, not so much. This part here, in the daytime, we got a lotta nice boys come in for lunch. They build things, they fix cars. Then they go home at night. Right here, this place, not so nice around at night."

"Why? What happens?"

"Eat, eat. You can eat while we talk. Your food get cold. This place. All these young… the tattoos, the loud music. They all look drugged up, you know? Eyes like they got the flu all the time. And they're all the time down there at that club. Kids and their toys. I don't like that place. Always trouble."

"But you've got your husband? He's around? And where do you live? Nearby?"

"We live upstairs. That's why we don't sleep so good at night. We gotta turn on the air condition, just to keep the noise out. You like those meatballs? You ready for some more?"

"If I had any more, I'd have to go take a nap. Speaking of which, there's a hotel around here someplace?"

She held up a hand right in front of her nose and sliced the air with it, cocked her head to the side.

"You see that light. You go straight through that light to the next corner, make a right, go up the rise two blocks and there's a little hotel right there across the street. It's a good hotel, not one of those nasty places. I know the people for years. You go that side, not the other way. Stay away from that nasty nightclub."

"OK. Well in that case, I'll take some more of this salad and another refill for this cup."

"That's my boy."

She took his plate back inside.

"I leave you that cup. You gotta finish that first."

Tate found the hotel, the Starlighter, in a neighborhood where it appeared little had changed for a generation. The open door led down a hallway off the street to a small foyer with a front desk. To the left, a darkened doorway leading to a bar. He ducked his head inside.

Somebody had spent years polishing the wood and the brass and the big mirror over the bar. Rows of wine glasses and beer mugs hanging from racks overhead. Shutters on the windows, heavy paneling on the walls. The tables and chairs were heavy too. Vintage movie posters on the walls. There was a wooden sailing ship on a tall shelf, a three-master with sails unfurled and a long row of cannon run out. There was a plaque underneath it: U.S.S. *Constitution*.

Next to that, a sign on a chalkboard read: Best Pizza in Town.

He got a room and spent the afternoon making calls. When it got to be 5 o'clock he quit. People would be going home.

Staring out the window, thinking hard about the thing lurking on the edge of his consciousness, the thing he'd been avoiding.

Tate was smart, one of the good guys.

Griffin was smart too, really smart. Plus, he was crazy. He kicked the shit out of anything he didn't like. He was quick and he was strong and he was ruthless.

Advantage Griffin.

But Tate had one other thing. Just lately he'd realized it. He was angry, angry enough he wanted to finish this up close, with his hands.

He lay down, watched the dark move in across the ceiling, took out a packet the prison shrink had given him. There was a list of characteristics:

- Grandiosity: Feelings of entitlement, firmly holding to the belief that one is better than others; condescension;

- Prone to feel slighted or insulted;

- Unstable, frequent mood changes;

- Impulsivity; lack of awareness one's limitations;

- Antagonism

The clock moved to 6. And 7. That night he had some of the best pizza he'd had in a long time. A couple of beers. Four men sat at the bar. They looked like regulars. A little girl on TV was about to sing the national anthem. The men stopped talking. Tate set down his fork.

After the song, one of the four turned to the bartender.

"Hey Ivy, take that guy a beer. It's on me."

Tate took his beer over and sat down at the bar.

"You don't have to do that. Besides, I haven't finished this one."

"Hey that's all right. Hey guys, meet… what's your name?"

"Tate, Tate Drawdy."

"Southern boy, eh? My name's Mooch. Just call me Mooch. Tate, you sit with us, unless you got a girl coming or something."

"No, I'm by myself."

"All right. That's OK. You can watch the game with us. Hey guys, this guy Tate from down south, he's gonna watch the game."

The other three nodded. They introduced themselves. It turned out they were all cops. And so was he. They offered a toast. One of the cops, a big guy, started ordering shots.

THE NEXT morning, there was a knock on the hotel door. Tate winced and struggled to his feet. He staggered to the door, pulled it open. A young man holding a tray brushed past him and set it on the desk by the window.

"Breakfast."

"I didn't know you served breakfast here. Or delivered it."

Words, a foreign substance in his mouth, slowly formed.

"We don't. My mom says, "Take something to eat to the nice young policeman.'"

"Your mom's the lady who checked me in? How'd she know I was a cop?"

"The guys told us. The guys from the bar."

Eggs, home fries, OJ. Canadian bacon and two English muffins. A carafe of good coffee. There were no grits. He wouldn't be getting any grits now. Tate gave the kid five bucks, asked him to find him a bottle of aspirin. The recognition was beginning to set in. He'd mistaken the booze for water and he'd been real thirsty. Something had unlocked a door that was supposed to stay shut. And what was on the other side was darkness and pain and anger and regret. The hammering inside his head would live on.

At least he'd slept.

At first it was work to get anything down. It needed to happen. He ate slowly, his head hurting so bad he wanted to call his mama. He forced his way through, then carried the tray downstairs after he showered.

He made more calls. And then it was time to visit Griffin's last known address. The lobby was empty when Tate walked outside. The sun, high in the sky, shone with a brilliance that sent shadows scurrying and seared the top of his head. The air had the feel of the north. He was enjoying the visit, thought he'd like to come back when he wasn't looking for somebody who wanted to kill him.

The light came from a different angle here.

He grabbed the car and turned the corner in the direction of Lawrenceville. It took him past his favorite lunch spot. Rose was already out front, sweeping the sidewalk. She was sporting a white apron over a dress covered with little red flowers, and a pair of dark green bedroom slippers.

The broom snapped at the concrete like a reprimand. He parked.

"Hey. There you are. You find that hotel?"

"Yup. Stayed there last night. Ate some pizza."

"Good for you. I got some coffee on. How about a nice cup or some cappuchino and a coupla cornettis?"

"Coffee sounds great. Can I just take it in a plastic cup, though? I need to run. What's a cornetti?"

"You don't know cornetti?"

The look, as if someone had just told her the earth was no longer round. She rose to her full height. Her eyes narrowed.

"You sit right there."

He could hear her talking to herself as she scurried back inside.

"What's a cornetti? he says. What's a cornetti?"

In a moment she was back. There was no plastic cup. She put the coffee down, along with a plate of pastries. They were crescent-shaped, golden brown. She sat down, pointed.

"Eat."

"Keep this up, I'll have to call you Mom."

She laughed. She raised her hands in surrender, high above her shoulders. Then she pointed, took on a stern look. He was about to be schooled.

"First you make the dough. Very important. You wrap it around the butter, roll it up, fold it, roll it up again, fold it, roll it up, fold it, then you chill, then you roll it out again, fold it, chill it some more."

She was gesturing as she talked, showing him the motions, kneading the air.

"Then you take it out, spread it out in a nice box, like so, cut it into little triangles, you see? Then you roll them up and put a cover on top. They're gonna rise now. I put a little marmalade on top. Very nice. Then I brush on the syrup, it's sugar and water, and then I put them in to bake... 400 for about 15 minutes until they're just nice."

She was laughing at him now. He'd been eating the whole time, stuffing them into his mouth.

"My God. I could never remember all that. But I am gonna get a bunch of these from you to take back."

"You eat cornetti, you put on some love handles."

He snorted, wiped the sugar off his face and pulled out the map.

"You know where this place is?"

She bent down, traced a finger along the crease, slowly, until she came to it. Then she moved her finger back, traced it again.

"It's pretty close. I'm gonna get you down to Liberty, take you through the Strip. Good place to go on down if you wanna see the river, you can hear some nice squeezebox. Get you down to Butler."

"Some nice what?"

"Squeeze... accordion. Go this way, you come to it. What's down there you need to see?"

"I just need to find this address."

"OK, you go ahead. Butler is very nice. Places fixed up. Where you're going is only a couple of blocks east of there, but mostly warehouses, row houses. Be careful. Lock your car up tight."

20

HE FOUND the neighborhood right away. It was full of shops and pizzerias, liquor stores, apartments overhead. An ancient bowling alley. An old government building converted into a bank. Tons of dark red brick. Houses crowded together.

Up a hill, a cobbled street. The place where Griffin had lived was blocks back. A warehouse at one time. There were row houses here, made of brick, with big windows.

The door was right on the sidewalk. Through the glass he could see a stairway. He tried the knob. It was locked. But there was a bell. He pressed it and heard a buzz. He pushed the door open and started up the stairs.

A guy in bluejeans stood at the top of the stairs. He was shirtless and had paint over his hands and arms.

"Help you?"

"My name's Drawdy. I'm a police officer. You mind if I come up and show you my ID?"

The guy was repainting the main room. His girlfriend had picked the color. She had a fancy name for it. Guy couldn't remember the name. Both he and Tate thought it would be fine just to call it blue. There was a small elevator with a mesh cage. He wasn't using it right now.

They hadn't moved in yet. He was working there a day or two a week.

He wanted to replace the windows first thing. It had been vacant a long time.

"I had the feeling a couple of times somebody was in here, you know? There's nothing to take, nothing looked different. All this furniture and stuff was here, though. I had the electric put on, cause we're doing a little work on it when we have the time. One day there was a pile of newspapers next to the bed. I don't think they were there before, you know?

"Yeah, how long ago was that?"

"A couple of weeks. Not long after I first started coming in here. I still feel like somebody's been here. But since then I haven't seen anything. It's just a feeling, you know? And that window would be real easy. It's not a huge deal cause I would secure the place real good before we moved in."

There was a fire escape, but it didn't look like somebody had jimmied the window.

"Any chance you still got that pile of newspapers? I wouldn't mind taking a quick look at em, see what that's all about."

"Really? So you're looking for something, somebody in particular, it sounds like to me."

"Yeah. I'm gonna be honest with you. I'm looking for a guy who used to live here and I came by just to see what the place looked like."

"What's this guy done? I mean, cause you're freaking me out a little bit."

Brian was his name. Skinny as a rail. Big knuckles on his hands. Big bones in his face. Big ears. He looked like a kid who hadn't quite grown in. He tended toward grinning. Self-deprecating.

Tate thought the kid might have led a sheltered life, but sometimes you couldn't really tell. One thing, he hadn't had much to eat in his life. Or he worried it right off. But he was doing some nice work. Knew his way around wood. He'd built an island for the kitchen area. Dark stain, a nice sweep to it.

Bunch of tools lying around. Good tools.

They were walking as they talked. The furnishings were pretty bare, but comfortable. The place had a decent feel. There was good wood on the floor. The walls, mostly brick, but somebody had nailed up some wallboard in one corner of the room. There was a big chair, a good place for a TV. In the middle of the room was a rough-cut bookcase. Some of the shelves were empty, but there were magazines and some books. Mostly old stuff that looked like discards from the public library. A lot of non-fiction, histories of the wars, biographies, some books on boating.

The bedroom looked about the same, the way some college guy might have left it. The bed was a mattress on top of a set of box springs, raised up on cinder blocks and 2x4s. There was a lamp by the bed. It still had sheets and pillows and stuff. The cover was one of those Mexican blankets you see for sale at a gas station.

"OK. Look, I don't think there's anything you need to be concerned about. But I'll make you a deal. You let me look around here for a little while. I'd like to poke around in the closet, see what kind of books are on the shelves there, those magazines. Just stick my head around in stuff, see what I can see. I won't get in your hair at all, won't stay too long. And just to say thanks, I'll go out and get you lunch, whatever you want, a box of beer, you name it."

Brian was ok with it. But he wanted the rundown... whose place it was, what the guy looked like.

Tate said ok.

"You change the locks?"

"Not yet."

Tate nodded. He started poking around in the bookshelf.

"You smoke?"

Tate held out his Camel filters. Brian took one. There was a shirt hanging off the top of the bathroom door. He pulled it down. They sat on the floor, backs against the wall.

Brian wanted to talk.

"So for all we know, the guy has been coming back here. He's probably still got a key to the door. Geez, I'm not sure my girl-friend's gonna be cool with all of that. And we already bought the place. I think you need to tell me what this guy did."

"He's a murder suspect. He escaped from jail in Savannah. That's where I'm from."

"I saw that on your ID. I was gonna ask you about that. So this guy is pretty mean or you wouldn't be chasing him around."

Tate didn't see much point in glossing things over. The guy could find out easily enough and do a quick computer search, put things together.

"Name's John Robert Griffin. I think he rented here for a couple of years and then he went to prison. Maybe what happened is, the place sat while he was gone, assuming this is all his stuff. I guess the other option is somebody else was in here. We're speculating. If there was somebody in here, coulda been anybody. I'm looking cause I wanna know whatever I can learn about the guy."

"Yeah, but if you were me, would you wanna be here... while the guy is loose, anyway?"

"No."

Brian put his half-smoked cigarette out on the floor. He asked for another. He buttoned up his shirt.

"Bubby's gonna freak."

"Bubby?"

"Barbara. She loves this place."

He stood, walked over to the refrigerator, pulled out a couple of beers. He pulled the tab on his, held one out to Tate.

"Still a little early for me. Thanks."

"Maybe I ought to see a picture of this guy, in case I ever see him."

"I don't have one. But I can get you one. Or if you've got a computer, I can tell you how to search it."

Brian was staring at the floor now. He tilted his head back and poured some beer down his throat, started coughing.

"Wrong pipe."

Tate sat with him a minute, then got to his feet. He started on the top shelf, pulling down every book, flipping through it. The magazines were a mix. Smithsonian, Popular Science, National Geographic, Car and Driver. A stack of old Proceedings, the Navy magazine.

"You keep looking," Brian said. "Then I'll ask you about this guy."

TATE STAYED awhile, and they talked more. Brian wanted advice. Tate couldn't offer much.

He was going to try to take Griffin off the table. Then there wouldn't be anything to worry about. Brian wasn't real happy with it.

"I'm going to talk with Barbara. She may wanna back off until this guy gets caught. That's sorta where I'm headed, anyhow."

"Makes sense."

"But what happens if he doesn't?"

"I don't know what to tell you. Guys like this generally get caught. In this case, I suspect it won't be long before I hear from him. He calls me every once in awhile, just to push my buttons."

"Can you ask him to not bother us?"

"Probably not a good idea to mention you, or that I know you. You guys don't wanna be connected to me."

"This some kind of personal thing between you two? I guess it is, seeing as how you came up from Georgia."

"Yeah. Well I wouldn't go too far with that. I'm just trying to wrap up a case."

They talked a little more. Brian wasn't quite ready to let go. Tate didn't blame him. It was like he'd just found out the place he'd bought carried some kind of infection and he might get exposed.

Later, Tate headed down the stairs, running his hand across the peeling paint and the rough surface of the handrail. There were splotches of paint all along the top and down the sides. They'd thinned the mix too much when they rolled the walls and hadn't bothered to sand the rail down afterward. Tate thought they should have put it up last.

When he got to the bottom of the stairs, he turned around and went back up. He'd had another thought, a strategy about how they might try to resolve the thing.

And that freaked out Brian even more.

They shook on it. Tate headed out, pushed open the door and started for the car. He heard the shot and saw the dirt kick up in front of him at the same moment. It had to have come from a rooftop. He ducked, spinning behind a parked car as he reached for his gun. And then he saw them, all four. They were out, guns drawn, behind a rust-covered Jeep Cherokee. It was dark green, dented fender, big tires. It was the guys from the bar.

Two fanned out, flanking. One sprinted for the door. One set up behind the Jeep, gun pointed at the roof. Tate couldn't believe his eyes.

"What the hell you guys think you're doing?"

Nobody answered. Tate ran awkwardly for the back of the house, feeling the hole in his hamstring.

He heard a car door slam. As he rounded the corner, a white Volvo sedan flew out from under a stand of trees behind the house. And then, standing alongside him, huffing, Mooch.

He pulled out a cellphone and hit one button.

"Dispatch... who's this? Hey, it's the Mooch. I got a white Volvo, 95, two-door heading north toward Butler and 45th. Cut him off. Armed and dangerous.

"Yeah, guy just took some shots at an out-of-town police officer. We want this guy right now. No, no plates. Get going. All right. Good. Call me back, this number."

He put his phone back in his pocket, reached out to shake Tate's hand.

"Hey, there you are. Let's walk back out front, see the guys."

Tate held his arm.

"You wanna tell me what's going on?"

"Yeah, well, me and the guys we decided maybe we'd tag along. After we heard your story. We know this town pretty good."

"So you guys haven't quite left the cop thing behind."

"Eh. And all of us retired? But we got a lotta juice, still, for the job. We got 97 years on the force. I was a zone commander. Goo, he was vice. Wynt, he was a patrol guy. So was Bobby."

They could hear the sirens now. It sounded like several cars, from different directions.

They were out front now, gathering there by the Jeep. Mooch's cellphone rang.

"Mooch. Yeah. We hear 'em. Right now I'm down on Abernathy. Yeah, we'll sit tight. We can roll to you, or sit tight right now. Good."

He turned to Tate.

"Description of the driver."

Tate told him.

"OK, here you go. Six foot one inch, brown hair, brown eyes, medium build, 30 years old. We don't know what he's wearing. Sounded like a pistol. Could have been a .38. OK. Call me."

Tate was about to speak when the big guy, Goo, put a hand on Tate's shoulder.

"You look like you're thinking about being pissed off at us, my friend."

One of the others, Tate wasn't sure which one, leaned in.

"It was the bourbon shots, Goo. I told you before."

Goo nodded.

"OK. Well, we all decided we would just get on board. Help you grab this Griffin fella."

"Yeah, I don't remember even talking about it. I obviously had way too much to drink," Tate said. "And I'm really feeling it this morning. And you guys can't be doing this."

"Hey, no sweat. We got 97 and a half years on the force between us."

"97 years, Goo." It was Mooch.

"We been through this. It's 97 and a half. But, seriously, what the fuck difference does it make?"

Goo was George Arbison. He was the vice guy. Goo stood six foot five and had about 270 pounds on him. He was wearing a flannel shirt, an orange vest, bluejeans and high-toppers. He'd been putting a Glock 21 inside the vest when Tate walked up. It was a .45, big kick, very nice gun. Goo looked about 60, a guy who used to be in shape. He sported a long-past-gray goatee and wore his hair long in the back, tied up. Goo palmed a basketball in the ninth grade and he had the look of a guy who'd been telling people to settle down for most of his life.

Wynton Bonds was about half Goo's size, maybe 5'8, 160 wet. Wynt looked like he was still pounding the pavement pretty hard. He wore track shoes, shorts and a T-shirt, the type who works out after meals. Wynt was a cross your arms and look skeptical kinda guy. He looked to have the patience of a gnat.

Bobby Mayo, the other patrol guy, appeared to be the youngest of the bunch. Medium height, stocky, arms the size of a cantaloupe, like he was still on the force, pumping iron every day. He had beefy hands, a heavy jaw and a voice that came from the rocky depths. You'd see a lot of fumbling fingers when Bobby asked for ID.

And Mooch. Dino DiMucci. Crinkly eyes, a hole in his chin, just like Kirk Douglas. The Mooch was tall, trim, distinguished, early 60s, enjoying his retirement. The kinda guy who wore hiking boots everywhere.

His phone rang once more.

"Mooch. Yeah. You telling me the fucker got away? Son of a bitch.

"Anything in it? Nah? OK. Tell em to sit still. We're gonna head up there, have a look for ourselves."

A long pause.

"Well thank you for that, darlin' but I am still married. And yes, I still expect certain people to jump when I pick up the fucking telephone. Yeah. I may be retired. You wanna tell me to fuck off? I didn't think so. I love you too... yeah, if I wasn't married, you'd be the first... Yeah.. you'd be the only. Now lemme go hon... all right."

"Rhonda?"

The guys were laughing.

"Yeah."

"I told you, you coulda had some of that."

"Fuck you, Bobby. How do you know I didn't? Now let's go see the man's car. He ditched and ran. Tate, you follow me. Goo's gonna ride with you."

There was no mystery. The car was Griffin's. There were a couple of CDs in the back seat, a spare tire and a case of warm beer in the back. Yuengling. In the glove compartment, a hairbrush, a bottle opener and bag of weed.

21

GRIFFIN HAD gotten away clean.

They had to drive downtown to file a report. It would give them a chance to talk about it. Tate climbed behind the wheel of his car. There was a light tap at the window. It was Goo.

"You mind if I ride with you?"

Tate leaned over and flipped open the door. As they started down the road, Goo reached over and thumped a fist on Tate's leg. Tate decided not to tell him he'd been shot there not long ago, unless it looked like he was going to do it again. Goo was grinning.

"Hey man, you don't have to worry about us. We enjoy the work."

Tate started to answer, hesitated. He felt a creeping tightness in his chest. These were good guys. Real good guys. And he had no right to involve them. He was embarrassed that he'd told them his story, and with so much gusto that they'd felt the need to come on board. He'd been drunk to his fucking gills.

Embarrassed that he came across so needy. Embarrassed by the fact that he didn't know what to do next, by the fact that they might get hurt doing his dirty work.

Whether he got hurt was not a big deal. Mostly he didn't want to lose. Not to Griffin. He'd play it out. And at some point, like Goo said, what the fuck difference did it make?

He wasn't real sure there was much he could do about it now. So they filled out some reports. You could tell the guys there weren't going to be real particular about asking Mooch and his team what the fuck they were doing. Mooch still carried a boat-load of clout in the room.

Still, it took a long time. Afterward, he and Tate walked outside.

Mooch turned to Tate. "Hey man. How about I buy you a beer and we talk about how we got this far up the creek."

Goo came along. They went to Tate's hotel. Mooch got there first. When Tate and Goo walked in, he'd already been talking to the bartender, telling him Tate was all bent outa shape about how a bunch of retired cops were getting all D'Artagnan about his story, how Tate was feeling a little contrite over getting drunk.

The bartender, Ivy, clearly sympathetic.

"Hey Tate. You want me to set you up with 900 beers, like last time?"

They were all laughing. Tate laughed a little.

"Maybe not quite so many."

Tate took a beer. They headed for a table in the corner.

"That guy's name is Ivy?"

Goo straightened him out.

"Any more, people say it like 'Ivy.' It really started out like I.V."

Ivy overheard that part, came over. He was a stick, with a shaved head and a thin moustache, like he could play the part of the big guy at the hacienda. He wore a light sweater over a T-shirt, casual pants. A guy who could see what was in back on the top shelf.

"Yeah, I used to drink. Don't anymore. Back then I tipped em at about 330. The docs told me it was time to pay for my plot at the cemetery. So I fooled em. Now I just serve the stuff."

Ivy pulled up a chair, set his coffee down.

"I was on the squad with Mooch a couple years. Had a wreck one night, on duty. I was toasted. Mooch helped me get this job, after I got straightened out."

They talked for awhile. Everything the Pittsburgh guys had in mind took time and involved a shitload of patience, not the kind of thing Tate found real appealing.

"Tell you what I'm gonna do. I've got the phone number for the guy who bought Griffin's place. I'm gonna ask him if I can stay over there. I'll park my car out front, make it easy for him."

Goo liked it, partly.

"Short and sweet. Fuck if that don't cut to the chase. You do it cause you think he needs to confront, like maybe he needs to talk face to face. It gets real short if he's gotten uptight and just wants you out of his life. Then he might wanna just put you down. I don't know how you could predict which way the guy's gonna lean."

Mooch dug his cell phone out of his pocket. He punched a couple of buttons and handed it to Tate.

"Push this button here and scroll. I got four or five pictures there. You guys take a look."

It was Griffin's house, from the ground and from up high.

"The place next door is vacant. I think we could make this work."

Goo reached over.

"Push those little buttons for me, Tate. I wanna see this too. What's this? Second floor front? And this is the roof?"

Mooch nodded.

"Yeah and there's a door on the back side, so you feel like you could get in and out without a lot of trouble."

"Guys, once more I appreciate it. But roping you guys in was not exactly what I had in mind here."

"Tate, here's how I see it. We can take care of this as a group, get it done, eat some pizza, then you invite us down south for some fishing. Or you can do this by-yourself thing and it maybe works, maybe doesn't or it doesn't get it finished, which would be bad."

"Yeah, I understand. And you guys are real confident. But…"

"Here's what I think," said Goo. "This is his town and he's got nowhere else to go. He's gonna make this happen. We just need to be there.

"And in the meantime, it's past lunch and I didn't have breakfast. What say we grab a bite?"

Mooch started to wave at Ivy, but Goo grabbed his arm.

"Nah. Come on. Let's go down to Rose's. We can be there in five minutes. She's already got stuff ready."

It turned out the little deli Tate had discovered around the corner was one of Goo's favorites. They piled into the Jeep.

Rose was singing along with Dino.

"Send me the pillow that you dream on…"

She came around the counter to give Goo a hug.

"Hey. My best customer. And there's my Moochie"

She saw Tate.

"Hey, southern boy. You know these guys?"

Mooch put an arm around her.

"We've recruited this Savannah boy into our little club. So we're gonna need some beers and some meatball subs if you please. Maybe we'll sit outside."

"Coming right up. You go. Rose is gonna bring it all right to you."

They went outside, got a table in the shade. Goo rocked his chair back and forth a couple times to see if it was going to hold up. She brought out steaming cups of minestrone and a basket of bread and beers in plastic cups.

"Oh, I wish you guys coulda been here last night. The noise… the horns and the people shouting all night. That damn place."

"Now I told you to call me," said Goo.

"I know. I know. And I will next time. Those damn kids."

She pointed to Tate.

"Didn't I tell you about that place when you came in first time? That damn toy place."

"I remember. What is it, a club?"

"Yeah," she said. "A club."

Tate was letting his soup cool off. He started in on the bread. Goo finished his beer in one long pull, grabbed a slice of bread and stuffed it in his mouth and walked inside.

Mooch lifted a spoonful of minestrone and blew on it.

"Goo's gonna go in there and get her to hand him samples of about 12 things before he eats. The club she's talking about... not far. Place has been there for a few years. Rough. Lotta ecstasy. Lotta trouble. Very successful."

"And it's close enough it keeps Rose and her husband up at night?"

"They've had a couple of shootings. Mostly I think it just creeps them out."

"Where is it from here?"

"See that old brick building there with the flat roof? Couple blocks over. That's it. First floor's a bar. So big they got maybe 10 guys working it. Upstairs is another bar. That one's just babes working behind it. They charge more for the same thing if you get it upstairs."

Goo came back out and stood in the door. He had three beers on a tray and a carafe of chianti.

"Hey guys, let's move inside. I wanna drink some wine and Rose doesn't want to."

She was bustling along right behind him.

"You shush. You go on out there with your friends. Take that wine with you. I got your subs coming up. You finish that soup now."

Goo set the drinks down. Then he went back inside, came out with a wooden chair and a mouthful. Rose brought out more bread.

Goo waited until she went back inside.

"Rose's husband's a light sleeper. She worries about him."

"Why does she call it that toy place?"

"Name of the club. Little Toys. They got all sorts of old gadgets hanging from the walls. Sleds and wagons, stuff like that."

Tate put up a hand. He was deep in concentration, trying to bring something back. They waited. He began to smile.

"I think we just came up with another option for Mr. Griffin."

Just then, Rose came out with a basket full of hot subs. She pulled up a chair.

"I'm gonna eat one too."

But Mooch stood, put a hand behind her chair.

"Rose, you know I love you. But we're gonna talk shop now for a minute here, ok?"

She jumped up.

"All right. That's all right. You want something, you come to the door and I'll get it."

"You're not mad at me, are you?"

She kissed him on the cheek and hustled inside.

Tate was stuffing food in his mouth and talking at the same time.

"Just a couple of days ago, I went back and listened to the tapes of all the interviews. There was something Griffin's sidekick said that didn't make any sense. Not until now. He was ranting about how Griffin was the ringleader. He was throwing shit on the guy, talking about his loft apartment and his fucked up... 'little toys.' I thought he was talking about something Griffin had, some trinket. Now I'm thinking it's something else."

"Could be messy. We'd wanna get him outside."

"Yeah, Mooch. You're right. Maybe I let him see me at the bar, follow me outside."

"Way too obvious."

"Sure. But he'll still go for it."

After they finished eating, they went over to the club. Outside, it was all brick with tall windows. The mullions were heavy steel, paint peeling up like seagrass swaying in the current. Two doors, maybe nine feet tall, with trim that had been slathered up with some kind of fluorescent paint. Little Toys was closed, but Mooch was real persuasive with the guy who came to the door.

They went in.

The floor was acid-stained concrete, worn down. That was slathered too, in spilled booze and puke. The ceiling was a good 14 feet. Big lamps in the shape of bumblebees hung down, interspersed with sound-reflecting board, cut up like amoeba. Hanging cockeyed were some old bikes, a toboggan, a wooden propeller, maybe eight feet long. On the walls, posters from the 30s and 40s. Neon signs for obscure beers. Yankee brews, Tate figured.

The bar, a remarkable extravagance. It was as if an old sailing vessel had been cut in half and glued to the wall, 40 feet of dark wood and rigging and brass. Gave the place an air of sophistication it probably didn't deserve.

The bartenders could walk along the deck, hand drinks over the rails. Beyond the bar was an open floor, half a football field wide. The ceiling here was open and, in the back corner, an enormous screen for projection video.

Tate turned to a guy cleaning up behind the bar. Squatty, beard, curly black hair. Some kind of bowling shirt, colored patches around the shoulders.

"Is that for broadcast?"

"Cable... DVDs... anything we want."

"How many people you put in here at one time?"

"We stop at 150. We got guys outside counting. 'Course, some people go upstairs."

"Is there another big screen up there?"

"No, it's like a loft. They see the same screen."

"So what are they watching?"

"Music videos sometimes. Or old movies. My boss likes to buy real old foreign stuff and throw that up there. So you might see a Japanese flick from the 30s. Or she'll find some vintage sports stuff and show that. It's pretty cool."

"Actually, that does sound pretty cool. So I'm guessing you guys make a ton of money."

He nodded.

"A ton."

"Where's it run from? Here behind the bar?"

"No. The boss doesn't want anything like that. Some guy got toasted one time and put something on there that he shouldn't have. Boss runs it from an office upstairs. If it's short, she might just loop it. Or the floor manager has a key."

Goo leaned over the bar rail.

"So where is the boss? She come in during the day?"

"The guy leaned down, like he was trying to scrub out a little spot on the bar.

"She's over your right shoulder, in the loft. You didn't feel a hole in your back?"

Goo wasn't amused.

"What kinda hole?"

"She stares at you long enough, you can feel it. She's up there."

She was leaning over the railing, hair tied in a bun on top of her head. She looked like a swimmer, all shoulders and back, long arms, long legs, not much flab. She wore jeans, sandals, a baseball jersey with the sleeves rolled up.

Tate took the stairs. Once you got close, the thing you noticed was the mouth, so small she'd wear out her knife at dinner. Dwarfed by her outsized cheekbones and suspended over a receding jaw, it gave her the look of a skeptical bird.

"I am Vasiliya Popov. Why are policemen interested in my place?"

"We think a murder suspect has been frequenting your bar," he said.

"Give me his photograph. I will have my staff keep an eye out for him."

"I think that would be a really bad idea. But I may need your help in another way."

"Let me see your identification."

She glanced quickly, handed it back.

"This is not your jurisdiction. You have no business here."

"I can make a call, get a whole bunch of cops here in about 10 minutes."

"Dear God, you watch too much television. Are all people from Georgia so tedious?"

She gave it four syllables. He laughed.

"I could spend some time persuading you with stories about how nasty this guy is. But I think I'll just explain it this way. We're going to bring some guys in here to wait for him. If you want to cooperate, I'll explain what we're up to and we'll fix it so he doesn't get arrested inside this building. If you won't help, I may have to grab him. It might…"

She pointed at the door.

"You're an idiot. Get out."

Tate leaned over the railing, waved the guys over.

"She won't help, says we have to leave."

Goo waved at Popov and smiled.

"I think you're making the right decision, ma'am. I wouldn't help that asshole either. Did he give you that old story about the crazed killer he's trying to catch? That's a good one. Tate, you quit trying to scare that woman. Come on down here."

Tate came down.

"Where'd Mooch go?'

"He went to the car, get some stuff. He'll be right back."

Goo went over to the bar.

"Gimme some beers. You got something good on draft?"

He pointed.

"Gimme six of those."

The bartender was conflicted.

"I thought I heard your friend say you guys were leaving."

"Yeah, we're gonna go. I just need a couple beers apiece real quick. Then we'll go."

Goo had six inches and 100 pounds on the guy. He got the beers. They carried them over to a table.

"I think I'm feeling that hole in the back the guy was talking about."

Just then Mooch came in dragging a big foot locker. He had a couple of Kevlar vests slung over one shoulder. He'd strapped on a .45. They crowded around as he lifted the lid on the foot locker. There were two M-16s inside. He handed them to Goo and Tate. Goo snapped in a magazine and began to sight across the dance floor.

"What the fuck do you think you're doing?"

She was coming down the stairs.

Just then a siren began to wail outside the door. Goo leaned over toward Tate.

"Mooch gots himself a remote for the siren. He loves to play with that thing."

22

IT FELT like it might storm. There was a faint rumble of thunder in the distance and the breeze was starting to pick up. The branches of a maple alongside the hotel driveway scratched against the side of his car. Leaves rustled across the lawn. Down the block, a screen door slammed. Banging and colliding glass. Someone taking out the trash.

He got into the rental car, drove to Little Toys, taking his time. It was the night he'd been waiting for and it occurred to him now that he had so little a plan he might have scratched it out on a matchbook cover.

He went inside, under the watchful eye of their new best friend, Vasiliya. Mooch was already at a table away from the bar. Goo, upstairs on the rail. Bobby was outside.

Tate was on his second beer when the phone rang. He went outside so he could hear.

"Imagine my surprise to find you sitting on a stool at my favorite bar. That's good detective work, my friend."

"I'm just a bloodhound. I'm glad you kept my number."

"Well, it was hard to miss, so big on the screen. 'John Robert, I'm sitting at the bar. Call me.' I can't believe they let you take over the place."

"Nah. I just gave the bartender 10 bucks."

"Yes, and you've probably got associates hanging around someplace. So let's bypass all that togetherness, shall we? Why don't you come down to my old apartment and we can talk there.

Remember how to find the place? And let's stay on the line, shall we? That way we can talk."

"You've been missing me."

"I really have."

Tate walked to his car, phone to his ear. The parking lot was jammed now. A hazy glow from the streetlights. He thought he could hear the electricity buzzing through the lines overhead. The sounds of the nightclub bubbling in the background like water tumbling into a bath.

He wasn't wired, but if Bobby was watching, he'd be able to see him from his car, parked in a driveway across the street. Tate climbed in, turned the key. Nothing.

"Your car won't start?"

"Seems to have lost its mojo."

"It's a short walk. Just head straight across over there and down that little incline. I'll show you a shortcut."

Tate hopped out, slammed the door hard.

He started across the street.

"It's starting to rain, John Robert."

"Yeah. Shame. I'm super glad you came up, Tate. I'm just brimming with gladness. You found my house, you found my bar, you found me. All roads lead to Rome, no?"

Tate didn't answer. He crossed the street and found an opening between a dense hedgerow. It seemed like the only option. It was half a shoulder's width. He left the phone open, put it in his shirt pocket, squeezed through and saw the faint outline of a narrow path into the woods. He was picking his way along in the dark. The ground sloped down, mossy and slick. Ahead, a stone stairway. Holding his hands out in front of him, ducking, moving branches out of the way, protecting his eyes.

"Did you reach the stairs yet? Watch the third step. It's a politician."

Tate stepped down. Two more steps. The stone rocked from side to side. He kept going. Now the path led off to the right. The branches were low here. The trail zigged and zagged between the trees. He could imagine children running along it, but it didn't seem like anybody'd spent much time there lately.

Tate was inching along now, barely seeing anything. Tiptoeing down the steps. And then he paused.

He was a fool. It was pitch black. The man could be standing next to him and he wouldn't know. He'd let Griffin control the situation, following his orders on impulse. He turned around and started back.

Above him, just at the crest of the stone stairway, he saw a wobbling flashlight.

The shot came from off to his right. There was a grunt and the flashlight fell. Tate froze, heard nothing. He started to run, got to the stairs and saw Bobby on the ground. Tate reached for his phone. A fist across the back of his head sent him sprawling.

"Get up. Leave your dead asshole friend where he is."

No more sweetness.

Tate rolled over and began crawling toward him, stopping to wipe his eyes. He'd lost his gun and his phone, couldn't see either one. Griffin was at the foot of the stairs. He could just make out the shape.

"Stand up."

Griffin was 10 feet away. There was nothing he could do.

He crawled slowly toward the stairs, moving his hands in front of him, feeling his way, feeling for something.

"You're going to stand the fuck up. Now."

Tate didn't answer. He crawled forward again, another few inches, his heart pounding. He wanted to leap for him, knock him to the ground, squeeze his neck like a dry sponge. But this wasn't his chance. It was dark, too dark. He was on his hands and knees.

The stairs rose above him like the entrance to a tomb.

"Tate, I do not know why you fall for this shit. Your pal here was just gonna follow me and you'd make the arrest? Sometimes I think you are one fucking inch old. And you can stand up now."

Tate, still moving his hands, searching, biding his time.

"Just so we're clear. It's not just you that I'm killing right now. It's your red-haired, green-eyed beauty. So quit fucking with me. Stand the fuck up."

There was an edge to the voice he hadn't heard before. No surprise. John Robert was starting to hit his stride. Tate, realizing he hadn't planned for this, how he'd act if things weren't working out.

He stood, slowly. He felt a hand lightly grasp his heel.

Bobby.

"Come this way. You can walk ahead of me. I have a few things I want to run past you. I've been wanting to get a cop's point of view."

They were moving in the darkness. Griffin seemed to know just where he was, but Tate stumbled and fell, bashing his knee against a rock. The rain, starting to come harder now.

It looked like Griffin wanted the confrontation to happen at the apartment. That was the good news.

"You know what really pisses me off these days, Tate? I want a stop to these people who let tiny dogs sit in their lap and look out the window while they're driving. How come you can let a dog sit in your lap? What the fuck is that? I can't fucking stand it, truth be told.

"Hey. I'm forgetting myself here. Do you think your buddy is stone cold dead? Let's make sure, shall we?"

Griffin walked back toward the stairs. He fired three shots, stepped back to admire his work. He put his hands in the air.

"Move along people. Nothing to see here...."

Tate leaped to his feet, charged him, wrapped his arms around him, struggling to take him to the ground. Griffin spun, smashed the gun butt across the side of his face. Tate collapsed in agony. And then Griffin was alongside, kicking him in the ribs, the face, the back, screaming at him.

"How's this feel, you mother fucker."

Griffin kept kicking.

It might be Tate's only chance. He reached out, caught a foot and twisted hard and then they were rolling on the ground, Griffin pounding the butt of the gun against Tate's head.

Tate rolling, on top of him now, pinning the pistol against the ground. Griffin threw a left, catching Tate in the throat. Drawdy was choking but he had no choice. Hang on, keep fighting. He threw punches, as many as he could and as fast as he could, still straining to keep the gun pressed to the ground.

He was losing.

Griffin kneed him in the groin and got the gun hand free. He fired one shot that sent dirt flying. Tate leaped to the side. He could hear Griffin crashing through the bushes, free and clear. He set out after him, moving as quickly as the darkness would allow.

Another stupid choice, but it was time to finish this.

Red-haired, green-eyed beauty?

23

JOHN ROBERT could feel the blood on his face. But he wasn't badly hurt. Tate had taken the worst of it, gotten that pistol pounded against his head four or five times. That was gonna leave a mark.

Now it was time to recalibrate. He'd killed somebody who was along for the ride, someone helping Drawdy, another cop perhaps, or a friend. Dead. Just like Tate Drawdy would be in just a few minutes, if he judged right.

If he recalibrated right.

Drawdy would be behind him, not far. No real dilemma for the cop. He was driven. He'd come along quietly. That was a good one. Come along quietly.

He wanted Drawdy in the light. He wanted to see his face, see the fear. Drawdy wouldn't beg. Not his style. But he'd know. He'd know he was about to buy it.

He'd only killed a few times. But always in the daylight. See what you're doing. That was his mantra. See what you're doing. See him die. See the bullet hit him in the chest. The look on his face.

Bye bye, Tate. See you, fella. Wouldn't wanna be ya.

He was feeling good now. He knew the trail. Here's where it leveled off, where you could stretch out into a nice run. A good pace. Passing the trees. Passing them by.

The first Marine went over the wall, parlez-vous.
The second Marine went over the wall, parlez-vous.
The third Marine went over the wall,
got shot in the ass with a cannon ball.
Inky dinky parlez vous.

Feels good to run. Might go for a long run after I shoot the cop. I like running in the rain. The sound of your shoes on the pavement. Makes a little smack, a different sound. Rather run on the street. But the grass is nice.

He stopped for a second, listening. Drawdy might be back there. He might be close. He'd be along soon.

Drawdy won't wait. He won't even go back and look for his gun. Never find it anyway. He's a stud cop. He'll try to outsmart me.

You wanna see a closet pedophile? Here's one. It's called a pistol. He'd go all Jimmy Cagney with him. Eat fucking lead, copper.

He stopped again to listen. Now he could hear him. Were all cops this stupid? He'd have to ask. He was nearing the end of the woods now, the trail dumping out on the back end of a side street, just a block and a half from his place.

Tate should be able to find it ok.

And, if he needed it, there was that little present he'd left behind. Tate had never asked him about the day out by the water, the day he blew his fucking cop car all to hell. Then, Tate didn't ask about much. He'd ask questions, but just to piss you off.

Shame Tate never got to meet his friends. Actually, the only guy Tate was gonna meet now was his Maker.

He was at the house now. He left the door open and headed up the stairs, turning on the lights as he went. The party was about to start.

He would confess to Tate, the honor-bound cop. He'd tell him the truth. I'm only human, he'd say. I have screwed up more than once. But shooting your ass is gonna make Johnnie feel better.

MOOCH AND GOO found Bobby at the bottom of the stairs, called an ambulance.

"Motherfucker shot me. Then he came back and shot me again. Damnation, I'm glad I had on this vest."

The first shot, at the top of the stairs, was a clean miss. Bobby had hit the ground and tumbled, waiting for his chance. Of the next three, two had struck the vest. The third was more of a problem. Right through the shoulder.

"So you sat here and waited for him to come back and finish you?" said Mooch. "Not sure that was real smart. What if he wanted a head shot?"

"Well he didn't, so…"

"Down here guys."

It was Goo, calling out to the rescue squad.

"We need some light here. We're gonna want to carry him up these stairs. He's got a bullet through the shoulder. Cop in pursuit of a suspect. We need to get him back to the hospital right quick, if you don't mind. We're not coming with you."

A second ambulance was arriving now. Two men stood up top, shining light down the stairway. They quickly strapped Bobby to a board and started up the steps.

Bobby grabbed Mooch's hand when they reached the top.

"OK with me if you return the favor."

"What… you want me to shoot his ass?"

"Please."

"You got it."

"We'll be by later. Soon as we finish this business."

Goo commandeered a big flashlight from one of the ambulance guys.

"I'm gonna need this," he said.

And then they were off down the trail.

"No point in hiding now. We need some speed."

Mooch took the light from his hand.

"You're too big a target. Lemme carry it."

"Whatever. Let's just go. I feel like we're wasting time here..."

Down the trail, jogging. Guns in their hands.

TATE SLOWED just as he got close to the house. He pulled off his shirt and wiped the blood from his face, caught his breath.

He could see lights going on inside. John Robert was preparing his welcome. But Tate didn't go inside. He ducked across the street.

"Over here."

It was Wynt. And he had an extra gun.

"He just got here. You OK to travel?"

Tate nodded.

"Why don't you go in through the upstairs window?" Wynt said. "I'll make some noise coming up the stairs."

"Nah. Let's do the opposite. He sees you, he might just shoot. If it's me, he wants to gloat some more. He'll let me come up. In fact, let's do that. I'll come in loud, you get by that window."

"Where are the boys?"

"Should be right behind us. I think Bobby took one, but he's still moving."

"Mebbe we oughta give em a minute. You OK to wait a sec?"

"Yeah."

24

TATE STARTED up the stairs, the gun loose at his side.

Griffin stuck his head around the corner, leering. Pointing a revolver.

"Just drop it there."

A lilt in his voice. Loud thuds as Wynt's .45 bounced and spun back toward the street. Tate rested his hands on his hips, looked at Griffin. He stopped to wipe his face one more time, put the bloody shirt back on, then started up, climbing slowly. Paint smears on the railing, still. A smell of cooped up sawdust. The sound of his footfalls on the stairway bounced off the walls, a tinny sound. Along with the sound of his heart pounding. He didn't think Griffin could hear, but there was no way to tell.

There were a lot of stairs. It was an old building. High ceilings.

He stopped halfway, looked back, trying to slow it down.

"What are you doing?"

Griffin, standing in the doorway now, hair matted from the rain, blue jeans, running shoes, flannel shirt, a gray sweater with some kind of design running up and down. Probably Christmas, from his mom. Bernadette, vainly struggling to see him as a frat boy.

The light from the stairs cast a hulking shadow behind him.

His hands were grimy. Some bruising and a little blood. But he'd weathered the encounter pretty well. Much better than Tate.

He was smiling, contented, feeling good about how things had gone, how they were going.

Tate puffed his cheeks, pushed the air out of his lungs.

"I just was looking at the steps. Sometimes an old building like this has more steps, you know?"

Tate's voice, thin, like he needed to swallow. He remembered that feeling. The ninth grade. There were violins that night, fingers lightly brushing the strings. A waltz. Then another. Then another. Collar nagging at his neck, one of his daddy's ties, his hair slicked, new shoes full of torture and blunder.

The girl was tiny, a feather. She leaned her forehead against his shoulder, tugged on the sleeve of his jacket. She wore some kind of floral scent and she danced well. He did not.

Here was another chance.

Griffin stepped back to let him into the room. He'd turned on a floor lamp, over by the window. It threw off a soft light, just the slightest bit orange, because of the shade. Discolored, from a junk shop maybe. It was toasty in the room. The heat was on. And some music, an old 50s thing.

See the pyramids along the Nile... Jo Stafford, from the Dorsey band. Tate, mostly a blues guy, but he loved the old standards. He remembered the title: "You belong to me."

Probably what Griffin was thinking right now. Little did he know.

Tate kept his back to him. He walked over to the bookcase, ran his fingers along the shelf, leaning against it. His hand, streaking blood on the molding.

"There are a couple of good titles here. You got a Dashiell Hammett. You got a couple of Graham Greene's. Now there's a guy who could stand some uplifting. You've got broad interests. And here's a Conan Doyle. Very smart."

Griffin smiled, waved him away with his gun, a .44 magnum, four-incher. Rubber grip, looked like a Smith and Wesson 29. Good gun, pricey, easy enough to find. It would jump when he fired it.

His chin low, as if he were staring over glasses.

"I like a good mystery. Guess how this one ends. Lemme shoot you a couple times and let's get this over with."

The room, losing its cozy feel. Short, halting steps toward the kitchen and the center island that his new friend Brian had rebuilt. His new dance was beginning. He turned to face Griffin, set his hands down, lowered himself gingerly to the floor. He could feel a trace of sawdust underneath him. Brian had done more work lately.

"Sure. Sit right there."

Tate scooched his butt back toward the island.

"I didn't tell you to slide around."

"Just looking for a place to rest my back. Do you mind?"

Tate, legs stretched out before him, rolling his head from side to side, loosening his neck. He used his sleeves to wipe more blood from his face. He had a tight place around the spine. He pulled his shoulders back, tugging his arms, working at it.

"This is quite the little physio drama you're putting on, Tate. You wanna wrap it up?"

"Gimme a break, friend. I just had my ass whipped."

"That was an ass-whipping, wasn't it?"

Tate had his hands up around his ears now, a grimace, grunting softly, hauling his arms back, a pained look to his face. He pressed his hands up against the bottom of the countertop. There was a ledge there. Brian had framed it in with an old bar rail, so it hung over. Tate, struggling to find his voice, lost somewhere in the back of his throat. The pounding was louder now.

He pulled his lips back, grinned hard at John Robert.

"I'm sorry."

Griffin shook his head, laughed.

"Nah, you go right ahead."

Griffin pulled a stool over, sat down. He was 10 feet away. He'd let the gun fall to his thigh, just resting there. The light from the lamp played with it, tossing a reflection that collided into a corner, then slid toward the floor.

"Do you pray when you run, Tate?"

"I don't have to pray."

"God showers me with ideas. Incredible ideas. They come gushing from the sky."

A new song was starting, from the 40s now, one of those frantic big band shuffles. The trombones were going at it, slashing against the trumpets, hurling the melody back and forth, all that brass like windows breaking. The drummer, pouring it on like an avalanche.

It played hell with his timing.

"The paintings… the paintings are nice here too, John Robert. I like the one of the woman's face. Kind of impressionistic."

"Yeah. I know the artist. Hey, couple things I wanna tell you about, before…"

Tate, still stretching, working his hands up under the bar, the detective's expression suddenly changing.

And Griffin saw the smile disintegrate, saw the gun, the flash, strategy and truth roaring toward him, felt searing pain. He flipped backward.

"My buddy built a little holder for me, put my .38 there. Cool, huh? Now it's your turn to stand up."

Griffin, screaming, stunned, struggling.

"Stand up, you little shit."

Griffin staggered to one knee, somehow got to his feet, in a rage. One bullet, not enough.

"You fucking cocksucker. I'm gonna…"

Weaving from side to side, beginning to slur his words. Seeing the gun, still pointed at him, understanding it all now.

"Finish me, asshole."

Tate fired another three, quick, nicely grouped. Dead center.

Griffin fell backward, swimming his arms like a drunk in a cheesy western, blood spurting from his chest.

There was a low whistle.

"There you go. That's good shooting."

It was Wynt, sliding the window up, swinging a leg over.

"Yeah. I needed him on his feet. Angle of entry."

Tate stood over Griffin's body. He slid the .38 into a back pocket of his jeans.

"Let's go check on the others."

"They're right outside, under the window. I gave a thumbs up when you sat down. What you figure were the things he wanted to tell you about?"

Tate, shaking his head. He walked over to the radio, turned it down. A small laugh.

"We'll never know. Probably just some recipes he liked, maybe some cool towns he'd seen."

"Yeah. Probably."

They could hear Mooch and Goo coming up the stairs. Wynt walked over to the body. He patted down Griffin's pants legs.

"Cellphone on the right. Dunno what this is here in his left pocket. Let's take a look here."

He pulled out a thin rectangle, dark metal.

"Hey, I don't like this..."

Mooch was just coming into the room.

"Hey... careful. Lemme see that."

They stood, the four of them, together. The thing looked like a detonator. Ignoring the body at their feet.

Goo was calling for the coroner. He hung up, started searching his phone for another number.

"I'm gonna see if I can get Keith Flynn over here to look at this. It looks you have to enter a coupla numbers or something. I don't like it."

"I'm guessing this thing might have a limited range," Bobby said. "Maybe it's here. Maybe it's the club."

KEITH FLYNN brought his dog with him. Bomb sniffer. Name was Bell, because it was Belgian. He'd thought about Blackie, too, because it had a black face. Goo said Keith wasn't real imaginative when it came to dog names.

"Good thing it wasn't a female," Goo said. "Otherwise, we'd be outside every morning… 'Here Bitch. Here Bitch.'"

They found the bomb in the bookcase. Bell found it right away. Flynn grabbed it, said it was routine stuff. So was the detonator.

IVY BROUGHT over another round of drinks. Tate buying. Wynt had just gotten done telling the story for the second time. Seeing Tate playing it cool, sliding back toward the place where the gun was stashed, letting Griffin get confident, popping him when he got careless.

And then popping him another three times front and center.

"That's the capper," said Goo.

Wynt stuck an elbow in Goo's ribs.

"Goo always likes to call it a capper."

"Yeah I do. A capper is when you close a case. Or when you close a guy. In this case, we done closed the case and Tate done closed the guy. Big time. And I respect that."

Mooch raised his glass.

"Here's to Tate mopping the mother fucker without causing more taxpayer expense."

"And having the foresight to have him stand first." This, from Wynt.

"Appreciate it, in more ways than I can tell. I'm not feeling bad about tonight. I guess that means I'm not in the wrong business."

Mooch spoke first. "Some guys are just messy. Your job is to clean things up."

"We don't like to think of ourselves as janitorial," Goo said. "But damned if it don't feel that way sometimes."

"Bottom line, guys," said Mooch, "you spend your life and you may only have a few opportunities to be a man. When they come, you take em. Plus, we told Bobby."

Tate raised an eyebrow.

"Bobby asked us, make sure to wax the guy," said Goo. "We don't like to let Bobby down, especially now. I mean, how do you think he's gonna feel? He wanted to come out drinking with us. His doc said no. Bobby was pissed, I gotta tell ya."

"Yeah, so we shot the guy that shot him. All I'm sayin,'" said Wynt.

Mooch held his hands up, asking for silence.

"The way I figure it, Bobby had the fucking poor taste to get shot. He had the unmitifuckingated gall to be a no-show tonight. We are celebrating the case and where is Bobby? So… he buys. And not just the next time. He buys tonight."

Mooch punched a finger in the air. Nods around the table. They were all agreed.

"Here's my idea," Tate said. "We have a few drinks. We offer a toast to the law enforcement brotherhood. We have one for Bell or Blackie or whatever the fuck the dog's name is. And then we go by and throw some rocks at Bobby's window."

"Tate, my brother. You're starting to fit in nicely."

This from Goo.

"So," said Wynt. "You got a girlfriend?"

"Come on guys. You gonna take advantage of me every time I get a beer in front of me?"

"Just wanna know what kinda long-term maturity curve we're looking at here. Most of us, we kinda divide our time between behave and not behave."

"Well I am spending time with a woman I like in Savannah. But I've been trying to keep it under wraps. A couple of guys tried to shoot me down there just recently. I figure it was Griffin, hiring out some help. I wanted to keep her out of the picture."

Wynt put his hand on Tate's shoulder, held it there.

"Back up pardner. Lemme hear that again."

"You mean, keeping her out of the picture?"

"No. Somebody was shooting at you? And you think it was Griffin, hiring out some help?"

"I dunno. I'm just guessing. Some guys came after me. Had to be Griffin."

"Don't wanna chill your evening, my friend. But give this some thought. Everything I saw the last couple days says Griffin wanted—no, lemme say, needed—to do you himself. Some guys are just wired that way.

"You might wanna be open-minded about this. Looks to me like maybe you got somebody else on your ass down there in Savannah. But leave that for tomorrow. Let's get back to the girlfriend. You got a picture?"

25

"SO WHERE is a good steak place. I mean serious steaks, where we can still walk in and get a table?"

Goo liked the idea immediately. You don't get to be 270 without making an effort.

"There's Mantini's... Morton's," said Goo, a smile creeping over his face.

"Sure, dude," Wynt laughed.

"Why is that funny?"

"We'll never get into Morton's tonight."

Goo leaned in, smacked his hands together, then raised them, asked for silence.

"Capital Grille."

Wynt translated.

"Tate, the Grille is great stuff, really great. But it will set you back, big time. Now maybe you don't care..."

"I do care. And if it's living large, then that's what we need. And I'm picking up the tab."

He could see the objections forming. He held out his hands, a teacher pleading for quiet.

"Time out guys. Let me put it to you straight. I'm very OK where money's concerned."

Goo translated for the group, said it looked like they could get drinks, the big Delmonicos, a couple of nice bottles, hammer the dessert tray.

"No reason to wait," he said. "I feel like we're wasting time here."

Tate drove. It was on Fifth Avenue, west of Steel Plaza. They parked on a side street. It was a gorgeous old department store, converted to luxury condos, offices and retail.

Nice place. On either side of the door, carriage lamps, lion sculptures.

They went inside. Dark wood, leather, mirrors. Along the bar, a small lamp every couple of feet. Deco chandeliers. Ambience.

Goo in his high-toppers. Mooch in hiking boots. Wynt, sweaty. Tate had thrown a sweater over his bloody shirt. They wore jeans. And they'd been running around outside in the rain. There was a little mud... shoes, knees for the guys. Tate, pretty much head to toe.

A hostess stepped forward. Shoulder-length hair, brunette, glasses with soft blue rims. She was young, in a low-cut black dress. She'd gotten the job because of the way she made the dress seem small. And because she could speak well. And, perhaps, because of the way she was able to exhibit her disapproval by scrunching her eyebrows, pursing her lips, turning her head slightly to the side.

She was doing that now.

Then the tallest of the four, a very large man, stepped very close. He looked down at her.

"We're going to need a table."

She quivered. They were seated in a small private room toward the back. Which was fine. It was late, but the place was still crowded.

When the waiter came around, they could see his eyes get big and a bit glassy. Wynt's gun, peeking out from under a jacket.

They got drinks all around. Tate ordered a couple of bottles of the Stag's Leap Petite Syrah. Glasses were clinked. A toast to Bobby. More nonsense about making him pay, making him suffer. Bad form to get shot by an asshole.

"Tate," asked Wynt, "you get to order the wine from now on. And, while we're on that subject, you said you felt pretty good about whacking the bad guy."

"Yeah. No qualms."

The waiter brought over the first bottle. He pulled out the cork, set it on a small plate in front of Tate, poured a taste into his glass.

Tate waved an arm.

"Go ahead and pour, if you don't mind."

Wynt held out his glass to the waiter, to speed things up.

"Like I was saying, I've been around a lot of shooters and a lot of shooting. I've seen guys get ready. Thing I saw about you... you really didn't care. What you wanted was to see the guy go down. But if you went down with him, not such a big deal. At least that's what it looked like to me."

Tate took a long swallow.

"You guys wanna get four of the Delmonicos?"

Mooch had his chin on his hand, reading the menu. He wagged a finger in front of his nose.

"Man asked you a question."

"Yeah. Well, I've been wanting to get my hands on the guy."

"Wynt's telling you something here you may wanna think about," Mooch said. "We're a lot older, got a lot more years on the ground. What you've got, my young friend, is real good instincts and some serious balls. Some anger is good. Why we keep going. Question is... are you careful? Cause careful is what smart guys do."

"Maybe I'll get more careful as I go..."

Goo, slowly waving his glass over the table, trying not to topple the glassware, moving his head from side to side, trying to see past his muttonchop hands.

Wynt reached over, patted him gently on the arm.

"What is it, Goo?"

"Will somebody pour some fucking wine in this bitty glass."

"The glass is full, man."

"The glass is not full."

Wynt topped it off.

Goo brought it slowly to his lips, holding it gently at the lip with his thumb and forefinger.

"I like a nice restaurant as much as the next guy. I just need a full-sized fucking glass. One of you guys, wave at that waitress. I need a glass."

The waitress hurried over.

"Can I get something for you? Some more bread?"

"Yes ma'am," said Tate. "My friend needs a large water glass, the biggest you have. And we'll have two more of these…"

He held up a bottle of the Stag's Leap.

"Thank you, my friend," said Goo. "And now, let's talk more about the explosion Griffin set off in Savannah. You guys are clear on how that needs to be looked at?"

IN THE MORNING, Tate drove out to the house. He'd put on a tie. He rounded the corner toward the little yellow cottage. The grass had been cut. The bushes were trimmed. There was a pile of branches tied up with string by the side of the road. The Mazda was parked under the carport, newly washed. A hose coiled neatly by the side door.

The sun was high now and he felt the heat as he got out of the car, the slow, heavy beat of his heart as he walked toward them.

Earl and Bernadette were standing out front in a spot of shade, their arms around each other. Bernadette came forward slowly.

"We put coffee on. We thought you might want some."

Earl and Bernadette were very understanding. They'd seen the TV. The local newshounds had been on the phone with Tate's boss. They knew about Precious Gardner, the girls, a little about the statements the girls had made to police. They knew about

John Robert's escape, the doctor's severe head injury, the policeman he'd shot. They knew about Tate's car, all blown to hell. The
TV people had brought up the other killing, the friend who'd had
his head shot clean off.

Their son was not depicted as a nice sort.

Bernadette went into the kitchen, came back a moment later,
wearing another apron. This one said: "If I didn't cook it, you
don't have to like it."

She was making some muffins. They'd be ready in half a sec.
Talk loud, she said, so I can hear in the kitchen.

It was too much television, Earl said. John Robert had spent
too much time in front of the television watching reports about
crimes. And then he'd started reading those detective magazines.

"Women with hardly nothing on. Big-chested women, their
clothes all torn up. And people getting killed. It was all that sex
and violence did it. It turned our boy."

Earl sniffled a little, but he was mostly over it, or reconciled to
it. Or numb. Bernadette came back with a plate of muffins, blue-
berry. She had Tate take two.

"I don't think so, Earl," she said. "I think Johnnie already had
stuff in his head. Maybe those shows and those magazines caught
his eye because he was already a certain kind of person."

She turned to Tate.

"What do you think, sir?"

Tate wasn't sure where to go with that. He shrugged.

"I'm just not sure about it."

"I want your honest opinion. You're a detective. You're a college man."

He was still hesitating.

"Please," she said.

He took a deep breath.

"I don't think TV or newspapers or magazines cause crimes.
For some people, people who have a fascination for it, they may

touch some kind of chord with them. But I don't think they create the need to commit crimes. The research shows that. Somebody who wants to do mayhem... that comes from inside. That's all anybody knows."

"That's what I think, too," she said. "He got there all on his own. We never dropped him on his head or anything. It was bad luck. He was the first in our line, on either side of the family, to go bad. The first."

They talked a bit more. Tate finished his muffins. He thought it was time to go. He put his hands on his knees. Bernadette stood. She clasped her hands.

"I find it very gracious that you would call us and come back out here. We both appreciate that gesture. I suppose you'll be heading back south."

"Yes."

He turned toward the door, paused.

"I guess there's one other thing I'd like to say."

They waited.

"I came here to arrest John Robert, take him back to face trial. And it was for a couple of very serious crimes. But... you know, we had talked a few times. I thought he was guilty and I thought he needed to go back to prison. But in a weird way, I kind of liked him. I thought he was a smart guy. I'm just sorry he didn't do more with his life."

Earl came up, wrapped his hand around Tate's arm.

"That's a damn nice thing to say. Damn nice."

Then he turned and walked back into the kitchen.

Bernadette went with him to the front door.

"You be careful going back."

26

COMING OFF the escalator he saw Barks standing behind the barrier. She had on a chauffeur's cap, black waiter's jacket, white shirt, black skirt. The outfit broke down when it got to the purple running shoes. She was holding up a sign that read: "Mr. Smith."

He walked up, gave her a squeeze and a peck. He'd told her not to come, that he was going to be careful just a little bit longer. But she was not an unwelcome sight, though she was collecting some attention.

"The disguise thing is pretty good, I gotta tell ya. But I noticed you got your shirt unbuttoned down to your waist and you got nothing on underneath . I don't see a lotta chauffeurs doing that."

"You should see me in the rain."

He stammered a bit. She stood, enjoying his discomfort. He picked up his bag.

"So where we heading?"

"Not far. You and I have a room less than a mile from here."

"I must be doing something right."

"I'll let you know."

They headed out for the car.

TATE WAS getting ready to head home when Char came to the detectives' office door.

"Cup of coffee?"

Tate thought Char was looking a little antsy.

"How about a beer instead?"

She nodded. They went down to the riverfront, got a table at Spanky's. Tate tended to stay away from the place these days, but it was Barks' day off. So she'd be off running around, looking in shops at old furniture.

Tate had participated in a couple of these outings and had discovered an essential truth about Barks, and, perhaps, about women as a species. Not to say he would never again step into an antique shop. Rather, he would pick his moments.

Char had changed her work outfit for a skirt and a shirt with flowers on it. She had on wooden shoes, like the Dutch. Somebody had said they were really good for your feet. For such little shoes, they made a lot of noise on the cobblestones. Tate, in his typical garb, tan pants, checked shirt, knit tie—blue, loafers.

"You been back here since you got shot?"

"Yeah. Not all the time."

"Doesn't freak you out?"

"Nope."

The waiter came. Tate ordered a beer. Char asked for a Diet Coke.

"I think you need a beer, too."

"No, that's OK."

"Looks to me like you got something on your mind. Get a beer."

She waved the server back and opted for the 22-ouncer.

"Stuff at the jail on your mind again?"

"Actually, this one is personal, if you don't mind."

She sat up straight in the chair, leaned forward, folded her hands. She was ready to tell the story.

A guy kept asking her out, a tall, good-looking guy from church. They'd had coffee a couple of times after the service, and then they'd started having breakfast beforehand. Then dinners. Now things were starting to feel a little different. He'd asked her to dinner. He'd made it sound important. It was freaking her out, just a little.

"How come?"

"He's smart, he speaks well, he's educated, he has a good job. He could go out with anybody he wants and he's asking me. It scares me."

"What kind of stuff you guys talk about?"

"Regular stuff. People, jobs, life, the city, the church, movies we've seen, books we've read, stuff growing up."

"Sounds pretty normal. You laugh with this guy?"

"Yeah we do, we laugh a good bit. He's pretty funny."

"He think you're funny?"

"He acts like it. He acts like it a lot. But here's the thing. I'm no Marilyn Monroe, you know what I mean? What if he's just slumming or something? I'm not used to some hunk who wants to go out."

"You gotta be willing to admit to yourself there are some guys who might look past skin-deep. Your instincts on the guy are pretty good in the first place or you wouldn't have kept meeting with him and you wouldn't have spent that much time. Or agreed to this last thing."

"Yeah. 1790. Friday. And that's part of what worried me a little. It's a nice restaurant."

"He's picking you up?"

"No, I said I had to meet him there cause I had a thing on the other side of town. I was just being extra-cautious I guess. I like him a lot."

"This happens to everybody, you know. You meet somebody you think is really great and you start having some doubts. Maybe I'm not good enough for this person. You are good enough, if you'll just be yourself. If it doesn't work out, it wasn't meant to work out."

She nodded, gulped down some beer, got a little teary. Tate reached over and gave her hand a squeeze.

"You know, I was thinking about going out on Friday. Haven't been to 1790 in a good while. I think I might see if I can't get a table for one, or maybe sit in the bar."

"You would? You will? You don't mind?"

"Nah. What's this guy's name?"

"Ken Fowler"

"OK. We need to have a signal for Mr. Fowler."

"What kind of signal?"

At some point, you may decide to let him drive you home, or back to his house, or somewhere. And you no longer want somebody following you."

She blushed, drank some more beer. They came up with a plan.

"Tate, what if this is because he doesn't want to date me anymore and he's just being nice?"

"So you move on. The dating thing is trial and error, both sides. For all you know, he's nervous too."

"Yeah, like that makes total sense. Like a guy is worrying whether I'll think he's ok. And you know what else? He plays golf. He plays fucking golf."

"So you don't play golf."

"Heck no. I can barely bowl."

"You know what? You know what he's saying right now? She arrests people. She fucking arrests people. I've never arrested anybody in my life."

Tate got another round. Char was still nursing hers.

TATE DRAWDY had made his bones. He'd whacked the bad guy, while on leave, for God's sake. He'd taken a trip, tracked the guy down and whacked him. A clean shoot. There was some distinction there. And there were beers to be consumed.

After he talked with the chief.

He was sitting in the office, now. He'd come early and the chief had met him in the hallway. A tall man who walked quickly. Crew cut. Gray, but still trim. He'd been a colonel, head of Criminal Investigation Command at Hunter Army Airfield, which had something like 5,000 troops. They were bound to get into some trouble. The chief, with a lot of years behind him, a lot of experience.

A double dipper, salary and a military pension. Chief drove a Seville. Spent his Sunday mornings up on Bull Street at the Oglethorpe Club.

"How's the leg? I think we're gonna have to put you back on active, seeing as how you're now the guy who shot Liberty Valance. Soon as the review winds up."

Tate grinned, but just slightly.

"No problem. I'm ready to get back in the swing. I really need to work, really, after a bunch of Italian food up there. Really good food."

"You're telling me. I married a girl from Sicily. Incredible cook. Do not piss her off. Anyhow, congratulations on getting this thing resolved quickly, and safely. And thank you for doing all the paperwork already. I didn't expect that."

"Best to get it out of the way. Let me know what else you need me to do. You've got statements from those guys up there. They're all former officers. So I can pull some other duty for awhile if you need me to."

"This won't take but a minute. Jimmy Patterson wants you back. Says he hasn't done squat while you were gone."

"Yeah. We've been talking about it. We've got some more interviews we wanna do. Some people who worked at the church. Nuns. See if anybody knew."

"I know. Let me give you a tip, son. You seem like your head's on pretty straight. But there will be guys who want to slap you on the back, buy you a drink. Let me tell you this, for down the road.

"You killed a real bad guy. Don't get real talky about it. You hear what I'm saying?"

"I hear what you're saying. I know some guys have come across looking kinda juvenile. Makes you a little uncomfortable."

He shook his hand.

"Thanks Tate."

Time to find Jimmy.

IF YOU wanted to see Robert Fuller, you headed for the basement. That's where Fuller lived. And had for years. Short guy, round, big beard, curly hair, looked kinda rough-cut, like a party animal, until he began to speak. Then you knew. Eyebrows leaping around on top of his face. Dweeb. Geek. The kind of guy who could recite the dialogue from Japanese monster movies.

Couple of drinks and he would walk around the room, arms outstretched, acting like he could huff and puff and set a city on fire.

Fuller had come on as a patrol guy, but his real value was crime scene analysis. Over the years, he'd gotten a title, administrative assistant to the chief, which meant he could keep doing whatever he damn well pleased and they'd be glad to have him. He'd been to FBI training schools, taken lots of courses and he had a bookcase full of titles like The Handbook of Crime Scene Forensics, Crime Scene Investigation and Reconstruction, The Science of Crime, Criminalistics and the Law. Read em all, he was quick to say. He knew his stuff.

He told Tate they'd talk on the phone. No meeting. Do not come by.

When somebody blows something up, he said, the experts gather up evidence at the scene, figure out what was used, mebbe even reassemble the damn thing. You'd be surprised how much is left afterward. Somebody blows up a cop's car, we're pretty quick to call in the bureau.

The bomb that blew up your ride, he was telling Tate, was simple, elegant, high order, meaning... the thing was good to go. Commercial detonator, commercial wiring, a nice timer, so there'd be time to get away. Nothing homemade.

So what was the stuff? Tate wanted to know.

Oh that, that was C-4.

"C-4? Where can you get C-4?"

"You can't."

"So what does that mean?"

"It could have come from a military base, which means somebody with access and authority stole it and took it off the property, which is about as likely as me getting a date with Princess Leia."

"So?"

"So... simple. He got it from us."

"You're serious?"

"Yup. And that is why I am filing a preliminary report that will say we're still evaluating. And why this convo never took place. Capisce?"

Later that afternoon, Jimmy registered zero surprise at Robert Fuller's take. Day in, day out, folks did their jobs, he said. Bad guys got caught, got put away. Law-abiding citizens got treated right. But guys who'd been around the department for awhile saw things, knew things.

"So people just look the other way?" Tate asked.

"One day, a lot of this stuff gets straightened out. The chief is a good guy. Don't assume he doesn't know what's going on. Between now and then, let's just not get killed."

Part Four

27

CHAR OPENED the oven door to peek inside. She'd been looking every 20 minutes for the last hour and a half.

Jimmy's kitchen. It was a standing rib roast and she'd gone to town... the butcher's nicest cut... garlic, rosemary, thyme, all-spice, tarragon, nutmeg, salt, pepper, Dijon. Potatoes and asparagus. It was an outstanding piece of cow, it was beautifully dressed for the evening and she'd be entertaining a couple of world-class meat eaters.

On the dining room table, a vase of white lilies, purple asters and green hypericum, her mom's favorite. She'd run home to fetch her frilly napkins and the silver she'd inherited when her grandma died. There were little plates for salad, bowls for fruit and some silver salt and pepper shakers she'd spotted in Jimmy's cupboard. She'd found a stainless steel wine bucket there too. For dessert, there was a cream cheese and carrot cake from the priciest shop in town.

She'd found a little bell, too. She put it in the middle of the table. No reason. She'd ring it a few times while they ate. Maybe she'd ring it every time they needed to try some more wine.

And that, too, was special. A unique blend of Zinfandel, Cabernet Sauvignon, Syrah, Petit Sirah, Charbono and Grenache. Or that's what the man said. Very special.

They ought to be here now, or soon. Time to open the wine. Time to say her goodbyes, although they'd still see each other. But it was a milestone, a new direction.

It was almost time to light the candles.

She heard a faint rattling downstairs. Jimmy must have decided to come in through the back, through the lane behind the house. Lots of the big houses downtown were built on the old grid, a street in front, a lane in the back for the help.

Then she looked at herself and laughed, realized she was still wearing the old sweatshirt she'd cooked in. She started upstairs to change.

There was that sound again. It wasn't a key in the lock. No, it was more like the door was rattling, shaking. A squeak. A stubborn latch?

She stopped partway up the stairs, a dishrag over her shoulder, pulling off the oven mitt.

"Jimmy, is that you?"

There was no answer. And then she remembered what he'd told her one night when she was getting a tour of the house. The only time he ever went into the basement was when he needed the good china for entertaining. Which was never. He'd had a good laugh about it.

Jimmy never came in the back.

The sound from the basement had stopped. She continued up the stairs, walking softly now in her stocking feet, beginning to hurry.

At the top of the stairs, she ducked inside the first bedroom, Jimmy's. Beams on the ceiling, wildlife prints on the wall, an enormous mahogany desk, huge windows, a fireplace at the foot of the bed, surrounded with rose-tinted tile and marble. Laundry basket by the door.

The bed, an elegant four-poster, made up snug.

She eased open the drawer in the bedside table. No gun. The bedroom she'd been using, at the far end of the hall. All the rooms had connecting doors. She opened them as she went, softly, leaving them ajar.

And now there was a noise from the bottom of the stairs, a foot scraping on the wood. She'd reached the last room. Her gunbelt, hanging over the bedpost. She put it on, her fingers fumbling, tiptoed to the door. She held onto the molding, ducked down low, turned sideways, pressed her nose against the doorjamb, closed one eye, inching her face out, just enough to look down the long hallway, like a child playing hide and seek.

He'd come all the way up the stairs. She saw the uniform, the badge, the gun. It was a familiar face, just not Jimmy's. And a familiar shape. No one else was that tall, that big around. He, too, was walking quietly, holding a 9mm in front of him.

He turned into the first bedroom. She took a chance, crept across the hall toward the back stairs, then slid as quietly as she could through the door to the attic, hands shaking, her breath coming in short, choking gasps. It was like hiccupping. She couldn't get enough air.

Slinking up the stairs, listening for any sound, using the hand-rail to pull herself along.

The attic was tiny, dark, a low ceiling. The air was stale up here, dried out. She looked for a place to hide, saw nothing. No refuge. She'd have to make a stand. Could she shoot him? What would she say? *One of my colleagues on the force seemed like he wanted to shoot me, so I shot him first.*

What would Jimmy do? He'd pull the trigger, no questions asked. She wasn't sure she could do it, wasn't even sure she could hit a target that big, not even from close range, not the way she was shaking. She'd fired a gun in training, poorly. She'd never fired it on the job, never fired it at a person. Footsteps now, in the hall below. She looked for anything close to hand she could use.

There was no more time.

On a chair near the top of the stairs, an old silver serving tray. It looked to be the real thing. Just beside it, a pine cupboard, missing several shelves. She lifted the tray. It was plenty heavy.

She ducked in the shadow behind the cupboard. He'd have to crouch when he got to the top step, not enough room for someone that tall.

Her hands were shaking uncontrollably now. A bead of sweat was beginning to trickle down her forehead. She shook her head, trying to keep it out of her eyes, squeezed the tray tight, slid her foot back, nearly shrieked in pain. A splinter in the side of her foot, as sharp as a knife, as the big man came halfway up the stairs, taking them two at a time. He must be able to hear her.

Downstairs, the oven chimed.

Holding her breath. Two more steps. One more. He stopped, listening. She couldn't wait any longer. With a gasp, she leaped high, straight at him, swung the tray as hard she could against his head, screaming as she hit him. He was stunned. She hit him again, and again as he fell. She leaped over him and fled down the stairs.

He lunged for her as she passed him, then threw himself down and through the door, his great body hurtling to the floor with a huge crash. She was running down the hallway.

He rolled onto his side, fired one shot. The sound bounced unmercifully down the hallway, echoing along under the portraits of Jimmy's ancestors.

TATE POPPED in a CD, one of his homemade blues collections. This was old stuff, mellow stuff. Ella Fitzgerald and Joe Pass... "Why don't you do right?"

Great song. He had the original Lil' Green version, and Peggy Lee's.

> I fell for your jivin' and I took you in
> Now all you got to offer me's a drink of gin

Taking his time as he drove back to Jimmy's, where Char was putting together some kind of special dinner. She'd been making plans with that guy from church. Char was quitting the force. The chief had tried to change her mind. Nobody was as good with the kids. But she said no. Had to be the boyfriend, a new life.

He would miss her. They'd become pals. Lunch, the occasional beer. Mostly she was one of the few in this town who didn't treat him like some kind of outsider, just because his family hadn't been here for generations. He was driving slowly. Big Bill Broonzy was coming up. He stopped in the driveway to listen.

Upstairs, Char was beginning to ebb away.

Her breaths smaller now, almost like a baby's. And then she heard Tate come in the front door. She began tapping on the floor, hardly had the strength to make a sound. He looked in the kitchen, called out.

"Char? Where'd you go?"

Finally, he came up the stairs, saw her there, face-down in the hallway.

He called 911, screaming at the dispatcher, ran to her, rolled her over, clutching her against him, the blood bubbling from her chest. The eyes, vacant, glassy. For a moment, she seemed alert, but unable to speak. A tiny whimpering, the only sound.

And then, seconds later, Jimmy had come in, the two of them on the floor with her now, begging her to breathe. Gently.

Lips, turning blue. She rolled her head from side to side, as if to shake loose from the growing dark and, in a final, brief moment, had reached out toward Jimmy, tapping a finger on his badge. Tate moaned, began to sob. He kissed her cheek.

They heard a clanging as the paramedics burst in the front door.

It was hours later, after the evidence techs had done their work, after all the statements had been given, after all the teams had hit the streets, Jimmy and Tate walked out of the hospital. The chief and Ken Fowler, still inside. Char Pinckney was holding on, barely. If she survived, she'd be paralyzed.

Back at the house. Jimmy took a plastic garbage bag from under the sink, held it open. Tate grabbed Char's elegant dinner, piled high in a glass baking dish, maneuvered it over the bag, tipped it in. Jimmy tied the sack, put it by the back door. He took the wine and a corkscrew. They walked out onto the front porch. Jimmy opened the bottle, took a long pull and passed it over.

"God," Tate said, "I wish she'd been able to say something."

"No wind. I've seen it a bunch of times. They get that hole in the lungs and it hurts like hell to take in any air. Talking is pretty much out of the question."

"I think I'm gonna have fucking nightmares on this for a long time. It was like a little sister dying in my arms."

Jimmy walked to the front of the porch, sat on the stairs, leaning against one of the big columns.

"The strap was still down on her fucking holster. Why would she never listen to me? My own fucking house. After all this time... At least she was able to tell us."

"Yeah. I got that too. As if we needed to know."

"I hate it that she was so fucking naïve. If she'd never said anything to the girl, if she'd acted like she never saw that coat in her cell."

"Or just kept on walking. No conversation at all. She made herself a loose end."

"Got an idea yet?"

Tate handed the bottle back.

"Force their hand somehow, nail 'em. At this point, I wanna take vengeance on the motherfuckers. But I need to know how far it goes. But you're not waiting on me for ideas, not this time, boss. How do you want to handle it?"

"They're watching us right now. And will be. We got nothing to worry about for awhile. Nothing too soon. But they'll follow us. And that's what makes it easy."

"Keep talking."

"Later. I'm gonna sleep on it. Firm it up. Right now, let's drink more of Char's fancy wine, offer a toast. Then we put those thoughts away. Get this business done."

They touched glasses.

"I've got a sneaking suspicion you're about to line up another kill, my young friend."

"Count on it."

That night he lay awake for hours, finally drifting off. And the dream came... a formal ballroom, an orchestra. Soft light from the chandeliers, playing off the instruments, the crystal. A long table stacked high. The crowd in tuxedos and long gowns. Tate, seated at one end of the table. At the other end, John Robert Griffin.

A waiter was asking if he wanted more wine. Tate declined, reached for his weapon. It stuck, somehow, on the lapel of his jacket, Griffin laughing at him, pointing. The others at the table, staring as he struggled. Finally, he got the gun free, fired at Griffin.

But the laughter went on. Griffin, leering, shouting at him. And then there were no bullets left.

TYREE WAS holding forth.

"I popped her once. Center shot. Shame to shoot another cop though. Don't much care for it."

The Noose was pissed.

"Look, we agreed on all this shit, right? What? You're trying to make us feel bad about the woman? We got no choice now. She was a fucking girl scout. She would have reported the whole thing. In for a penny, all right? The good news is she can't talk and she's got like a zero percent chance of making it."

The concrete paint on the floor around Newsome's desk was peeling, had been for some time. Tyree scraped at a piece with the toe of his boot. He scuffed it loose, pushed it under the desk.

"Look," Newsome said, "don't get sketchy on us here. We need to know you're solid. Or maybe something bad happens to you, too."

Tyree just lifted his head. His eyes narrowed.

"What did you say?"

Noose didn't answer.

Tyree stared a moment, right at him, then at the others. He was sitting up straight, his hands hanging loose at his sides, his fingers tickling the floor, like a parent in a tiny chair in the nursery.

"You worried I might testify against you guys? Not my style. If I decide I don't want any more part of this, I will come to you face to face. And I will settle it. My way. The chief, or Drawdy or Jimmy Patterson… those are not the guys you need to be worried about.

"You boys understanding me? Cause what I'm seeing here is not tough guys."

Noose stretched out his arms, trying to muster a quorum.

"Be cool, ok? We're fine here. We got nothing to fuss about. And we got money. We're good here, guys. Am I right?"

Nods around the room. But they were looking for sureness, backbone. And the Noose wasn't bringing any. Tyree took a long breath, settled in the chair.

"All right. Let's start dialing it back. I want to make a list of everybody who's a part of this, a part of any of it. Anybody who paid. Anybody we watched after. And then I want to look at what we have on them, whether it's enough.

"You wanna be chief of police?" Newsome said. "There's no money to be made as chief. What this for, man? Everybody's cool."

"This is what for. I look around this room and everybody I see looks nervous. So I think we get down to what it is that might make us less nervous. For one thing, it's figuring out for sure that everybody in the deal has as much to lose as we do. Which means they don't talk. If we got a list and everybody on that list looks like they won't talk, then we start to feel better.

"And I want to start dialing it back. We're not sending any of our people out for awhile. Any objections?"

There were none. The dynamics had changed. A new leader was born.

Tyree pulled his feet under underneath him, stood slowly, looked at each of them, then left the room. It was quiet for a moment.

One of the deputies asked the Noose what his problem was.

"The fucking country was glad to have me risk my life in Nam. Hey... no problem. But get behind on your taxes and what happens? The IRS wants to lock your ass up. Fuck that and fuck those guys."

TATE HAD scarcely knocked on the door before it came open. Ken Fowler was unshaven, hair mussed, bleary-eyed. Clearly hadn't slept. Holding a tall mug of coffee. It was a mid-sized colonial, couple of square columns, garage around back. Lots of azaleas in the yard. A hedge across the front. Fowler was old Savannah.

One of those elf statues by the front walk.

"Ken? Looked for you at the hospital. Thought I'd see how you're doing."

Fowler, squinting in the daylight, started to speak, then couldn't quite manage it. He took Tate's hand. Tate patted him on the shoulder, eased his way inside, leaving Fowler standing at the front door.

Chair rails and bookcases, some of the original tile and brick on a back wall, a chandelier made with pink glass, wrought iron in front of the fireplace. The curtains were pulled tight in front of the picture window.

"How's that coffee? Ready for another?"

He turned to look. Fowler nodded.

Tate poured himself a cup. Fowler held out his. Tate took it from him, refilled it and handed it back. It appeared that the kitchen might be the newest part of the house. Glass-front cupboards, granite.

"Great kitchen."

"She loved it. Sorry... loves it. She wants to stain the wood a little darker, take out a couple of shelves and add one of those wine things."

He sputtered, trouble getting the words out. The voice, like he'd been banging Southern Comfort all night.

"Ain't that just like a woman. Loves it, still gonna have to make changes."

Fowler looked like he was ready to collapse. Tate reached out, squeezed an arm.

"Why don't we walk across the street? I saw a couple of benches out there. Might do you some good to get some fresh air."

"I'm a sight," Fowler said. "I don't think..."

"Anybody looks sideways..."

Tate was about to say he'd shoot 'em, thought better of it.

They walked outside, Tate keeping a hand on Fowler's shoulder, guiding him along. The sun was bright coming through the trees. Squatting by the side of the road, a couple of ducks, like they were waiting for a bus.

They sat without speaking. Heavy coats of paint on the benches, bronze plaques on the ground for the families that had donated. Someone had raked a cluster of pine cones into a pile under a tree.

Fowler had something he wanted to say. He'd suck in a long breath, let it out slowly, puffing his cheeks, staring. After a couple of tries, he put his face in his hands and began to sob. Tate put an arm around his shoulder. They sat.

It was like that for a time.

Fowler cleared his throat, sat up straight.

"She said you were her best friend on the force. Her best friend."

Down the street, some kids playing kickball in a side yard, shouting over who got next; it mingled with the sound of the traffic and the birds, a guy next door playing a radio talk show in his garage. A block over, the rhythmic beeping of a big truck backing up. Everyone cooking under the same sun.

"And she's mine. She was never that thrilled with being a cop, you know? But she thought she'd stay on, stay with it. She had a whole different life in mind before she met you. But then she told me she didn't want to come home from a day of nastiness, didn't want to have to carry that with her. But she wanted to stay in it, somehow, with the kids, find a way to keep working with the kids."

The occasional car driving past, kids going by on their bikes, some cardinals flitting from one tree to the next. Down the street, a hissing from an electric lawn mower. Must be a small yard.

"I think I want to go inside now."

They started back. Fowler squared his shoulders, turned to look at Tate.

"I don't know how you guys live with it."

Tate nodded.

"It's hard."

238

28

THEY DIDN'T WAIT. Tyree driving. The Noose in the front passenger seat. Russell was in the back, on the right side, unbuckled, one hand on the latch. It was a big DeVille with heavily tinted windows. Texas plates. A car seized from a doper in a drug bust, then reported stolen from the police impound lot. Bulk. Horsepower. Anonymity.

"Here he is. Stomp it."

The Cadillac accelerated sharply. The Noose shouted.

"Now. Coontag him."

On another day when he wasn't distracted, it wouldn't have worked. Tate would have seen the car waiting, wouldn't have left himself so vulnerable, would have leaped aside at the last moment.

But Tate was thinking about Ken Fowler, about Char, the look in her eyes as they lost focus. Walking underneath a high sun shining through the oaks and the pines, head down from the heat and the glare. The breeze, spinning leaves over the ground as he stepped onto the curb.

He turned just as the car raced alongside, saw the rear door fly open. It caught him just behind the hip, the impact throwing him into the air and onto someone's front lawn. A stunning blow. A home run that sent an eruption of pigeons from the trees.

Russell and the Noose leaped out, grabbed him, shucked him into the back seat. The car roared away. Broad daylight on a city street. No one saw a thing.

"**NO BROKEN** bones? What a disappointment."

Tate was just coming around. Unable to move, somewhere damp, too dark to see. His head was throbbing.

The muscles in his lower back, his butt and his hamstrings, cramping severely. He began to see shapes. Somebody's basement. His hands and feet were tied to a heavy chair. The chair was wicker, with an oak frame. An old chair, solid. There was nothing he could do but endure the pain.

"Speak up, tough guy. What? Nothing to say?"

"That you, Noose?"

"Yeah, it's me, brother. You recognized my voice."

"Actually it was that retarded accent. You make it through the fifth grade? Brother?"

Noose flipped on a light.

"You're gonna find out it's not smart to fuck with me, Drawdy."

The Noose, sitting several feet away. Behind him, a wooden stairway. A washer and dryer underneath. Boxes, paint cans, rusted yard tools, a small stepladder, more boxes. Hand-written labels on the boxes: Paint thinner. Insecticide. The Noose could spell.

A bare bulb hanging from the ceiling with a string pull and a metal shade. It left deep shadows across the room. There were shelves along one wall. Under Tate's feet, a drain.

"Enjoying your surroundings, I see. Get used to it. You're gonna be here for the duration, if you know what I mean."

The Noose stood, began to pace. He wore grungy overalls and a flannel shirt, like he was getting ready to work outside. Those boots with the thick soles you see in the hardware stores. That telltale reddish glow to his face.

"I was looking around down here, trying to remember all the crap I've got in these old boxes. Looking for something good to fuck you with, Drawdy. Check this out."

He came closer, held out his hand. It was a utility knife, the old retractable kind. The Noose pushed the slider forward with his thumb. Age spots on his fat fingers. Ink in his hair.

"Look at that shit. This thing's covered with rust and who knows what else. That's gotta be nasty."

He held the point against Tate's cheek. And then, snarling, he pushed it hard against Tate's face until the skin parted. Tate screamed, jerked his head back, afraid for his eye. The Noose dragged the blade down to the chin, cutting a deep gash, blood spurting over his hands and the blade.

"Face stuff is always bad. Even if they can fix it, you end up lopsided. I've seen a ton of it, worked patrol for years. Car wrecks, back in the day, when people didn't use their seatbelts. Always shredding their faces on the glass. You hate to see it with kids, women, young women especially. In your case, it's pretty fuckin funny, if you ask me."

Tate leaned his head forward, blood still gushing. Tasting it.

"They're gonna put you away for the rest of your life, Newsome."

The Noose pulled his chair over close. His breath, hot against Tate's forehead. He stood, slapped Tate hard. He had a score to settle.

"You're getting blood all over my floor you asshole."

Suddenly he reached down, grabbed Tate's left hand, held it tight while he sliced deep into the palm.

There was nothing Tate could do but scream.

"That's gotta hurt like shit. Keep yelling my friend. Ain't nobody around to hear you. Except for me."

He reached for the string and turned out the light. Tate, moaning, waiting for the footsteps, hearing nothing. And then the voice, close against him. He could feel the Noose breathing into his ear. The scent of whiskey, pastrami, old cigar. Noose's personal fragrance.

"How's it feel, college boy? You and I are gonna have some good times here, brother."

And then he heard him clomping up the stairs in those big boots. The door slammed shut. Darkness. The pain, deep, piercing, floating in waves across his neck and along his arm. He could feel his shirt getting soaked from the shoulder down his chest. And on his leg, under the hand. It was filling up in his shoe. He leaned his head back, turned his hand upward toward the ceiling, hoping the blood flow would begin to slow, tried to make a fist but couldn't. It hurt too much.

He wouldn't have minded going out in a blaze, putting up some kind of fight. Dying with some kind of dignity. But here he was, strapped in. He tried to stand. His legs were tied so tightly, he couldn't make any headway, couldn't get himself straight up and down.

Worst case, he could lunge forward, once, but that would topple him onto the floor.

He pulled hard against his bonds. No give. Perhaps he could scoot the chair across the room to something sharp, something he could rub against. He'd have to wait until the next time the Noose was here, with the light on, to see.

He'd have to wait until the next cutting.

Hours passed. He lost track of time. Sitting there in a stupor, weighing his odds. He'd been careless. Mooch would be pissed. So would Jimmy. He'd let them down. His mom and dad would be crushed. If they ever found him, if people ever found out what had happened to him.

It came again that afternoon, or that night. Feet on the stairs. Leather soles, hard heels. It was Noose, had to be. He'd traded the boots for something else. His basement. Who else was involved? Were they party to the torture? Or was this a private party?

This time it was a fluorescent, a big light over the stairs. The Noose stood before Tate, feet apart, hands clasped in front of him, as if he were about to pray.

"How's my buddy? Resting quietly? Building up your strength? Tate, I gotta tell you. You're some kind of stupid. You coulda played ball with us. You could even have had a little bit of that very nice piece of ass in the cell. What? Not good enough for you? The bitch is prime and you know it.

"Now some guys, they see anything young, they think it's prime. Some of you college shits like to think you're better than that. Woman has to be special. Well you fucked up, didn't you?"

He slapped Tate across the back of the head, then slapped him a couple more times, like he couldn't get enough of it.

"I've been thinking about what you said, Tate. About how you thought maybe I never got out of grade school. Got a surprise for you, pal. I've had plenty of schooling. I've got one of those word of the day things on my desk. You know what today's word is? Symmetry.

Noose walked to the bottom of the stairs, picked up a pile of clothes. He was going to change first, before the fun began, keep his good clothes nice.

"I like the symmetry idea a lot. It means I need to gash up the other side of your face. The other hand. That'll be next. Then the bottoms of your feet. That's what they did in Nam. Severe long-lasting psychological effects, the doctors said.

"You won't have that problem, not that it won't be severe. Just not long-lasting."

He laughed hard at his joke, then made another about keeping it personal. Bullets weren't personal. Neither were arrests.

Now pain... torture... that was a different story. You had a stake in the process, like creating equity in your home. You made an effort, you worked hard, you built something, you took all the right steps to inflict bodily harm, to screw up another man's brain. You invested in his pain.

He'd put on a yellow sweatshirt, faded, covered with paint smears, jeans, those work boots. And now he pulled on a pair of canvas gloves and began to punch Drawdy in the face. Punctuation for his little speech.

He pulled his fist back tight against his waist, leaning in with each punch, driving the knuckles deep. He circled him, punching hard across the back of his head, battering his ears, his temples, nose, eyes. Grunting from the effort. The sound, like a slider slapping into a catcher's mitt.

"The blue wall, Tate. Every hear of it? You don't rat out your comrades. We're supposed to be a family. Brotherly love. You need to start giving a shit about the other guys on the team.

"I'm glad that bullet missed you up in Pittsburgh. I'm really gonna enjoy this."

Every second or third word, another pop. Tate worked at pulling his head back upright after each impact. Blood pouring again from his wounds; trying to tell himself not to squeeze the arms of the chair. Not with his left hand.

His head was bouncing. He tried counting the blows. Wondering what he'd done to earn them. Was it the big sins that took you down? Those three bullets he'd so carefully sent through John Robert's shirt pocket?

Funny. He could have pictured John Robert shooting him in the leg, or the knee, something to give him pain. He'd never contemplated being tortured, not here, in genteel Savannah.

Hard to keep a train of thought.

"You want me to stop, brother? You want me to quit? Speak up. Tell me how sorry you are that we got sideways with each other."

Tate slowly opened his eyes. Coughing, trying to catch his breath. His voice, like sandpaper.

"You ever have sex with a woman, Noose? Or did they all get a good look at you first?"

More blows to his head, his face, again and again. After a time, he drifted. A bucket of cold water brought him around. He threw up, clenched his eyelids shut.

His head, slipping from side to side. Tiny lights, flashing. He'd seen them before, when he'd had his bell rung. Once, in a high school basketball game, he'd leaped for the rebound and had his legs cut from beneath him by a rampaging forward. He'd landed hard on his back, slammed his head against the floor.

The lights shone brightly that day.

After a time... he had no idea how long... the Noose wore out and crawled back upstairs.

Tate, drifting again, a numbness slowly creeping over him. He slept.

Now there was light coming through a window well, a soft light, seeping through the window like a gentle fog, the slightest color on the concrete floor. Dirt, swept into a pile in the corner, a pair of shovels by the door.

Was it the second day? The bleeding had stopped. There was just the throbbing from the cuttings, and from the beatings and from being tied down. There were moments when he thought the pain in his butt and his legs was the worst of it, wishing he could just wipe his face of sweat and blood. Wipe the smell of puke from his clothes.

A faint noise from outside, a car, birds chirping. The Noose had lied about no one being able to hear. He'd have to try. It was a small chance. Someone would have to be standing next to the house to hear him. So he shouted, sparingly, saving his voice. His throat, like he'd swallowed a mouthful of sand.

It took all he had to muster a call for help.

It grew dark again without a visitor. He was weakening. They'd left him there to die, in Noose's private little country club.

He tried to picture Barks absorbing the news. He hoped she would leave town, start somewhere new.

She wouldn't.

Outside, the city grew quiet. Families turned out their lights, locked their doors. Birds cooed and whispered to each other, their feathers ruffling in the quiet breeze.

HE WAS SWIMMING. It was night and he was far from shore. His shoulders, aching, his strength, failing. His legs and back, cramping as if they were tied in a vice. Floundering in the water, the waves pushing him back, forcing him back into the deepest part of the ocean. Kicking, struggling to lift his face out of the water. He could hear a gong, in time with the waves, rocking him, echoing, bouncing inside. With every ring, a jarring flash of light and pain. Salt water pouring into his lungs. Waves crashing over his head, pounding him under the surface.

Laughter, somewhere off along the shore. He kept swimming. Losing the fight. There was nothing else to do.

More cold water. Daylight barging in.

"Did you lose me for a second there, pal? I think you did."

Noose set down the bucket, pulled his gloves tight, preparing for another round. Tate closed his eyes.

"Lemme tell you something Noose."

The words, stumbling out of his mouth, like he'd become a prideful drunk. His tongue, clammy with dehydration and pain and inevitability.

"You've got me tied up, pal. But lemme tell you. My buddy... he's gonna stomp you..."

His head was spinning. Tears pouring from his eyes now. He was losing touch, seeing the end. The pain, pushed aside. Something that almost felt like gratitude began to wash over him. No more mysteries to solve. Going under.

Acceptance.

Another fusillade of fists.

"Fuck you, Drawdy. And fuck your friend. Aint't nobody gonna help you now."

Noose took a breather, standing there by the washing machine, then came toward him again, began throwing new blows to his shoulders, ears. Suddenly, he stopped, looked up. Footsteps overhead. He'd left the door open at the top of the stairs.

Tate shook himself from his stupor. He mustered a croaking shout.

"Whoever you are, get out of the house! Run! Call 911. Tell them 'officer down.'"

Was it loud enough?

The Noose grabbed a bottle of detergent, swung it hard against Tate's head, turned and raced up the stairs. The light went out and, for a moment, there was no sound. Then a thud, bodies hurtling together. Scuffling feet, banging against something… furniture, cabinets. Hard at it. The door at the top of the stairs crashed shut as someone or something slammed against it.

Grunts. Shouting.

Why was there no gunfire? The Noose, older, but with plenty of beef. He could be trouble. Fists now. The sound of knuckles against cheekbones, ribs. A hard contact, then a shout. The door flew open. Someone racing down, then more crashing. Two bodies tangling at the bottom of the stairs.

He could just make them out. Standing apart, facing off. Noose, shorter, stockier, clutching a knife. The other man, bluejeans, tall, wiry.

Jimmy.

They were circling, struggling to see, to adjust to the darkness. The Noose was closer now. Tate gathered himself, leaning forward to put the weight on his feet. He lunged toward them. The chair fell. Barely enough for a distraction, for an instant.

Noose turned toward the sound. Jimmy leaped to close the distance and then they were on the floor. Too dark to know who was on top. Seconds... it seemed longer... locked. The struggle, almost silent. And then there was a cry. Small, birdlike.

Tate, lying on his side, still strapped tight to the chair. Jimmy, taking him by the shoulder.

"Lift your head. That's it. Easy. Can you lift it? That's better. Now where's the fucking light switch, asshole?"

"String. Over your head."

Newsome was on the floor, a knife in his chest. Jimmy flew back up the stairs. Tate could hear him talking to another officer. Jimmy'd brought backup.

Tate, astonished, managing to croak out a puny insult.

"You just gonna leave me here like some kinda fucking fish on the dock."

His voice, smaller than he remembered it. Jimmy called down from upstairs.

"Kinda busy right now. Hold your horses."

Jimmy found the light switch at the top of the stairs. He walked toward Newsome, bent down, pulled the knife from his chest and used it to cut Tate's bonds.

"You've looked better partner. Actually, kinda reminds me of that Ethiopian girl we busted doing the botox on herself in the garage. Remember? Didn't she look like shit."

Tate, gushing blood again, trying to move a leg, an arm, anything at all. Hoarse. Babbling.

"You rescue me? Then tell me I look like shit?"

"Rescue, that's the key word, pal. Now let's get you upstairs. I got an ambulance coming."

Tate couldn't walk, couldn't stand, couldn't open his eyes. Nothing was working. The pain, as bad as it had been, increasing even now as he tried to straighten his legs. His head, spinning.

Jimmy holding him tight, easing him back down to the floor, telling him to wait for the guys with the stretcher. He opened the dryer, found some clean clothes, soaked them in the sink and began washing Tate's wounds.

"I may be going out on a limb here, brother. But from the looks of it, the Noose didn't like you much."

Tate, a sputtering cough, began to shake.

"How'd you figure it out?"

"All this blood and shit. I'm a trained investigator."

"No. How you found me."

His head was spinning harder now. His control, dissolving. He was falling, deep into it, like toppling off a ledge, nothing below. The pain was taking over, like shards of light bursting in through chinks in the timber. He could feel air rushing, taking him by the shoulders, the ground slipping away beneath him. The shaking was worse now. Tears spilling out. Words spilling out, colliding as they left him.

"Noose's house… basement. Got a knife. Gloves. Find the gloves. Find the gloves?"

Jimmy had him on his back. He covered him with towels from the laundry, stuck a few under his head and under his feet to keep the blood high.

"Lie still bro. Quiet now."

He put a hand on his chest.

"Lie still. Help's on the way. Get you a nice bed and a doctor and mebbe a beer later. Glad I finally found you. I was following those guys, one after the other, spotted that black Caddy. I had em day before yesterday, but they lost me. Then I caught up to the Noose today. You were out of sight. So I figured I better look around. When Noose tried to kill me, I figured I must be in the right place.

"Lie still now."

Tate found Jimmy's hand, squeezed it.

THE BULLET that would put Char Pinckney in a wheelchair had entered roughly halfway between the spine and the shoulder blade, about midway between the neck and the waist. Just the right height to pierce the lung. It had torn an artery, then come out the front of her chest, why they'd seen blood bubbling. A sucking chest wound.

One shot. It wreaked havoc on her body.

Jimmy had found the doc who had been seeing to Char at the hospital, and asked him to come by Tate's room, get them caught up.

"There's penetration damage," the doc said. "That's the damage from the bullet. Then there's cavitation damage. Think of the bullet like a bomb hitting the body. There's a shock wave. It does bad things. In her case, the bullet passed on through, and it didn't fragment, so there weren't bullet remains. The penetration damage. And the energy of impact... those were the issue."

Tate hated hearing it. But there were things he needed to know. There were stitches in his face. He'd been told not to move. Nothing but liquids through a straw for the time being. He formed the words slowly.

"Why couldn't she speak?"

"I can't tell you for sure. It was painful to breathe. She'd just been shot. She was losing blood. I suppose she probably felt she was dying."

TYREE WAS gone, and Russell.

After the ambulance had arrived, Jimmy put out the word. Nobody talks about the Noose. But it was past the point of control. The TV crews were there. Footage of Tate being wheeled out. Footage of another stretcher, the body covered in a sheet. The word was out.

There would be warrants, interviews. But the first clue, the first indication of who was involved, was immediate. Some guys just disappeared, gone. And some others wanted alone time with the chief, right now. Each wanted to be the first to roll over on his colleagues.

By the end of the day, it was taking shape. Cops covering up for dopers, taking a cut.

"Why do you think Elliott Ness wouldn't tell anybody what he was doing? He had no idea who he could trust."

Jimmy was talking to Tate. He'd been out in the hallway, talking on the radio, getting reports, sending guys out. But he kept coming back into the room to talk with Tate.

This time, Barks stopped him at the door.

"I'm telling the nurses not to let you up here anymore. He's supposed to be resting. You act like this is another day at the office. Get out before I take your gun and shoot you with it."

Jimmy thought that was pretty funny. He still hightailed it.

She'd had the nurses aside for a little chat. We don't want his cop buddies coming in here unsupervised. They can come by for five minutes at a time, a few of them. But no bags or satchels or backpacks or carry-ons or lunchboxes or anything else. The cops were all like frat boys, she told them. They'll be bringing him six-packs and straws.

There was no reason those cops couldn't behave for a couple of days.

The docs were going to keep him for a bit. One of the docs had given him a nickname. Harry Hematoma. Bruises, nasty cuts. A serious concussion. After the swelling went down, there would be surgery to try to minimize that scar along his cheek. For now, it was antibiotics, cleaning the wounds. Drugs to kill the pain, to erase the memory. She sat alongside his bed, holding his hand.

Tate, drifting, contemplating his sins.

Was it Griffin? Or that day in middle school, when a couple of guys decided to kick the ass of the new kid behind the gym? Tate saw it, declined the invitation to join in. Kept walking. But he'd seen it. He could have stopped it. But that wouldn't have been cool.

The kid had been scared. Knowing guys wanted a piece of him was worse than getting his ass kicked. Tate spoke to the kid in the lunch line one day. Maybe that was setting things straight, penance. He didn't really think that. He just wanted to feel like he'd made some kind of effort.

There were other sins. He'd stolen some shit. Magazines, CDs, a book or two, when he was a teenager. Rich kid, stealing. Maybe that was why he was here now. Or perhaps it was just an accumulation, a scorecard of failing to think about someone else when the opportunity arose.

What was the worst thing? Being held accountable? Or being tied to a chair, the helpless victim? He'd been afraid of the punishment. But he'd been afraid, too, of dying too soon, before he was old enough to understand some things.

Now he might have another chance. He slept.

29

TYREE JUMPED to the front of the class, right after word got out about the Noose and his tucked-away torture room.

Lamonica called the agent in charge of the FBI office in Atlanta, which covered all of the state. He was ready to spill, ready to deal. He was wasting no time.

Tyree had covered himself well. He had a file. He could tell them who was smuggling dope, who paid for protection, who got the money. The FBI really wanted a handle on all of those things.

And that was about enough to send Jimmy Patterson right over the edge. The chief had called him in for a briefing. A handful of street cops had already made a pitch to roll over. Most of the Noose's crew wanted out.

The feds would hold the trump card. And, as it turned out, Tyree Lamonica had the kind of documentation the prosecutors covet. Dates, names, places.

The guys working drugs in Savannah were hooked into Brunswick. Savannah was the big port, but Brunswick had its own import scheme. Containers from Belize, the Bahamas, Jamaica and Trinidad... too many to check.

And cars... Jags, Porsches, Land Rovers, Volvos. There was always something extra in the shipment.

The feds were good. They routinely found tons of coke stuffed under the rocker panels, wrapped inside the spare tires, crammed into phony tailpipes bolted to the undercarriage, taped underneath the console, inside the stuffing in the seatbacks.

But tons got through, they knew.

Savannah had its own setup. One of the biggest container ports in the country. More than a million tons of sugar came into the port every year. Palm oil and beer flooded into the port. But the best hiding places were in the sugar and the onions, the shrimp and the canned pineapples, the frozen fish and the tea. Panama, Malasia, Thailand, Mexico, Guatemala and Peru. Coke in shipping containers. Leafy khat listed on the manifest as tea.

Tyree knew stuff about where and when and who.

He'd offered a teaser to get them interested. He gave up a shrimper from Thunderbolt, a guy who was bringing pot back from Colombia, 10 tons at a time. They were offloading to smaller boats in the Bahamas, occasionally running the dope straight into Frogmore, off Beaufort. Tyree knew where. And he told them to look for a bunch of coke buried in the back yard of the shrimper's daddy's house.

The feds dug a hole. And found the coke. And now they were drooling.

AFTER FOUR days, Tate had been released to home rest. Char would be there at the hospital for awhile, a good while. Tate and the rest of the crew, along with Barks, had put in a good many hours sitting by her bedside. It looked like she might pull through, although she still hadn't spoken.

And now Tate was home, sitting in a hot tub, soaking. Drinking a beer. Barks was there, watching over him like a hawk. The docs had told him not to smoke. He was ignoring it.

She jumped. "What is that?"

A black spider about the size of a dime had crawled to the edge of the tub, giving Tate the eye. Lifting one leg. Another. Back and forth.

"It's just a spider," he said.

"Don't move. Lemme get something."

"No. No. It's all right. He's not doing anything."

"I don't like it. It could be a black widow."

"It's OK. Really. This is probably his bathtub. He would prefer if I don't disturb his stuff."

She knocked over the stool she'd brought in from the kitchen.

"This is crazy."

"It's just a spider."

"No. You. Your life, or what's left of it."

"Not sure what you mean. Maybe you're just creeped out by his eyes."

"You think? You asshole."

She leaned against the door, stared at the ceiling. And then she cut loose.

"The guys who shot you are dead. The guy who threatened you is dead. The crazy nun is dead. The biker who tried to stab you is dead. The guy who kept you in his basement and cut you up and beat you is dead."

He started to say something. She shook an arm at him.

"Now don't give me any macho bullshit about how this is no big deal. This is nasty violent shit and you've come close to getting killed yourself—what... five times? In the short time that I've known you? I can't keep count. I don't know if I can live with this. I don't even know if I want to know about this. I feel like I ought to move to California."

He reached out for her. She backed into the open doorway to the kitchen.

She was angry, not anywhere close to tears. He was feeling self-conscious about the puffy mass of bandages on his face and the gauze and the tape wrapped around his hand.

"I don't know if you even understand," she said. "I'm worried about you being killed. I'm worried about you turning into some kind of hard-case asshole, just to keep your sanity. And I worry that it will drive me crazy, or that I'll have to live with it after you're six feet underground. This is absolutely insane."

He hesitated, cleared his throat.

"Anything I say about how most guys never fire their gun would just piss you off. You'd think I was trying to downplay it."

She picked up the pack of cigarettes from the edge of the bathtub and stormed into the kitchen. He could hear the garbage disposal running. When she came back, she picked up the ashtray and threw it through a window. It was a big window.

He climbed wearily out of the tub. She was standing in the doorway, hands on her hips. He picked up the towel, started to dry off. She refused to look at him.

"I don't think I'm ready to quit this job," he said. "Maybe at some point, but not now. If you need to go, or you want to go, I don't blame you."

Probably not the right thing to say. There was no right thing.

THAT NIGHT, Jimmy and Tate took a drive out toward Isle of Palms. Along the Skidaway River, where the old shrimp docks once had been. Now, docks for speedboats. Colonial mansions and yachts.

Tyree's place, set back from the road. Heavily wooded lot, not far from the river. Tall pines, a few big oaks. A dilapidated shed off the side of the driveway.

The last of the day's sunlight edging through the trees. Still a bit of glare. Not much. A bit like the day Tate and his friends were riding bikes along the Chattahoochee. The sun, easing from purple to green, back to purple. A hot day. They'd thrown the bikes on the ground and jumped in the river with their clothes on. Flocks of birds mushrooming out of the trees as if there'd been an explosion.

No one was home at Tyree's. They parked in the driveway.

Alarm system on the doors and windows. Jimmy stood on the front porch railing, tugged on the gutter. It felt OK. He pulled himself onto the roof, clambered in through an upstairs window. The code for the alarm was written on a post-it note over the keypad. He turned off the alarm and let Tate in the front door. A big screen TV in the den. Wood paneling throughout the house. Some old paintings on the walls, antique shop stuff. Flowers in the kitchen.

Woman's clothes in the bedroom closet and her stuff in the bathroom. Jimmy was going through drawers.

"Girlfriend's a little on the wild side."

"Lemme see."

Jimmy held up a thong.

"Not much in the way of coverup."

And then Tate said: "You know what I'm thinking?"

"Yeah. Maybe we can find her, use her to get Tyree out in the open."

"Exactly. I'll start rummaging through the desk."

Bills, some receipts, pay stubs, rubber bands, paper clips, a couple of screwdrivers, bunch of pens. On top of the desk, a very nice calculator.

"Jimmy. Check this out."

It was a picture of Noose and Tyree, leaning against a Porsche. In the Noose's outstretched hand, a set of keys.

"And look, here's a stamp collection. Funny."

They searched awhile longer, found nothing interesting, went through the kitchen into the garage. There was a plywood floor nailed down above the rafters. Tate pulled a ladder over and they climbed up. Under a tarp, a pair of heavy duty plastic storage bins, locked.

"I saw a lopper on the wall," Tate said. "Won't cut the lock, but we can rip the plastic handle off and see what's inside here."

In each bin, four M16s, looking barely used.

"Surplus stuff," said Jimmy. "Same as we have downtown. And let's get over here."

Under another tarp, another set of storage boxes, also locked. Inside, C-4... nicely stacked, with all the necessary accessories.

"Clears some shit up, don't it?" Jimmy said.

"Is this what you were talking about when you said I would find out about some things?"

"Well, I didn't know guys were hoarding hardware, but I could see pretty clearly some of our brethren had gone over to the dark side. It started with the drugs. Guys would go into a bar, off-duty, plant a stash, then find it and threaten to shut the place down. A bunch of the owners went to Noose, offered to pay up regular if he'd stop the shakedowns. We've got quite a bit of cleanup ahead of us."

"I don't wanna see Tyree skate," Tate said. "Five bucks says he was the one at your place."

"Agreed. Problem is, Tyree's got a handful of guys with him. I'm not sure who we can count on right now. You gotta put guys against each other. And there's the bikers."

"Be nice to have some guys from the outside."

"Exactimundo."

"Lemme make a call to my guys from Pittsburgh."

"You might have to sweeten the pot with some fishing and some beer," Jimmy said.

"I'm guessing they'd like nothing better than this, mebbe with a little fishing thrown in."

They found some decent beer in Tyree's fridge, sat out back and hatched a plan.

Once again, Tate wasn't totally sure he wanted to involve the guys, but resources were getting short and it was time. He called the Mooch.

"You guys still looking for trouble?"

"Always. What you got in mind?"

"Couple of rogue cops. Might be more than a couple."

"Not surprised. You getting over that shellacking?"

"I mighta lost half a step, but it's temporary."

"What you want from us? Bobby's still a little sketchy, but he's gonna wanna be in."

"Jimmy and I need some backup, some guys we can count on. We'll try to leave you out of it, but it would help to have a little confidence, if you know what I mean. In the meantime, talk to the guys, see what you wanna do. We need you pretty soon, if you want to come. I'll get you first class round-trips down here, some serious wheels, rooms at an old mansion downtown.

And once we wrap this thing, a charter trip out to the Gulf Stream."

"Sounds great, my friend. And it also sounds a little on the pricey side. And, you know, Goo's gonna want to eat."

"I think I mentioned this before. I am very OK where money is concerned. Can you guys get hardware on the plane? We've got stuff here."

"Yeah, no sweat. All right. I'll get back to you."

The guys were good. Tate sent a limo to the airport. Better if he and Jimmy weren't seen. But it wouldn't be long before the word was out.

TATE TOOK the call in Jimmy's office. Laura wanted to meet. There was something back at Tyree's house that he would be coming back for. It was so well hidden, the cops would never find it, unless she showed them.

Laura wanted out.

Tate told her to look for a guy on a park bench on the north side of Forsythe, along Gaston. Just after dark. He knew it was her when he saw her coming. Tall, hourglass, walking on air. An old gent in lime green pants was walking the other way. As she passed him, he stumbled for a second, turned, put his hands on his hips. He watched for her for 20 feet or so, then his shoulders leaped up to his ears. His hands shook, like he'd stuck his finger in a socket. Pulsating there, watching as she sat. And then he walked on, woozily. Just alongside of him, a family snapping flash pictures from a horse-drawn carriage.

Tate was wondering what she saw in Tyree.

She was wondering whether she'd be in any trouble. And she was worrying about whether Tyree'd changed his mind about her.

"I could see stuff was going on. I told him I didn't want anything to do with somebody in that kind of trouble. This is getting way out of hand. I like Tyree a lot, but I'm not a damned criminal... anything beyond speeding."

Tate cut right to the chase.

"You ever suspect anything, before all this stuff came out?"

"Yeah, but only because he'd be, you know, quiet about some things. That, and the fact that he was loaded."

"So now you want to get out from under, make sure you're not connected to him when people start going to jail."

"Yeah, exactly. All I ever did was live with the guy. I don't know anything about what he did or when he did it or who he did it with. There were never any other people at the house, or when we went out for a drink. When he wanted to talk on the phone, he'd go outside."

She'd confronted him about it. Just how much trouble was he in, she wanted to know. He'd gotten angry. And she'd gotten very scared.

"When?"

"Just lately. It was like he was getting all wired up. Not sleeping well. Talking a lot outside."

"But things were OK between you, other than that?"

"Yeah, mostly. I mean, he eats a ton of Mexican and then he farts like a creaky door in a horror movie. And sometimes he forgets which fork to use. But he's very sweet and he's a complete gen-tleman. I think maybe if he hadn't grown up so damn poor, if he hadn't had such a hard life growing up, he might have been OK.

"But there's a place where he hides stuff. I haven't looked there, but I know that's where he keeps records. It's at his house. I think it's important. And he hasn't been back. He's going to want that stuff."

The first shot kicked up dirt at her feet just as they heard the sound. Tate grabbed her hand and they ran, ducking behind trees. He wasn't sure where the shot came from, but there weren't many choices. They bolted for his car.

"Get in," he shouted.

Another shot pinged off the hood as he accelerated away.

"He could have had us both in the park."

Tate threw the wheel over, down a side street, making for the river.

"I guess I ignored the signs," she said.

30

THE FLEETWOOD raced through the darkness, gliding along like a child's sled skimming over ice.

The faint blue of the dashboard lights rolling upward, bouncing off his chin like moonlit waves tumbling onto a rocky beach. Trees drifting past, mailboxes, a few houses set back from the road, the big Cadillac snugged in tight. The others, a caravan off his wings, a miniature phalanx rushing into the black.

A light fog lingering just over the pavement, thicker along the shoulders. Tyree, out in front. Just behind him, two sedans, an old muscle car.

Tate could hear it rumbling as it accelerated behind him. At first, they had pulled tight against him, drafting inches from his rear, the Cadillac a hulking menace. Tate, forcing the pedal down. And then they drifted back, content to follow.

The caravan sent Spanish moss floating skyward, leaves scuttling away from the road. Hissing from the tires on the pavement and the wind rushing past. Fifty feet now, no closer. There was no other traffic. Hard to know why. It was beginning to cool. The moon, peeking through the tall trees at the end of the road, lighting the way.

Tate took a hard right, then another. He had a place to go. He called Jimmy.

"I've got maybe half a dozen of 'em behind me, heading east, out toward Tyree's place. Looks like somebody wants to wrap this up."

"Quicker than we thought. Not bad, though."

"No."

"Leaving you room?"

"Enough."

"All right. See you in a minute."

He pushed hard on the accelerator. The gap widened. The sky, darker still as they traveled farther from town, a cluster of small ships disappearing over the horizon, on through the fog and into the gloom beyond. He pulled his seatbelt tighter.

Laura, not speaking, her eyes glued to the floor, clutching fast on the door handle and the seat.

The headlights of his pursuers collapsed into a single pair of beams behind him as a delivery truck rumbled past in the other direction. And now it was beginning to rain. Rain from far out to sea had come in. She wondered why he didn't use the wipers. A minute passed. It felt longer.

She whispered, so quietly it took Tate a moment to realize she was speaking. She never dreamed he would want to hurt her. It left her so frightened she could hardly breathe.

Once again, he remembered that slow waltz. The band was about to pack up and head home. Here he was, tempting the devil once again.

He punched it, powered through a turn, roaring down the long, final straightaway, knifing through the fog. A long run ahead of them. He kept the pedal down, gaining distance, separation. Skidded into the driveway. They burst from the car and ran for the door. Tate, carrying a shotgun he'd thrown under a blanket in the back seat. She followed, stumbling. He kicked open the door. Heard an owl, off in the trees. The old house was quiet now.

Find a closet and tuck in, he told her.

She staggered three steps and dropped to the floor, her breaths coming in brittle staccato bursts, moaning like a child exhausted after a tantrum. She clamped her hands under her arms and began to rock, fore and aft, fore and aft.

Take a second, he said. Then you need to find a place to hide.

He stood at the window, seeing the faint green-gold of the marsh, the lights reflecting off the water from the houses across the river, shadows under the trees like long dark pools. He felt a tiredness sweeping over him as if he had suddenly confronted a long-held grief.

Headlights looming larger.

In a moment, engines, doors slamming. There were seven of them. They'd stopped out by the street, coming through slowly. Tyree out in front, a good 40 yards from the house.

Tate bent down, tugged on her arm.

"They're getting close. Come on now. Get up."

But she wasn't moving. Just there on the floor, back, forth, the moan turning into a wail that rose and fell as her head dipped toward the floor and swung back toward the ceiling, so loud they could hear it outside.

Tyree's men, carrying M16s. Shots kicked up the dirt in front of them. Shots from the trees. They hesitated.

"It's an ambush," one screamed.

But then Tyree shouted: "Keep moving."

One of the men cut loose into the woods, a long fusillade. The others joined in, firing indiscriminately. And then they began to pepper the house. Standing erect now, like sentries, firing round after round through the trees and against the house.

The bullets tore into the shingles on the roof, gashed splinters in the siding, ripped the spotlight at the corner of the house. The bullets took chunks out of Tyree's desk, the drawer where he kept his broker's statements, his stamps and his tiny tweezers. They smashed lamps and snatched pictures from the walls. They ripped a door from its hinges, shattered crystal, cleaved bricks from the fireplace. Glass and photos and flowers and pottery crashed to the floor.

And then, for just a moment, there was silence. Tate, lying flat alongside her, holding Laura tight, pushing her deep into the carpet as if there were safety there.

Out in the river, a 40-foot fisherman heeled over, sliced through the water, accelerating now to get away from whatever was happening onshore. The gunfire, echoing across the water for miles and, downtown, telephones were beginning to ring.

A hollow clank as a clip fell to the driveway, the smack of another sliding home. And then it began again, bullet holes filling the room with moonlight. Laura, screeching, clawing at the air, at his arms, at the floor, nearly choking. Only seconds had passed and they were covered with bits of glass, wood splinters, wallboard dust. He began to crawl, pulling her with him, staying low. Laura's eyes, glazed over, whimpering now as the men outside continue to fire.

And then, another shot from the trees and one of Tyree's men fell to the ground. For a moment, the shooting stopped. A voice called out.

"I will count to five."

Two men turned, ran for their cars. The others raised their weapons, firing again into the house, into the woods, raking fire clear into the scaffolds of the trees. Another of Tyree's men reeled backward.

And now there were three. They loped toward the house, firing as they went. Another fell.

Tate, half carrying her now, smashed a shoulder into the back door and then they were outside, running for the trees.

The air was thick here, down by the water.

Above, stars in a clear sky, moonglow cutting through the fog like smoke, lending a timid green cast to the ground at the water's edge, broken by ferns and the gnarled pine walkway that reached into the river, skeletons of grandfather oaks giving way to erosion and time.

Tyree, crouching, edged closer to the house. Soft light, filtering through pine and Spanish moss, in from the marsh, sifting through the shredded lace of his curtains, wafting through clouds of dust and destruction, echoing through his collapsing home.

He closed in. Suddenly, something struck him across the head. He ducked, reflexively, and then swung an arm as something smacked his head once again. Blood streaming over his face.

Out back, Tate pushed for the trees, dragging her behind him, like running through muck.

No more warning shots.

Tyree, stunned with a round to the shoulder, regained his balance, kept firing. And now his last companion bolted for the street. Tyree, struck again across the top of his head. Feeling a piercing pain, something raking the flesh from his scalp. He swatted the owl away, still moving forward, thinking of Cadillacs and fine restaurants, torn plastic stretched over the windows of a tar-stained mobile home, a woman screaming in fear and the money he'd never spend.

Another shot spun him around. He stumbled into the house and fell.

FOR LAURA, it was like regaining consciousness after a heavy sleep. She walked gingerly toward the street, Goo holding one hand, Bobby the other. Wynt, walking ahead of them. When they reached the street, he turned, bowed slightly.

"I'm Wynton Bonds, ma'am, and I'm single."

She smiled and took his hand.

"So am I."

In the trees just beyond the house, a pair of headlights came on. An SUV pulled toward them.

Bobby turned to Tate. "Mooch really likes that rental you gave us. Might want to take it home."

"For what you guys did tonight, a new car sounds about right."

They helped her inside. The others got in.

"You guys go ahead," said Tate. "I'm right behind you."

They could hear sirens in the distance. Jimmy jogged out from behind the house, a rifle and a set of keys in his hands.

"I'm gonna ride back with you, partner."

The car pulled away. Tate reached out to take Jimmy's arm.

"How's Tyree?"

"Just winged," Jimmy said.

"But he's not going anywhere."

"No. Fraid not."

He paused.

"I dunno if Char's going to understand all this."

"Might not."

They climbed into Tate's BMW and were half a mile down the road when the explosion rocked the air and sent a brilliant white and orange flash into the sky.

Jimmy chuckled.

"Boy must have done something wrong with all that stolen C-4."

"Yup. Shame."

31

THE PHONE rang. Barks took it.

"Yeah, this is Tate's phone. He's in the shower. You want me to tell him something? OK. Who?"

She walked into the bathroom and called out.

"Guy on the phone wants me to pass along some info. Says his name is Moochie. Oh, sorry. It's just Mooch…"

Tate was laughing.

"Tell him I'll be right out."

"No. He says I can tell you. OK. Go ahead.

"You probably ought to spell that for me. How much? V-A-S-I… OK. Tate, you talk to him. Everybody has a funny name."

Tate got out, took the phone.

"Mooch."

"Yeah, we'll come up. Yeah, both of us. Who is she? Name is Barks. Right, B-A-R-K-S. No, she's not. OK."

He cupped his hand over the phone, turned to her.

"Mooch says you should talk about funny names."

He talked to Mooch awhile, laughed a lot, hung up. He came out to the kitchen, looking for Barks. Wearing a towel.

"So," she said, "tell me…"

"Well the woman with the funny name is Vasiliya. She owns the nightclub where we caught Griffin. Turns out she has been going to lunch a couple days a week at Rose's little café. Rose is the Italian lady I told you about. Anyhow, Rose and Vasiliya have become good friends and Vasiliya has started closing her nightclub at 1 am, instead of 4, so it won't be such a nuisance in the neighborhood.

"And she gave Rose a house."

"A house…"

"Yeah. Turns out Vasiliya is a fucking multi-millionaire. She didn't want Rose staying in that little apartment upstairs."

"Nice."

"Real nice."

"And what was that thing you said to Mooch about me?"

"What thing?"

"You spelled my name. And then you said… "No, she's not'"

"Oh. He wanted to know if you were a dog."

"And that was the best you could come up with? No she's not?"

Tate tried a charming smile. Didn't work.

ACKNOWLEDGMENTS

This book is a work of pure fiction and any mistakes are mine. Nevertheless, I relied upon support and invaluable technical and literary advice from:

Sgt. Karla Baldini, Atlanta Police Department

Dr. David Baker

Sonny Cohrs, Savannah-Chatham Metropolitan Police

Henry Pierson Curtis

Donna Eyring

Dr. Lawrence Golusinski

L. John Haile

Josh Homan, Isle of Palms Fire Department

Lynne Bumpus Hooper

John C. Huff

Justin M. Keen, Assistant State Attorney, Florida 18th Judicial Circuit

Lynn Kittson

Jacob Preston

Nancy Thigpen

Vice Detective Jared Watkins, Atlanta Police Department

Sgt. Neil Welch, SWAT bomb technician, Atlanta Police Department

David Wersinger, The Daytona Beach News Journal

Maj. Rick Zapal, Savannah, Chatham Metropolitan Police Dept.

ABOUT THE AUTHOR

MICHAEL LUDDEN is a former Deputy Managing Editor at the *Orlando Sentinel,* where he directed an investigation that won a Pulitzer Prize. He's written for magazines, advertising and marketing firms, edited books and been a senior writer/editor at CNN's *Headline News.* He lives in Atlanta, where he's working on another Tate Drawdy thriller.

Check out our website at:
www.michaelludden.com

And see Michael Ludden's blog "Tales from the Morgue" at:
https://michaelludden.net

EXCERPT:

Alfredo's Luck

PROLOGUE

TATE DRAWDY popped in a CD and headed for the interstate, keeping it good and loud during the vocals, cranking it up hard for the breaks.

It was sunny and cool, the sky the sort of blue southerners like to claim as their own. He'd thrown on a baseball cap, a flannel shirt, jeans, pair of old running shoes. It had been days since he'd bothered to shave.

He pulled alongside an old couple in a big Beemer. The light went red. Tate tilted his head back, cigarette dangling, adopted a pose suggesting imminent death and played air guitar until the light changed. They stared, shaking, helpless. He could see their crooked little fingers scrambling for the windows.

In the back, his hands cuffed, Herbert Dodds, the human refrigerator, stared out the window, flinching every time Tate reached for that knob.

Tate had volunteered to take him north. He owed a guy a favor. He'd gotten one of the department's unmarked cars, wedged a big boom box into the front seat, headed up the road. Traffic was heavy. He caught Herb's eye in the rear-view mirror.

"Johnny Winter."

Tate, shouting.

Herb was beginning to understand the consequences of crime, the meaning of remorse. Tate turned off the music.

"Where you from?"

"My name's Herb. I'm from Okeechobee. I stole a car."

"And you got stopped."

"Yessir."

"Cop needed surgery, am I right? You crushed his hand?"

"Didn't mean to. I just reached out, took hold of it, squeezed too hard. I got scared is all."

"What were you scared of?"

"Thought he was gonna arrest me."

"What about that thing in the jail? Heard you pulled a TV off the wall."

"Yessir."

"And threw it out the window."

"Yessir. I wished I hadn't done that either. They was playing this game, where somebody asks these people a question and while they're thinking about it, this music plays. It got to driving me a little nutsy."

Tate nodded. He hit the button on the CD.

Herb was gonna keep his mouth shut. But he was miserable.

"Wonder if I might ask, this being a long drive and all. Maybe every so often we could take a breather from that music. Just for a minute. Just a minute. Then you could play it some more. I'm just asking... real respectful."

"That's good thinking Herbert."

Herb was looking more pound puppy than dangerous cargo. Then Tate saw the Chevy, a big Suburban pushing through the traffic, coming up fast. He'd seen it once already this morning, sitting in front of his office.

Another right behind it. Both were black, with heavy tint on the windows.

Broad daylight in the middle of town. Tate didn't think it would make much difference. They were about 10 cars back. Herb was saying he liked a cool breeze.

"Herb... shut up."

He fished a key out of his shirt pocket, held it behind his head.

"Get the cuffs off."

He was looking for a side street. Herb was working on the cuffs, not asking. Tate pulled the shotgun out of the rack on the dashboard, held it back to him.

"Two Suburbans… half a block back."

Herb turned to see. The Chevys were banging fenders now, forcing people out of the way. There wasn't much doubt. Couple of folks seemed to think blowing their horn might help.

"I popped a couple of dopers yesterday. Somebody wants to object."

Herb was twisted around, looking, neck spilling out over his shirt collar, his fingers wrapped like tree roots around the gun barrel. The air was still now.

The big man shook his head. "Geez."

"We don't have a lotta choice here compadre."

Herb turned back to look at him. Sweat began to trickle down the sides of his face.

"I never done nothing like this."

"Just don't shoot any women and children."

The Chevys were two cars back now. One of the drivers was leaning out, shouting something. He was waving a gun. There was a crunching sound. The car behind them suddenly lurched up onto the sidewalk.

"Do we wait for em?"

Tate slammed it into park.

"Come out low and fast. Straight at em."

Later, he would remember it. Spinning from the car, the pavement glistening in the sun, digging hard against it, stunned the big man was keeping pace, a scream, horns, a burning deep in his throat and behind his eyes, the recoil as he pulled the trigger, the sudden explosion of glass and metal, shards floating past him like ornamental birds.

It was a surprise, them coming out of the car like that. Tate got the shooter. The driver opened the door and ran. Herb let out a scream, put a shot in the air, got both his guys to put their hands up. And then the place was crawling with cops. As soon as things were under control, Tate got Herb back into the car. Herb snatched up the cuffs, wrapped them around his wrists and held them against his stomach.

"Forget the cuffs. Hey, I bet you scared the Starbucks crowd real good, coming out shooting in that orange jumpsuit."

"I hope there's not a lot of trouble about it. Mebbe I could just say I sat here while you took care of it."

"Don't think that'll work. We had about two dozen witnesses. And what was that Johnny Weissmuller thing?"

"Huh?"

Sure enough, The chief thought giving a con a shotgun was the worst thing he'd ever heard.

"Let's call it improvisation," Tate said.

Tate's perfectly coiffed boss spit hard enough to crack the concrete.

"You got to be kidding me."

"I don't blame you for being pissed off. You can roast me. Or maybe you get real upbeat about how no citizens got hurt and you don't condone it, but this is the kind of war we're fighting."

The chief worked his jaw real hard.

"Get outa here. Take the man to FSP. Do not say squat to anybody. Then I want you in my office. And find a frickin razor before you come to see me."

Tate hopped in the car, threw on the blue light and got through to the interstate. It was a Crown Vic, so people tended to get out of the way when they saw it in the mirror. Tate liked to run up behind somebody real fast and wave em inside with a snap of the finger. Hey, enjoy the perks of the job.

"What's gonna happen? We're in for it, right?"

"Dunno. Good chance. Let's stop for a bite, what do you say?"

"That would be real good. You know, I don't have any money on me right now."

"I can cover you."

Herb thought about it for a minute. He looked at his hands.

"I tend to want to eat a good bit. You just say when it gets to be too much."

And so began the friendship between Tate Drawdy, tough guy detective, and Herbert Dodds, a young man who'd spent much of his life carrying things other people couldn't manage, picking them up in one house, setting them down in another. It was a life without complication, until now.

Herb was headed for Florida State Prison, the place they call the End of the Line.

—꩜—

To read the rest of Alfredo's Luck, visit:

www.michaelludden.com

Made in the USA
Middletown, DE
25 November 2017